THE IMPOSTOR

DAMON GALGUT

Atlantic Books
LONDON

To Alison Lowry

First published in South Africa in 2008 by Penguin Books (South Africa) (Pty) Ltd.

First published in hardback and trade paperback in Great Britain in 2008 by Atlantic Books, an imprint of Grove Atlantic Ltd.

This paperback editon published in Great Britain in 2009 by Atlantic Books.

This novel is entirely a work of fiction. The names, characters and incidents portrayed in it are the work of the author's imagination. Any resemblance to actual persons, living or dead, events or localities, is entirely coincidental.

1 3 5 7 9 8 6 4 2

A CIP catalogue record for this book is available from the British Library.

ISBN: 978 1 84354 783 9

Printed in Great Britain by CPI Bookmarque, Croydon

Atlantic Books
An imprint of Grove Atlantic Ltd
Ormond House
26–27 Boswell Street
London
WC1N 3JZ

www.atlantic-books.co.uk

Author's Note

Terms like 'Coloured' or 'Bushman' are fraught with the tensions of South Africa's history. Used for a long time as slurs or for purposes of racial classification, in recent years they have to some extent been reclaimed and neutralised. It's in this spirit in which they appear here, with no intention to hurt.

Acknowledgements

Big thanks to Riyaz Mir, whose cooking and companionship have kept me going, and to my friend Sheila Coggon, for lending me her Goan hideaway for at least one draft's worth. Likewise to the Civitella Ranieri Centre in Umbria, where these pages were completed. On the editorial front, I am indebted to the formidable talents of Alison Lowry, Toby Mundy and Ellen Seligman, as well as Tony Peake and Nigel Maister, whose critical observations have sharpened this book. I'm also grateful to Helen Bradford and Lance van Sittert for some useful conversations.

YOUR HINTERLAND IS THERE

– Inscription on a statue of Cecil John Rhodes
The Company's Garden, Cape Town

BEFORE

1

The journey was almost over; they were nearly at their destination. There was a turn-off and nothing else in sight except a tree, a field of sheep and lines of heat rippling from the tar. Adam was supposed to stop, but he didn't stop, or not completely. Nothing was coming, it was safe, what he did posed no danger to anybody.

When the cop stepped out from behind the tree, it was as if he'd materialized out of nowhere. He was clean and vertical and peremptory in his uniform, like an exclamation mark. He stood in the road with his hand held up and Adam pulled over. They looked at each other through the open window.

Adam said, 'Oh, come on, you can't be serious.'

The cop was a young man, wearing dark glasses. He gave the impression, in all this dust and sun, of being impossibly cool and composed. 'There is a stop sign,' he told Adam. 'You didn't stop. The fine is one thousand rand.'

'Wow. That's a lot of money.'

He smiled and shrugged. 'Your driver's licence, please.'

'Can't you let it go? Just give me a warning or something?' He searched for the man's eyes, but all he got was dark glass.

'I have to follow the rules, sir. Do you want me to break the rules?'

'Uh, well, it would be nice if you stretched them a bit.'

The man smiled again. 'I could get into trouble for that, sir.' After a pause he added, 'You would have to make it worth my while.'

'Sorry?'

'If you want me to break the rules, you have to make it worthwhile.'

It was spoken so casually, in such a conversational way, that Adam thought he'd misheard. But no: it had been said, exactly as he thought. He was stunned. He'd heard about this sort of thing, but he'd never had to deal with it himself. He sat rigidly behind the wheel, trying to think it through, his sense of time frozen in the vertical white light, while the man stalked around the car, looking at the headlamps, the tyres, the registration. When he got back to the window, the cop said, 'And I notice your licence is out of date. That would be another thousand. So, what do you think? Let's say... two hundred, and we can forget the whole thing.'

Adam was suddenly outraged. 'No,' he said.

'No?'

'Absolutely not. I'm not paying you one cent.'

The man shrugged again. The smile was still there, flickering faintly around his plump little mouth. 'Your driver's licence, please,' he said.

*

Adam managed to read the registration number of the cop's car, which was parked behind the tree, as he pulled out, and he recited it to himself as he drove on. But he didn't have a pen and paper to hand, and by the time he reached the next service station, a few kilometres further, he wasn't sure any more whether the sequence of numbers was correct. Nevertheless, he wrote it down on a scrap of paper he got from the waitress in the tea-room adjoining the garage. He was repeating it, trying to match it to the memory in his head, when Gavin and Charmaine came in. They had pulled over when he was stopped and had watched the whole scene in the rear-view mirror. 'What was all that about?' Gavin said.

'He wanted money. He just asked for it, straight out like that.'

Gavin snorted. 'How much did you give him?'

'I didn't give him anything.' Adam glanced anxiously at his brother. 'What would you have done?'

'Well...' Gavin said, moustache twitching. 'It's a lot cheaper than the fine.'

'That's not the point.'

'Okay, okay, whatever.' Gavin looked around. 'I've got another problem. I'm wondering if we're actually on the right road. I was pretty sure till the last turn-off. But all the road signs are mentioning some other place with a name I never heard of.'

'*Ja*, same place,' said the waitress, who happened to be passing. 'Just the name's changed. It's because of the new mayor. He changed it a year ago. A lot of people are upset about it.'

'I bet they are,' Gavin said. 'They're doing it everywhere. Big waste of money. Now they've got to reprint all the maps.'

Adam only half-heard this conversation. His mind was still preoccupied with the cop. No threat had been made, yet the man felt somehow threatening. He stood like a dark gatekeeper at the door to Adam's new life, blocking the path, one hungry hand extended.

As it happened, the town was only a kilometre or two further on. The road had been wandering aimlessly over the plain towards a distant line of mountains, as if trying to find a way across. But not far beyond the service station it went over a rise and on the other side was the town. It was built in a low valley, so that the landscape concealed it. There was a brief glimpse of a scattering of buildings, none more than a storey high, except for the church steeple, which rose like a strict, admonishing finger. On the far side of a river in the middle of the valley was the township, connected to the main town by a single concrete bridge. Across the top of a nearby hill the old name of the town had been spelled out in white stones, but somebody had started to rearrange them into the form of the new name and abandoned the job halfway through.

They turned off the road they were following and into the main street. The first and only stop was outside the church, where they pulled over. Some of Adam's unease, which had lingered from the encounter with the traffic cop, seemed to find a focus there. The street, with its single supermarket and bank and butchery and post-office, its beauty salon and hotel and bottle store, clenched at his heart. Although it was the end of August, there were Christmas lights hanging tiredly on the streetlamps, still left over from last year. The road, which they had been following for so long, narrowed at its end on a vista of yellow scrub, in which a drunk man fell over, got up and staggered a few steps, then fell over again.

Gavin got out and came over. 'Cheery, hey?'

'Well,' Adam said. 'It is Sunday.'

Gavin blew through his moustache and shook his head. 'Let's go take a look at the house,' he said.

The house was a shock. It was out at the edge of the white town, where the roads were untarred and the ground sloped steeply upward to the rocky crest of a ridge. It was very bare and basic, with a slanted tin roof. The windows had a blind, blank look to them. The paint was faded and peeling. The fence was overgrown with creeper, and the creeper had twined through the gate.

Gavin ripped at the creeper, clearing it. He was muttering to himself in a low, vehement voice, but he went silent as they stepped through onto an old slate path. The path ran through an orchard up to the front door, and the trees had grown out of control, their branches twisting and spreading. The slate was covered with a thick layer of rotting fruit, which gave off a haze of fermentation and flies. They picked their way, slipping and sliding, through fumes and a heady stink. Gavin took out a big iron key, which looked as if it should open a medieval monastery. But it slotted easily into the lock and twisted.

Adam let Gavin and Charmaine go ahead, as if they belonged here and he was the visitor. But as he stepped over the threshold he could feel the house pulling at him, drawing him in – claiming him. It was almost a physical sensation.

The air inside was dead and heavy, as if it had been breathed already. The furniture was a depressing mixture of old, clunky pieces interspersed with the tastelessly modern. The four rooms were functional and barren. There was no carpeting on the concrete floor, no picture on the walls, no softness anywhere. All of it was immured in a thick, brown pelt of dust. There was the distinct sense that time had been shut outside and was only now flowing in again behind them, through the open front door.

Gavin was furious. He stalked silently through the house, leaving his footprints marked out clearly on the floor. A bird had come in through the chimney and died and he pushed at it angrily with his toe.

'I warned you,' he said eventually.

'I know.'

'But I'll admit, this is even worse than I thought. It's pretty rough.'

'It's okay,' Adam said bravely. 'I'll get it cleaned up.'

Charmaine had gone off on an exploration, opening doors, peering into cupboards. Now she came scurrying back, her voice low and breathless.

'There are *presences* here,' she said.

'What?'

'I'm a little bit psychic,' she explained to Adam. 'I can sense presences from the past. This house is full of them. It must be very old.'

Gavin sighed. 'I don't know how old it is,' he said gruffly. 'There's certainly a lot of dirt present.'

'When were you last here?' Adam said.

'Not sure. Years ago. Just after I bought it. To tell you the truth, I almost forgot that I own it. I don't remember it very well, but I think it was in better shape than this. I only came here a couple of times.'

'What made you buy here?' It didn't seem like the sort of place his brother would go for.

'God knows. It was very trendy at the time, having a little place in the Karoo. I think I had a girlfriend who wanted it. Dirt cheap, I can tell you that. Stress on dirt.'

'I sense an old woman,' Charmaine said. 'Very old and very sad.'

'Jeez, babe. Give it a rest.'

'Mock if you want. But I do.'

'Oh, boy,' Gavin said. 'Take a look at this.'

He had opened the back door out of the kitchen. There was a small cement *stoep*, from which steps led down, and then the yard stretched away. It was choked with tall brown weeds that had died long ago and set solidly in the baked ground. They were thorny, massed together into an impenetrable wall. For some reason, those weeds were overwhelming. All the neglect and abandonment took form in them. There was a tall windmill and concrete dam to one side, but they were diminished and eclipsed by the weeds.

The two brothers stood shoulder to shoulder, staring. A wind came up and hissed through the dry stalks.

'Mother of God,' Gavin said softly, 'I feel so depressed.'

Some part of Adam was moving forward into the weeds. He had to shake his head, to clear it and return to where he was standing.

'Well,' Gavin said, clapping his hands together, trying to sound brisk. 'We can't stay here tonight, that's for sure. Let's go take a look at the hotel.'

'Oh,' Adam said, surprising himself, 'I'll stay here.'

They both blinked at him. 'Don't be crazy,' Gavin said.

'I seriously think,' Charmaine said, 'that you should do some sort of cleansing ritual first. Exorcize the place. I know somebody who could do it for you.'

Adam couldn't speak; he only shook his head.

A spark jumped in Gavin's eyes, but he spoke coolly, with a shrug. 'Whatever,' he said. 'You can do what you want, you're an adult human being.'

*

Alone in the house as night fell, he didn't know why he'd insisted on staying. The dust and disuse were everywhere. There was no power. He found an old candle in the kitchen cupboard, but the wavering puddle of light only amplified the darkness. The bare mattress was dirty and he couldn't bring himself to lie down. The place was old and many different acts might have happened in these rooms. Murder and birth might have left their traces. In the daytime he was a rational and sceptical man and he didn't believe in presences. But now, at night, with strange walls enclosing him and a strange roof creaking overhead, a lot of things seemed possible. It was as if another person, from another time, was buried under his skin. This person was squatting by a fire, with a vast darkness pressing in.

The branches of trees in the orchard rubbed against each other. Something splatted softly outside – a fruit, or a foot.

In the end he took a pillow and went out onto the back *stoep*. It was a little better here. A faint breeze moved over him, there was a brilliant frieze of stars overhead. On the far side of the valley he could see the lights of cars and trucks on the road bypassing the town, stitching back and forth with comforting indifference. There was a larger world out there.

He woke just before dawn, his face burning and swollen with mosquito bites. He had a sense of dark and troubling dreams receding back into himself like a tide. In the first light the mountains stood out like a strip torn from the sky. He sat up slowly and all of it returned to him: the unused rooms, the twisted trees, the weeds in the back yard.

Then, for the first time, he noticed the house next door. It entered his consciousness by degrees, like a photograph developing. It was a small house, in layout and shape almost exactly the same as Gavin's – except that it was different in every other way. It was brightly painted and neat and immaculate. The garden at the back was green and clipped, ordered into regular lines. A huge amount of toil and effort had gone into maintaining the place; and at this moment Adam saw a small human figure, turning over the soil with a spade.

His next-door neighbour was an older white man, dressed in blue overalls. More than that couldn't be seen at this distance, except for a general air of frenzy that the man gave off. He was hurling himself at the earth with dedication or fury, talking to himself, while a cigarette glowed redly in his mouth, like the light of an engine, but suddenly he became aware of Adam and he stopped work instantly, as if he'd been switched off. His stillness was almost unnatural.

Now the two of them looked at each other across the wire fence between them, while pretending they were not. There was no reason for them not to greet each other, or wave a hand, or nod, but neither did. It was as if they were waiting for something to happen. Then the man in blue dropped his spade and ran to his back door and went inside.

*

Adam was in a frightened, irritable mood when he walked down to the hotel a little later. This was a big, blockish building opposite the church, with an imposing, balustraded façade.

In its proportions and design it resembled an old saloon in a western.

Gavin and Charmaine were at a table on the front balcony overlooking the street. A big man in an apron was serving them breakfast and Adam heard him say, as he came up, 'It was the voice of God, speaking like I'm speaking to you now.'

'Amazing,' Charmaine said, shaking her head.

'This is my brother,' Gavin said. 'Adam, this is Fanie Prinsloo.'

Everything about the big man was meaty. Even his face, with its dull, minimal expression, was like a slab of steak. But the movement with which he dried his fingertips on the apron was surprisingly delicate. He repeated his name significantly, as if it should mean something, as he shook hands with Adam.

'I believe you are coming to live here,' he said. 'Welcome!'

'Thanks.'

'I was just telling your brother how I came here three years ago. My wife and me, we were attacked in our house in George. In the middle of the night. Tied up, hit over the head. I lost a tooth – look here.' He bared a black gap in his smile. 'And while I was lying there, with the rope around me, thinking I was going to die, I heard a voice. Just like I'm talking to you now. 'Fanie, go live in the country.' That's what it said. 'Go live in the country.' So I came.'

'It's incredible,' Charmaine said. 'Those moments when the barriers break down.'

'I used to come here for holidays,' Fanie Prinsloo said. 'Me and the wife, in my caravan. But I never thought of moving up here. Not till that night. But I packed my bags, I sold my house. My friend, I never looked back.'

'You own this place?' Gavin said. His eyes had narrowed, becoming cold and thoughtful. 'You do all right up here?'

'*Ja*, these days. Now with the new road and the pass over the mountains, there's a lot of traffic going through. It didn't used to be like that. This used to be the end of the road. But things have changed.'

'When God speaks,' Charmaine said, 'you should always take His advice.'

The big man laughed heartily. '*Ja*, it's a beautiful place,' he said. 'The mountains, the sky, just like our Heavenly Father made them. You won't be sorry, Adrian.'

'Adam.'

'And what can I get you for breakfast?'

When he'd gone lumbering off to the kitchen, Gavin said, 'Do you know who that is? Only one of the greatest forwards in the history of rugby. And he's living up here.'

The conversation had thrown Adam. He was full of insecurity about what he was doing, the whole move up here, the big change in his life. When he answered his brother, he spoke too vehemently. 'I don't care about rugby,' he said. There was a silence, and the mood around the table dropped.

'You've got red bumps all over your head,' Charmaine said, trying to be cheerful.

'Mosquito bites.'

'Well, you wanted to stay there,' Gavin said. 'In that dirty house.'

'It's *your* dirty house.'

'Nobody's forcing you to stay there.'

They stared off in different directions while Fanie Prinsloo brought the coffee and toast. Afterwards they ate without speaking. Both brothers were thinking about things that had happened in the past, which had nothing to do with their conversation. There was a lot of friction, a lot of *stuff*, between them, which had played itself out in recent weeks. The sound of chewing and swallowing was very loud, but the antagonism slowly drained away, till only its brittle shell remained. Gavin wiped his moustache carefully and, without looking at Adam, said, 'We shouldn't fight. It's all ancient history.'

'I agree.'

Gavin got up. 'Come on, babe. We'd better hit the road.'

Adam walked out to the car with them. But his brother had a last little speech to make. He had obviously prepared these thoughts, though the heart had gone out of them now. Looking down, his expression sulky, Gavin said that if Adam wanted to change his mind, if he wanted to come back to the city with them, now was the time to speak. There was still the offer of the job, if Adam wanted to reconsider...

'No,' Adam said. 'I want to be here.'

Since arriving the day before, he'd been unsure. He'd been wavering. But now, as he spoke, he was startled to discover that he meant it.

Gavin sucked on his moustache and glared at Adam in sad resignation. 'So you're set on being a martyr.'

'It's not like that.'

Gavin threw out his hands, palms upward, to show how helpless he was. But when he said goodbye to Adam he put his arms out and embraced him. It was out of character, a peculiar gesture for him, and despite himself Adam felt like crying. For weeks now, he'd wanted to get away from his brother. But when the red sports car had gone, he had an unsettling pang. Now he really was alone.

2

A set of unfortunate circumstances had led Adam to this point. In the normal course of things he wouldn't have been here at all, but his life hadn't been normal for a while. Everything had unravelled for him a few months before when two things happened at the same time to undo him. First he'd lost his job and then he'd lost his house.

He shouldn't have been surprised about the job. All the signs were there but Adam was oblivious, and it was a deep, cold shock to discover that the young black intern he'd been training for the past six months was, in fact, being groomed to replace him. His boss had been apologetic, talking about racial quotas and telling him it was nothing personal. But how could it not be personal? It was he, Adam Napier, nobody else, who had to pack up his desk and take his pictures off the wall and walk through the door for the last time. Afterwards, remembering this scene, what he felt most keenly was humiliation that he hadn't seen it coming.

The house was a different story. It had been clear for a long time how things were going. The area of Johannesburg in which he'd bought – trendy and vibrant and multi-cultural when he'd first moved in – had been sliding badly for a few years. All his friends who lived nearby had been selling up and getting out, and they'd urged Adam to do the same. But for some reason, some passivity in his character, he hadn't done anything about it. He'd just sat there, watching it all go to pieces: the gangsters taking over, the squatters moving in, the crime and drugs getting worse and worse, until it was too late. He couldn't find anybody reliable to rent the house and nobody wanted to buy it. In the end he couldn't even give the place away. The bank didn't want to repossess it and they only took it when they saw that Adam was in no position to keep up any repayments at all.

It was a real mess, a real stroke of bad luck. In just a few months he'd found himself stranded – alone and futureless in the middle of his life. Eventually he'd had to turn to his brother for help. Gavin was three years younger than Adam and had always done things in a very different way. He was down in Cape Town, at the other end of the country, and they had stayed only tangentially in touch over the years. But since Adam had got into trouble, Gavin had been calling a lot, affecting serious concern.

'Why don't you move down here?' he said now. 'You could take your time, stay with us till you find your feet.'

'I'll think about it,' Adam said. But he didn't have to think for too long. He'd been hoping, in fact, that Gavin would make the offer. He was tired of Johannesburg, tired of his life up there. The idea of a big move, a completely fresh start, was appealing.

It was amazing, when he packed up his life, how little there was. The bank had taken all the furniture along with the house. He was left with his clothes, a few household implements, some boxes of books. All of it fitted into his car.

*

As a young man, Gavin had been muscular and powerful, but he was running to fat these days. He had an affluent, satisfied look to him. He wore expensive clothes and jewellery and he had cultivated a smug little moustache. He'd recently moved into a huge penthouse apartment on the top floor of a fancy block of flats that he owned.

From Adam's bedroom window there was a spectacular view of Table Mountain and Lion's Head. A certain unreality attached to this vista, which reflected the unreality of Adam's position. Here he was, without prospects or cash, living like a king.

Gavin rubbed it in. 'Relax, no hurry,' he told Adam. 'I can afford to look after you, until you get things worked out.'

There was irony in this. Until just a few years ago, Adam had been the staid, dependable, predictable one, while Gavin was financially straitened and directionless. Now they seemed to have changed places. But the history went back further and deeper than that and it didn't take long for Adam to sense that Gavin was using his weakened state to try to settle some obscure moral score. He was constantly on his case, wearing him down. 'You've got to pull yourself together,' he told Adam just a day or two after he arrived. 'Look at you, you're a wreck. There are food stains on your shirt.'

'Who cares? Oh, all right, I'll change the shirt.'

'The shirt's not the point here, Ad. It's you. You're letting yourself go, you're collapsing. Why don't you fight back? You can't just give up. So you lost your job, big deal. Get another one.'

He made it sound so easy. That was the way Gavin thought: you side-stepped bad luck, you rolled with the punches. And maybe he was right – maybe Adam was indulging himself, giving in to self pity. In his place, Gavin wouldn't be folding up like this; he had proved it before. He had changed jobs a few times already, without suffering the slightest self-doubt. He had been through two marriages, both ending in ugly divorces, but the experience hadn't stopped him from getting involved with a series of unlikely women, the newest of whom was hanging on his arm now, chewing gum and staring at Adam. Her name was Charmaine.

'I've got a friend who's lonely too,' she put in. 'I could introduce you.'

'I'm not lonely.'

'That's your problem right there,' Gavin said. 'Denial. You've got to confront this thing. Get up, get out. Don't lie around, staring at the ceiling.'

'I'm different to you, Gavin. I reflect on things. I'm Hamlet to your Laertes.'

'What? What are you talking about? All I'm saying, get out and socialize a bit. Why don't you come out with us tonight? We're meeting some of my buddies for drinks.'

'No, thanks.'

He'd met some of Gavin's friends already. A bunch of them had come over for a *braai* in the garden downstairs a few nights before – big, boozy men with simpering wives, who talked about business deals and cars and insurance, and made jokes about blondes and blowjobs. One of them had asked Adam what line of work he was in, and when he'd answered that he was unemployed, a hot, scratchy silence had fallen.

As they got up to go, Charmaine said to Adam, 'I can read auras. Your aura is very dark.'

'Jeez, babe,' Gavin said. 'Leave my brother alone.'

'I'm just observing. You need to clear yourself,' she told Adam. 'You need to change your life.'

He thought about that the whole evening. He didn't know about the aura, but she was right about the rest of it. He did need to clear himself, he did need to change his life.

*

This idea was still on his mind a few days later when Gavin took him to visit a building site. It was a scene of frenzied activity. Hundreds of men were toiling with machines to raise a massive concrete structure from the ground. It was while they were up on the top floor, both wearing hard-hats, Adam beset by vertigo, that Gavin offered him a job.

'Nothing too big or high-powered, obviously,' he said. 'You're not qualified. But you could come and work at the office. I need an assistant. I could train you, show you the ropes. No, don't answer now, just think about it for a few days, all right?'

Gavin had made a fortune in just a few years out of property development. He'd started out up the west coast, getting involved in a marina and surf resort that had destroyed a wetlands conservation site. These days his energies were mostly focused on Cape Town. He was teamed up with people who were buying old buildings and gutting them or ripping them down and putting up shiny modern apartment blocks in their place. Some of these deals were unscrupulous and Gavin had pointed out proudly to Adam that one of their company directors was a black man who was paid a healthy retainer just to stay at home in Gugulethu while his name on the letterhead brought in legitimacy and investment. The sums of money involved were staggering.

More than anything, it was the idea of the money that swayed Adam. He'd never been seriously poor before and it wasn't nice. In recent years there had appeared a new phenomenon in Johannesburg: white people at the traffic lights, wearing old clothes and a hopeless air, begging. He wasn't anywhere near that state himself, but the possibility of it pulled at him with a powerful gravity. Losing everything, having nothing – the notion stirred contradictory feelings of panic and excitement.

So he did think about Gavin's offer. It was tempting. Later he would realize that Gavin had chosen his moment carefully: the view from the top of the construction site was heady, full of the promise of industry and power. It was only when they were back down at ground level that the real world returned. While they were walking to the car he heard his brother having a vehement conversation on his mobile phone. 'Rip it all out,' Gavin was saying. 'All the old fittings... *ja, ja*, I've got a buyer for the stuff... no, we'll put in copper... the cheapest, I told you, it's got to look good, that's the point... I know a guy, he'll handle it... take out the silver, put copper in...'

A blue melancholy rolled down over Adam. Cheap fittings. Copper instead of silver. No, he couldn't do it.

Although he'd agreed to think about it for a few days, he spoke to Gavin that night. It was better to talk while the urgency was there. He felt full of moral clarity, a sense of freedom and release. 'I want to make a contribution,' he said, 'not a fast buck.'

Gavin was instantly set bristling. 'What, I'm not contributing?'

'Well, how?'

'I employ hundreds of people. Construction work – that's a lot of jobs. It's good for bosses and workers, it's good for everybody. And it's all part of opening up the country. Where's the problem?'

It was a difficult argument to answer. But Adam remembered that, in the years leading up to South Africa's big change, Gavin had been gloomy and frightened. He'd even spoken about emigrating. Adam had been the positive one, full of hope for the future. It didn't seem right that it should have worked out like this: with Adam unemployed and homeless, and his brother talking loudly about opening up the country.

'The way I see it,' Gavin finished angrily, 'you're not in any position to refuse.'

'I'm grateful for the offer. Really. But it's a matter of principle.'

'Oh, right. It's like that. Great to keep your principles while other people are looking after you.'

'You offered,' Adam said. 'I didn't force you.'

'Out of interest, what will your principles allow you to do?'

He hesitated, but then he answered. 'I want to write poetry,' he said.

As a very young man, Adam had published a book of poems. The collection had been called THE FLAMING SWORD, a title he had taken from Genesis. It had been a small local publication and had sold only a few hundred copies, but it had attracted some attention, mostly because of his age. The poems were about the natural world, ardent and intense and romantic, and he felt quite embarrassed by them now. He had never written or published anything since, but he had always – secretly, inside himself – thought of himself as a poet. It had felt more like a condition than a vocation, especially while he was holding down another, ordinary job, trying to make his way in the world.

Now that the other job and life had fallen away, the poet in him felt renewed. It seemed to him that he'd returned to his true calling. Accordingly, he'd started to conceive of this crisis he was going through as something he'd willed upon himself. He hadn't lost his job; he had given it up. He hadn't lost his house; he was shedding his possessions. He was paring his life to the core.

Till now, he hadn't voiced these thoughts to anybody. He had barely acknowledged them to himself. But Gavin's offer of a job, and his reaction to it, had brought the whole issue into focus. He had reached a moment of truth.

'*Poetry*,' Gavin said. He made it sound like a perversion.

Adam blushed. 'Yes,' he said, feeling more certain than ever. He resolved that from this moment he would declare it to anybody who asked: that was what he was – a poet.

Charmaine was nodding at him. 'I think that's so amazing,' she breathed.

'Maybe it's amazing,' Gavin said, 'but it doesn't pay the rent.'

'The rent isn't important.'

'It is, if you don't have it.' Gavin glared at his brother. 'Look,' he said, 'things are good at the moment. The country's rolling along. There's a lot of money flowing, if you just know where to look. You've had a bit of bad luck, that's all. But there's no excuse for a white man to go starving here, whatever anybody says.'

'I'm sure that's all true,' Adam said. 'But I'm not after money. I'm after something else.'

'What?'

How could he explain? His brother would never understand. For Gavin, the goal in life was money and power, and he judged everybody by that standard. He assumed that everyone shared his aim, but of course that wasn't true. Adam believed in beauty for its own sake: Beauty with a capital B. He couldn't talk to Gavin about Beauty, but he saw his way forward clearly in that moment. He was a penniless poet, with nothing to offer anybody except words, but he was the real soul of the country. He was at the centre of things.

His feeling of exultant certainty lasted the rest of the day. In his room that evening, he studied himself in the mirror. He had a theory, which was that people's faces gradually became set around one overriding expression. There were satisfied faces, angry faces, sad faces. His own expression, he'd realized, was one of disappointment: it seemed to be the dominant theme of his life. But now, as he gazed at his image in the glass, he imagined he could see a transformation in his face. The little defeats, the compromises, had burned away. What remained was his essential self.

Adam was still a good-looking man. He didn't have the lush handsomeness of his early years, it was true, with his wild locks and saturnine stare; he had really looked the part of a poet back then. His hair had greyed and thinned, he had put on a bit of weight, there were creases next to his eyes. But the basic outline, the shape, was still in place. His intrinsic

nature showed through, his creative, bohemian spirit. The young man had matured into something less dramatic, but he was still pleasing on the eye.

He fell asleep that night secure in his conviction. But he woke in the small hours into doubt. He lay there for a long time, with the lights of the city spread out below the window, corroded by questions. What was he playing at? Who did he think he was? Thank God he hadn't used that line on Gavin, about being the real soul of the country. It didn't feel true any more. Of the two of them, perhaps it was Gavin who stood closer to the core of things. Maybe the soul of South Africa wasn't a poet; maybe it was a crooked property developer, obsessed with cheap fittings.

*

'I've got an idea to put to you,' Gavin said. 'No, no, not the job. Something different.'

This was a few days later. Adam had lapsed into a more normal state meanwhile, neither triumphant nor despairing. He knew what he wanted, but he wasn't sure he was right. In this cautious frame of mind, he paid attention to his brother, and the proposal he was listening to gradually took hold of him.

A few years before, Gavin said, he'd bought a house in a tiny Karoo town, about eight hours away. He'd meant to fix it up, to use as a place for long weekends and holidays, but somehow he'd never got around to it. So the house was just standing there, empty and unused, slowly going to pieces.

'You could go and stay there, if you like. I bought it complete, with all the furniture and everything. It wouldn't cost you much – just the electricity and water. You say you want to write poetry. Well, this could be the perfect spot for you.'

When he'd finished speaking, Gavin watched Adam with a little smirk on his face. There seemed to be some challenge in the look. It was only afterwards that Adam understood: Gavin was throwing down the gauntlet. In his mind, it was a crazy proposal. He was saying, in effect, 'you talk about writing poems. Well, let's see how badly you want to do that.'

Adam saw himself sitting at a window, a vista of rolling hills and fields outside, words proceeding from his pen in a long, unbroken flow, and it was exactly where he wanted to be. '*Yes!*' he said. 'I'll do it.'

Gavin's face fell and almost immediately he tried to persuade his brother why it was a really terrible idea. But every argument that he put forward – that the place was rough and old, that he hadn't been up there in years, that it was miles from anybody he knew – only made Adam more determined to go. It felt to him that his life had narrowed in on a tiny point of fate, on the other side of which lay regeneration and renewal. He had been worshipping false gods, but all the old idols were broken now. What would take their place was unknown, but it was almost in his grasp.

Which was how, not long afterwards, he came to find himself driving into the countryside on a Sunday morning in his old Fiat, following behind Gavin and Charmaine, who were speeding along in Gavin's red sports car. Once he was out of the city, he felt that he could breathe. He opened all the windows to let air into the car and it was like a new, fierce wind blowing through his life. He felt lighter than he had in years, as if he was leaving all his old, cumbersome baggage behind. He was sloughing off his previous life, like a skin that didn't fit him any more. His few remaining possessions, piled on the back seat, and even the car itself, didn't matter to him – he could let it all go.

Like a physical symbol of this change, the landscape they were driving through resembled nothing that he knew. He had seen the Karoo before, of course, but always in passing, on his way to Cape Town or back to Jo'burg. He had never given it his full attention till now. There were sun-blasted stretches of plain, then sudden eruptions of oddly-shaped hills. The emptiness was powerful and strange. It had the feel mostly of desert, but it was springtime and in certain fertile valleys, where there was water, the green was vivid and intense. Sometimes there would be a farm-house, with a scattering of buildings, a few stick-like human figures. And sometimes there was a tiny dwelling, no bigger than a room or two, in the middle of a huge desolation. It didn't seem possible that anybody could live there.

He had even begun tentatively to consider the poems that he might write. His early work, from the first collection, had been rooted in a very different landscape. Those were African poems: hymns to the bushveld. The stark, stripped-down countryside he was passing through now was of a different order entirely. It wasn't African; not in any conventional way. It was more like the surface of some arid, airless planet, or perhaps it was the bottom of the sea. But still, he could imagine that one might come to love all this vast vacancy. One might respond to the hugeness of the sky, or the brilliance that a blossom took on against the pale severity of the scrub. Up close, it was probably teeming with its own versions of life and vitality. Its beauty would be more valuable for having to be learned. No doubt the enormous spaces would fold the spirit inwards, on some core of contemplation and insight. Yes, it was a religious sort of landscape; and he felt a corresponding rhetoric stirring in him.

He was actually on the verge of a promising phrase, something he could build a stanza around, though its full cadence remained just out of reach, when the cop stepped out into the road.

3

He started by cleaning out the house. It was a big labour. He hadn't been this industrious in months, washing things and setting them in place, then changing his mind and moving them again. It seemed important to arrange the furniture in a new configuration. He took the curtains down and washed them in the bath. The bed-linen and the table-cloth too. He got down on his knees and scoured the floors. As he wiped and brushed, old colours emerged that had been dimmed under dirt. It was satisfying to push the dust back outside from where it had invaded, grain by grain.

This satisfaction was most complete in the evening as it started to get dark. He had been to the municipality to get the power connected and he switched on every light. The warm yellow glow renewed the little rooms. He walked through the house, exhausted but triumphant, and sat down on the back steps. At the edge of the light he could see the front line of the weeds, massed like a besieging army in the yard. There was still that enemy to overcome.

But he knew how much hard work was involved in a project like that. It wasn't easy to subdue the natural world. His neighbour, the man in the blue overalls, spent hours and hours outside each day, hacking and digging and pruning. Over the next week or two, Adam observed him as he toiled in solitary fervour. There was never a repeat of that strange incident from the first morning, when the man had gone rushing inside. But there was a mutually suspicious awareness between Adam and his neighbour, which grew more complex as the days went by.

They were always watching each other, in a sneaky sort of way. And one evening, as he sat out on his *stoep*, Adam noticed the man standing outside his back door, smoking a cigarette. There was a spill of light from inside the house and it caught the brooding presence of him, so silent and intense there on the grass, the red glow of the cigarette going agitatedly back and forth. It was twilight, the end of the day: a natural moment for reverie. But Adam felt uneasy – as if the man was waiting for something; wanting something from him – and this time it was he who jumped up and hurried off inside.

After that, they avoided each other. When the man was outside in his garden, Adam stayed indoors, spying on him from behind the curtains. But there wasn't much to see. The blue man – which was how Adam thought of him – was always working, always anxious and frenetic. On the rare occasions when he was standing still, he would be puffing on a cigarette. Nobody ever came to visit him; he appeared to be as lonely and singular as Adam himself.

Although he slaved away furiously in his garden, he had another job too – or perhaps it was a hobby. He did metal-work. There was a small shed behind the house and for hours every day a horrible noise of screeching and welding came out of it. When he worked at night, Adam could see a spray of fire inside, like the glow of some infernal industry. The blue man was making burglar bars and security gates. They were often propped up outside for the paint to dry. Later he would load them up on a *bakkie* and drive off to deliver them.

*

The poems didn't come. Or not yet. There was a big window in the lounge with the view that he'd imagined: rolling fields and hills, the dark bar of mountains in the distance. But in the foreground was the windmill, towering over his psyche, making thumping, threatening noises as the blades turned in the wind. It was broken, he could see; the water it fetched up blurted out in jets from a missing section of pipe. When he'd set up a desk in front of the window, with his notebook and pen on top of it, all he could see and hear was the windmill, churning uselessly against the sky. It stood between him and the poems, which stirred invisibly beyond it, out of reach.

He told himself he needed time. He'd had a major upheaval, a big shift in the foundations. He had to take it easy, allow himself to adjust. In a couple of weeks the windmill would recede into the background and the poems would take its place.

Meanwhile he tried to settle into this new life of his. He took himself off on walks to explore the town. But the heart of it was really that one main street. And whenever he walked down its length, popping into the shops, trying to make friendly conversation with the locals, the same feeling from that first day rose up in him again: that he was trapped somewhere that was nowhere, in which the light was too blindingly stark, and in which it was always Sunday afternoon.

What he felt – it came to him after a week or two – was the absence of history. There was the sense of a white deadness before the lightning strikes. In this electric lull, the hands of the clock didn't move. There was only the land, rolling and vast and elemental, in which time was measured out in the shadows of clouds passing over, or the minute scrabbling of a beetle among grains of sand. Human events were elsewhere. In Johannesburg or Cape Town, there was a sense of turmoil and ferment; South Africa's big change was evident and tangible. But not here. Here the way things were seemed inevitable and natural, as preordained as the weather. There was the old racial division, all the whites on one side of the river, in their spacious and expensive properties, and all the coloureds on the other side, in the township, in their crowded little houses between pot-holed, neglected streets. Two or three times a day there would be a knock on Adam's front door and it would be somebody looking for work. There was deference and desperation in the way they appealed to him, the men holding their hats in their hands and the women avoiding his eyes. He felt a curious mixture of pity and anger towards them. Couldn't they see that he had nothing to offer, that he had lost control of his own destiny too, that his future was up to fate?

*

One night he went down to the hotel in town, the place where Gavin and Charmaine had stayed. He'd seen the bar in passing and remembered it, and now the thought had come to him that he might go down there, have a beer, maybe chat to a couple of people.

It was almost empty. Five or six customers at most, not counting Fanie Prinsloo. The meaty ex-rugby player welcomed Adam loudly. But his heartiness was close to aggression, and the assortment of rugby jerseys hanging on the wall, amongst tarnished trophies and faded team photographs, were like the flags of a club that had refused membership to Adam.

After he'd set down his beer, Fanie Prinsloo said, 'So, Alan. What is it you do?'

'Adam.'

'Sorry?'

'My name is Adam. I write poetry.'

A gaunt older woman with a leathery face leaned towards him. 'I didn't catch that. You do pottery?'

'No, no. Poems. I write poems.'

Silence descended on the room, while Fanie Prinsloo flipped through channels on the television in the corner.

A thin man with glasses asked, 'You make a good living out of that?'

'Um, no, not really.'

'Didn't think so,' the man said.

The leathery woman leaned in again. 'Where do you come from?'

'Jo'burg. Well, more recently, Cape Town. I'm new here. I arrived a couple of weeks ago.'

'You know where he's staying?' Fanie Prinsloo said. 'He's staying in that old *vrot* place up the hill, with all the dead weeds outside.'

Somebody whistled and somebody else laughed.

'That place?' the thin man said. 'You not scared, living in that place?'

'No, why should I be?'

'I've seen lights moving around in there. In the night-time.'

'No, that's me,' Adam said. 'I light a candle sometimes at night. To keep me company.'

'You should clean that place up, man,' Fanie Prinsloo told him. 'Get those weeds out the back.'

'Yes, I plan to.'

'Get a boy to do it. Hire yourself a couple of boys.'

The thin man asked him, 'So how do you like it so far, living up here?'

'It's all right. A big change from the city.'

The older woman shifted closer. Adam saw that she had a glass eye, which he hadn't noticed till now. The half-dead stare unnerved him, as she told him, slurring just a little: 'I've lived here my whole life. I was born here. This was always a quiet place. Now they've made this fancy tar road that goes past. They've made a pass that goes across the mountains. The traffic that goes through now! It's ten times what it used to be.'

'Twenty,' the thin man said.

There seemed to be general agreement on this, though Adam couldn't work out whether they liked the traffic or not. Then a little dried-up man with ginger hair, who hadn't spoken till now, suddenly declared shrilly, 'There are prostitutes now. Girls from the township sell themselves up there, along the new road. To the truck drivers going through. There didn't used to be trucks. There didn't used to be prostitutes.' He slurped fiercely at his drink.

'Not only to truck drivers,' the older woman said, and the ginger man sank between his shoulders, because he took this as a reference to himself.

'Now crime is starting here too,' Fanie Prinsloo said gravely. 'Two robberies last year. Never had that before up here. That's also the road. It's people passing through.'

A sad-looking woman spoke up from behind the bar. She'd been sitting there the whole time, but Adam only now realized that she must be Fanie Prinsloo's wife. 'It isn't our coloureds,' she announced. 'Our coloureds behave themselves.'

'Except for the mayor,' Fanie Prinsloo said, and silence fell again.

In recent years, Adam had been experiencing a curious ambivalence when discussions of this nature came up. In the distant past, he had always been clear about his moral position, but that wasn't the case any more. These days, he found himself taking the opposite stand to whatever political point had been raised. If people liked the new road, he would start to wonder what vices and problems the road might bring. On the other hand, if people said the road was a bad thing, he would think of it as progress and development. His ambivalence was genuine; there seemed to be both a radical and a reactionary buried in him. More than anything, it was this fault-line in his psyche that he thought of as his new South African self.

In this particular conversation, the people in the bar were too uncertain themselves about the merits or dangers of the road for him to take a contrary position. But now that the mayor had been mentioned, the focus of the talk hardened. Everybody in the room seemed to dislike the mayor.

'You have a coloured mayor?' Adam asked, astounded. It didn't seem possible, not here.

'Oh, yes,' Fanie Prinsloo said. 'He's with the government. An angry *hotnot*. Always shouting about this and that. Nothing is ever right.'

'It's because of him they've changed the name of the town,' the thin man said. 'Everybody was happy with the old name. So the place was called after a Afrikaner hero – so what? Everybody's got their heroes. You start taking away people's heroes, then you're in trouble.'

'That's what they're doing,' Fanie Prinsloo's wife said. 'Taking away our heroes.'

'Now the town's got a African name that nobody can pronounce,' the thin man said. 'What's the use of that? What do we want a name like that for?'

There were nods and exclamations of dismay. What was happening was terrible; it shouldn't be allowed.

'But the road,' Adam said. 'Surely you're grateful to the mayor for the road?'

The silence came again, but it was charged now with suspicion. After a few moments Fanie Prinsloo said darkly, 'The road came before the mayor. The mayor's got nothing to do with the road.'

The conversation unravelled again into monologues and moody introspection, and not long afterwards Adam paid up and left. He didn't want to hang around with these sad, lost people, nursing their bigotry and their drinks. As he slipped out the door he heard the gaunt woman saying, to nobody in particular, 'I don't like the road. We got along fine before the road was here.' The television rimed her face in an icy blue frost.

He didn't go back to the hotel again, but there weren't a lot of other options for entertainment. At the far end of the main street he discovered a bed-and-breakfast place run by two women from the city who had recently moved up here. They had a bar too, but the clientele there upset him in a different sort of way. They were mostly visitors passing through, though there was a scattering of local people too, and all the talk was of crystals and energy lines and reincarnation. Charmaine would have felt at home in this company. All of these people, in their vague and apolitical way, thought that the mayor and the road and the new name for the town were good and positive things; any change, in their opinion, could only be for the better. And Adam found himself disagreeing with them on every count. To his own discomfort, he even recycled the arguments he'd heard in Fanie Prinsloo's bar, about the sudden arrival of prostitution and crime in the town.

Afterwards he stayed away from this place too. He kept to himself, and drank on his own at home in the evenings. But he was lonely, and there was too much time on his hands.

One day, to keep himself occupied, he took a drive out of town, heading towards the mountains. He wanted to see the new road and the pass for himself. As he left the buildings behind, he passed the spot where the old road went away on the right. It had been sealed off with barricades and screened with a row of trees, but he could still glimpse it from time to time, wandering over the landscape in the distance. He supposed that it continued to meander like this till eventually, much further on, it found a way to skirt around the mountains, or else petered out in some other godforsaken little *dorp* somewhere.

The new road, by contrast, was clean and big and blue. It had a forward-looking air of purpose. The land here was open and untrammelled and, except for the trucks, there wasn't much to slow you down. It was only after twenty minutes, just before the first slopes lifted, stark and sudden, out of the plain, that the way was abruptly blocked.

There was a toll booth, a heavy metal boom across the road. A woman behind a window confirmed what a painted sign informed him: that he would have to pay fifteen rand if he wanted to go any further. He had wanted to drive up into the mountains, maybe park in a spot where there was a view, look out over the plains below and think about things. But he was too poor right now to pay fifteen rand in both directions just to while away a few hours in contemplation. He pulled over to the side and watched a series of trucks going through, the drivers handing over their cash, the boom lifting to let them pass.

It took him a while to notice another sign nearby. '*This toll road is a proud project of Liberty Vision*.' He didn't know who or what Liberty Vision was, but somebody was making a lot of money out here in the sticks. He felt dully, uselessly angry, but the feeling faded. No point in protesting; he would just have to turn around and go back.

Behind the toll booth, almost part of the background, was an odd collection of buildings. It was like a tiny township, with rows of replicated houses, except that care had been taken over appearances: there were tarred roads and rudimentary gardens. The houses themselves were built in imitation Cape Dutch style, which couldn't disguise the fact that they were small and very basic. It wasn't quite poverty, but something close to it, dressed up as gentility and correctness – an impression deepened by the name on a board at the turn-off to the settlement: *Nuwe Hoop*. And in a certain way, the place did seem new and hopeful. But the human figures moving between the buildings looked leaden and aimless.

It was very curious. There was no explanation for this peculiar settlement, sprouting here in the middle of nowhere.

As Adam watched, there was a change of shift at the toll booth. The woman he'd spoken to climbed out of the little box and was replaced by a man who'd come plodding over from *Nuwe Hoop*. Both of them were wearing khaki uniforms. She hurried off to where the man had come from and became one of the nameless figures moving between the houses.

*

There was a knock at his door one late afternoon and when he went to answer there was a man outside, in white shirt-sleeves and a necktie. He was younger than Adam, with a fresh, aggressive energy. It was obvious that this man was of a different order to the ragged people who usually knocked on the door, looking for work. He was quite possibly collecting donations for the church.

'I noticed somebody had moved in,' he said. 'I thought I would stop and have a word. Your garden is a mess, sir. It is against municipal regulations.'

'Yes, I ... yes. Actually, this isn't my house.'

'We have been writing to the owner. Repeatedly. To date, we've had no answer.'

'I don't know anything about that.'

'I can show you copies of the letters. They are all on file.'

'It's my brother's house,' Adam said. 'He lives in Cape Town.'

'That may be. But you are resident. I'm sorry to inform you, but it's now your responsibility. The place is an eyesore.'

'And you are ...?'

'I am the mayor, sir.'

'*You're* the mayor ...?' Adam said. He didn't know what he'd been expecting, but it wasn't this small-boned, big-eared man, with his intense manner. He'd imagined somebody more in the city mould, with vestments and finery.

'Yes,' he said, looking Adam in the eye. 'I am the mayor.' He seemed to be staring down all the derision and rancour that his appointment had stirred up.

A day or two before this, when he'd gone to apply for a telephone line, Adam had passed a group of protesters outside the municipality. They were coloured people from the township and they were making a big clamour, dancing and singing. He'd thought the days of protest were over; he couldn't make out what they were angry about. When he was inside, he asked the pimply white girl behind the counter what was going on. She vibrated under her martial hairdo and said, 'They always want something. Whatever you give them, they want something more.'

'But what is it they want?'

'No, they want houses. They are upset because there is this new place, *Nuwe Hoop*, out on the highway. They say those people got their houses quickly, and they are still waiting. They want the council to give them houses right now, like this.' She snapped her fingers. 'But what can we do? *Nuwe Hoop* is a private development. Here we do not have money. We are waiting for the government to give us money.'

This conversation, and the song-and-dance outside, had renewed Adam's interest in the mayor. He seemed to be the figure on whom all this commotion was centred. But the man in front of him now looked too ordinary for all this excitement.

He said, 'Right. Well. Yes, I've been planning to get rid of the weeds. It's just… I'm alone, I have to do the work myself.'

'It's not only the weeds. There are unwanted aliens in your front garden that have to come out.' When he saw Adam's expression of confusion, he went on: 'I'm speaking about those trees there. They are not indigenous. Under new government regulations, they must go.'

'Okay,' Adam said. 'I'll attend to it.'

'Let me point out which trees I mean, sir.'

While the offending trees were being shown to him, Adam felt his resentment grow. This fervent little man, with his rules and regulations – who was he to give out orders like this? He made Adam feel like an unwanted alien himself.

But at this point the mayor softened, became personable. He seemed to notice Adam properly for the first time. 'You're alone here, you say?'

'Yes, I moved here recently from the city.'

'You're doing all the labour yourself? All right, listen. As long as the place is cleaned out in the next two months, I won't take action. But tell your brother he's lucky. I could have fined him.'

'I'll pass that on,' Adam said. 'And thank you.'

'What work do you do?' The mayor's tone had lost its insistent edge; he was making friendly conversation.

'I write poetry, actually.'

'Oh, *ja*? Listen to this.' He pulled himself very upright, his arms at his sides, and began to declaim stridently. The meaning of the harangue passed Adam by, though the angry hectoring rhythms were inescapable. As suddenly as he'd begun, the mayor broke off and said, 'That was one of mine. I used to write poetry myself. I was a well-known people's poet. You may have heard of me.' But when he said his name, it meant nothing to Adam.

'And do you still write poems?'

'Not any more. I wrote resistance poetry, to make my contribution to the struggle. But then I realized it was useless. We needed guns, not poems! So I went into exile for ten years. I was with Umkhonto in Tanzania. And when I came back I got arrested. I spent three years in jail, under the state of emergency. What about you?' he asked. 'What kind of poems do you write?'

'Uh, lyrical, about nature, I suppose.'

'Nature?'

'Yes, animals, you know, trees ...' He faltered, then added, 'Beauty!' too emphatically, like a gun going off.

The mayor smiled and nodded blandly. 'Yes,' he said illogically, 'I have put poetry behind me.' He said this proudly, as if he had outgrown some childish activity.

Adam was left disturbed by this conversation, with a lingering sense of accusation hanging over him. When his first collection had come out, he'd been astounded by one especially vitriolic review, which had charged him with deliberately avoiding the moral crisis at the heart of South Africa. He'd had no ideological project in mind with his pursuit of Beauty, and he'd been stung at the suggestion that he was indifferent to suffering. But in his weakest moments he reflected privately that maybe it was true; maybe he didn't care enough for people. Maybe he shied away from history. When he looked at the state of the world, he always shrank away in helplessness and horror; it seemed almost a duty, an artistic obligation, to replace politics with aesthetics. The fact that his life was empty of protest could feel like redemption at certain times, and at others – such as now – like a cause for guilt.

Yes, the mayor had got him stirred up; but he was troubled in any case by his inability to write. The poems just wouldn't come. He tried; he really did try. He forced himself to sit at the desk by the window. He resolved that he wouldn't move until he had the solid beginning of a poem. Just one would be enough. But there was always the skeletal presence of the windmill outside, with its blades and struts, its weird minatory noises. When he drew the curtains he could still hear it. He moved the desk to the back room. But from there he was disturbed by the sounds of the blue man in his workshop, cutting metal.

It was the windmill, that was the problem. Or it was the blue man, he was the problem. But when everything did go quiet, he sat down at the desk, pen in hand, and the poems still wouldn't come.

He lacked inspiration. That was it. He had moved out here to the country so that he could write about what surrounded him. Yet he'd spent no time in nature since he'd arrived. He needed to steep himself in the natural world.

He started taking himself for walks into the *veld* on the edge of town. Just a few steps, and all the signs and trappings of human settlement fell away. But it was the wrong time of year for this kind of wandering. The season had passed from spring into summer: the stony earth was exposed to a burning sun. He stumbled around among the *koppies*, gazing at the desolation, trying to take its emptiness into himself. But it didn't work: instead of inspiration, he brought a headache and sunburn home with him. He could see, in theory, how beautiful this landscape was, but it remained outside him, resistant to poetry.

It was the wrong landscape, that was the trouble. He had come here with an idea of what poetry should be, but it was based on the landscape of his youth, the part of the country he'd grown up in. Against that backdrop of fecundity and plenty, buzzing with life, his early poems had poured spontaneously out of him. He responded to lushness and growth, not all this arid spikiness. The past pulled at him through the memory of steamy green forests: that was his heart-landscape, the place where he truly belonged. He was starting to hate this parched, hostile place he'd landed up in. But what could he do? He had made such a show of his poetic mission that he couldn't backtrack now; Gavin would never let him forget it. He had to get on with things, make his peace with the Karoo, find a way out of this impasse.

He decided to set himself a task. He would take an object – any natural object his eye fell on outside. He would force himself to sit and focus on that object. Then he would write about it, however ineptly; a few lines of doggerel, even, just for practice. Afterwards he would go and find another object and do the same thing again. He had lost confidence; his technique had rusted up. Well, that wasn't so surprising: he'd had a twenty year break from it, half a lifetime. What he needed to do was start slowly, sharpening up, a little bit every day.

He picked up a stone outside the front door. It was a jagged lump about the size of his clenched fist. When he'd carried it in and put it down on the table, he sat and looked at it for a very long time. But the stone remained mute. There were things he could say about it; there were metaphors he could apply. But the lyrical ease floated high above the ground, while he stayed earthbound in a self-conscious tangle of anapests and spondees and iambs. Describing something in obvious metaphors – that wasn't poetry.

Poetry was syllable and rhythm. Poetry was the measurement of breath.

Poetry was time made audible.

Poetry evoked the present moment; poetry was the antidote to history.

Poetry was language free from habit.

Poetry was beyond him.

He recoiled from this last thought, jumping up from the table and striding around the room. It wasn't true! It couldn't be true – he knew, all the way down to his innermost being, that he was a poet. It was how he had always thought of himself – it was why he had come here. He shouldn't push himself. It was bad to force anything, especially something as abstract and delicate as a poem. If he was patient, if he just bided his time, the spirit would speak when it was ready.

So he stopped trying. He didn't go near the table or the pen any more. The stone sat on top of the paper, and it didn't speak a word.

4

The world shrank very quickly to the size of the house. He hardly ever went out, unless it was down to the supermarket or the bottle store. He started drinking in the afternoons, to make the evenings come faster. There was no cell-phone reception in the valley and he waited weeks for the land-line to be connected. When that finally happened, he sat and stared at the telephone for a long time, wondering who to call. There was only his brother, but he already knew the conversation they would have.

One night, when he was drunk, he did make a disastrous call to a woman he'd been engaged to briefly a long time ago. The engagement had been a big mistake, and they'd both been happy to escape so cleanly, no kids or property, no major damage done. They hadn't spoken in years, and he had to ring a few other people to get hold of her number. It turned out she was living in Durban now, married to somebody else, with two children. He had learned this in advance, but it didn't stop him from calling. For the first couple of minutes she was chatty and effusive; she sounded happy to hear from him. But then a silence opened up and his own mood turned. He realized now that she'd been talkative because she was nervous.

'Adam,' she said eventually. 'What is it you want?'

'I don't know. Just to catch up, I guess. Find out how you are.'

'Well, I'm fine, Adam, I'm fine. My life is good. And how are you?'

But she'd already asked him this; he didn't feel like lying again. 'Pretty shitty, actually. I've kind of lost my way. Midway on life's journey, as Dante has it.'

'Adam. That's awful. I'm sorry to hear it.'

'I'm living in my brother's house out in the country. I've got no money. I've got no job.'

'If it's money you want …'

'No, I don't want money.' He was furious for a moment, then ashamed; and then full of absurd, unbearable sadness: at himself, at her, at the road not taken. 'We should've stuck it out,' he told her, 'we should've made a go of it.'

'I can't have this conversation, Adam. I've got a husband, I've got a life.'

'It should've been me.' He was almost snivelling.

'I think you're drunk. I'm going to put the phone down in a minute.'

'I'm sorry about everything, I'm sorry it didn't work out.'

She put the phone down. He cursed at her, and then broke down sobbing, at what exactly he didn't know. The best, high point of his life was already behind him somewhere, though he didn't know when it had passed. He had started to dislike people younger than himself, wrapped in clothes and styles and values that he didn't understand. He was turning into the kind of person he'd always dreaded becoming: small-minded, focused relentlessly on himself. He foresaw an old age of tiny obsessions as his body gave in, bit by bit, and his sense of tragedy shrank to the scale of his own life. His compassion would also contract, but his intolerance would grow. Already he sensed his opinions crimping inward, on a hard core of endemic disapproval.

In the morning he remembered the conversation and was appalled. How could he have done that? And why had he been so full of grief over something he didn't really regret – didn't really ever think about? For a while, he thought about calling again to apologize, but decided that would only make it worse. He resolved instead to keep control of himself: no more drunken calls to people from long ago, no more chasing after the past. You couldn't bring back what was gone; you could only move forward, however imperfectly, into the future.

*

In the beginning he had swept and cleaned the house every week, to recharge the sense of satisfaction that first cleaning had given him. But now he started to let it go. He told himself: *tomorrow. Tomorrow I will do it.* The dust crept back, crunching delicately under his feet. It lay in a fine film over his paper, the pen, on the desk.

In just a few weeks he had lapsed into inertia. It was very hot; a massive weight of sun pressed down on everything. The light at noon cut human faces to the bone. The effort required, even for simple daily tasks, could seem too much.

He spent hours and hours entirely on his own. In his old life, in the city, everything had been arranged around particular points in the day. Now those points had gone. Not long after he'd arrived he had taken off his wrist-watch and left it somewhere, intending to pick it up later. But there had never been a reason to pick it up.

Time changed shape. Now he could sit and ponder something for what seemed like a moment, but when he came back to himself, several hours had gone by. It happened more and more that whole days disappeared behind him without trace, measured in the atomic drift of dust, the creeping progress of branches as they stretched towards the sun. And the sun itself, in its vast stellar motion, became a blotch of light that moved imperceptibly across the wall. He watched the light move. Or he saw a fig fall from a tree, and it fell and fell without ever hitting the ground.

On that first day, when he'd arrived, he'd felt time flowing in through the front door behind him. He'd brought time back into the house. But now he could feel a different time – old time, dead time – trapped inside, unable to pass back out, into the current. It had become shaped to the rooms, looping back on itself, piling up in compacted layers so dense and heavy that they were almost substantial. It didn't seem implausible that people or actions from long ago might be here, very close to him.

Sometimes the past was almost apparent. He would catch a movement out the corner of his eye, or he heard the sound of breathing from the room next door. One night he went to bed early, but struggled to sleep. When he did eventually fall into a hot, shallow doze, somebody sat down on the bottom of the bed. He was between waking and sleeping, just under the skin of time, and even after he'd jolted into full consciousness again he wasn't sure whether it had happened or not. He lay there rigidly in the dark, hearing his heart. Then he lunged sideways, fumbling for the lamp. He knew, before the light came on, that nobody would be there. But it felt as if someone was watching.

So he was alone, but he didn't feel alone. He remembered what Charmaine had said about the house; about presences. It wasn't quite like that for him. It was more the accumulation of tiny signs into a single presence: the presence of the house itself, made of time and neglect and leftover intentions.

It wasn't real, of course. It was only a shadow with no particular shape of its own. He thought of it as part of himself, a stray section of his mind that had ranged itself against him. It moved around the house as he did, behind him or off to one side, watching him. Listening. He could sense its attention, like a small, cold vacuum drawing substance towards itself, possibly out of him.

He began speaking to it. Not in a serious way – he didn't seriously believe in it. He just chatted, his manner off-hand, to amuse himself. There was nobody else to talk to, after all.

'Hey, are you there?' he might say. 'Hello, hello? Calling outer space – can you hear me?'

Then he imagined how it might answer. *Yes, I'm here. Always here. Reading you loud and clear.*

He thought of its voice as soft and dry, almost inaudible. A burr of static, made of all the lost sounds drifting around out there.

'Don't you get bored, watching me the whole time?'

No, no. On the contrary. I was bored before you came. You've given me fresh life.

'Come on. I'm not that interesting.'

Oh, don't be so sure of that.

And he laughed – at himself, because it was himself he was listening to. There was no spirit, no presence, no *thing* there in the house. Of course he knew that.

'I'm the only one here,' he announced. Very loudly, so that the words rang back at him. He listened after the echo. Nobody answered.

Except me.

*

Occasionally it occurred to him to doubt his mind. He had allowed a slow slippage in, a change to the way he thought about things. Perhaps he ought to be worried about himself. In the end, he did ring Gavin, looking for reassurance, though he assumed a nonchalant tone. 'Just thought I'd call and say hello. There's nothing much to report.'

His brother was in a cheerful, bullying mood. 'Finally we hear from you. I was starting to think I had to drive up to check on you. How's it been going? Writing lots of poems?'

'Uh, not really, not yet. But I will. I'm just getting ready.'

'Getting ready? How long does that take you?'

'A while.' He shouldn't have called; it was a mistake. 'You can't just switch it on and off like an engine.'

'It's been five weeks, Ad.'

'Has it?'

'Of course. What do you mean, you don't know what day it is?'

'Uh, I've kind of lost track a bit.'

'Should I be concerned about you? I mean, what are you actually *doing* there? How are you spending the days?'

'Thinking, mostly.'

'Thinking? You shouldn't think too much, Ad. It isn't good for you. You need to stay active. Have you done any work on the garden yet?'

'Not much.'

'How much?'

'I haven't done anything, to be honest.'

Gavin sighed. 'Get out into the yard, Ad. Go and dig up the weeds. You'll feel a lot better afterwards.'

The conversation left him irritated. But when he'd put the phone down he went to the bathroom and looked at himself in the mirror. Unshaven, a bit dirty, a feverish glint in the eye. Maybe his brother had a point. He was spending too much time idle and alone. Believing in ghosts was the symptom of a deeper malaise. His mind was a little loose, a little displaced on its foundations. It wasn't a bad feeling, to be sure – and that was the danger. You went a bit further and it felt okay, so you went a bit further still. This was how people lost track, the mental rivets popping out one by one. It crept up on you, the slow dereliction of the senses, till one day you were holed up in a ruin, beard all the way to your knees, defending your territory with a shotgun.

He must do something to push back. Any effort would be good. He filled the tub and got in and cleaned himself up. After a wash and a shave, a change of clothing, he already looked better. The way you looked was half the battle. Then he went onto the back *stoep* and glared at the weeds. He'd been avoiding it and putting it off, but the moment had come. Clearing out the back yard would be like ordering his mind. And he would start right now. No more of this *tomorrow, tomorrow*.

He got into the car and drove down to the farming co-op. He needed tools, though he wasn't exactly sure of what. He walked up and down the aisles, studying the bags of seed and fertilizer, the cisterns and pipes and fittings, and all the other peculiar items whose purpose he couldn't guess. He felt like an obvious fraud: anyone could see he didn't belong here, amongst the paraphernalia of a vigorous outdoor life. He was something else, a pale indoor creature, made for books and indirect light.

He chose a fork and a spade. He thought about the thick, thorny stems of the weeds and picked out a pair of heavy gloves. Once he'd loaded his purchases up in the car, he stood there for a long moment, feeling anew the oddness of his fate. His job, his home, his familiar life – all the old stars by which he'd steered his way – where had everything gone? What was he doing here? How had this happened to him?

Somebody nearby said, 'Nappy.'

GONDWANA

5

Adam jumps. 'Nappy' is a name he hasn't heard for twenty-five years, but it re-attaches itself to him instantly, with a jolt of shame. It's like being hit by a fist.

The man who has spoken to him is plump, about the same age as Adam, wearing short pants and a T-shirt and tennis shoes. He has a very odd expression on his face – somewhere between happiness and weeping.

He says, 'I've been waiting for this moment. I knew it would come, sooner or later.'

Adam peers at him. But the face means nothing at all. Bland and sandy skin, almost colourless. The only distinctive feature is a pillowy upper lip, which seems to button down over the lower one, like the flap of a purse. The short, wheatish hair has receded badly, giving an oval, egg-like quality to the head – one of those Easter eggs on which a child has painted a simple expression.

'You don't remember me,' the man says. 'I don't blame you. I've changed. But you, Nappy. You look the same. You haven't aged at all.'

'Oh, no,' Adam says, 'that's not true.' He gestures at his own face to indicate what the years have done, but he's just stalling for time. He realizes that he is wearing an idiotic half-grin and wipes it off.

The man comes up close to Adam, jangling his car-keys in his hand. He has a strong personal smell, sweat over-laid with aftershave. 'I'll give you a clue,' he says. '*Cloakroom.*'

'Cloakroom?'

'Think about it.'

Adam has started to wonder if the man isn't mentally deficient, an impression exacerbated by the beatific expression on his face. But at this moment the expression disappears, to be replaced by something more petulant. He seems disappointed not to be recognized.

'All right,' he says. 'I'll tell you. It's Canning.'

'Canning,' Adam says. 'My God.'

They shake hands. Canning has a moist, warm, insistent grip. When he finally lets go, he slaps Adam hard on the shoulder, unbalancing him. 'Nappy,' he says. 'Old Nappy.'

They blink at each other, unsure of what should come next.

'Do you live here?' Adam says at last.

'I live outside town. With my wife. I have an amazing wife, Nappy. How about you? Are you married?'

'No,' Adam says. 'I'm not married.'

'But you live here?'

'Yes, I... moved here recently. To write poems.'

Canning's face becomes solemn, and he nods. 'I read your poems, Nappy,' he says.

This is very unexpected.

'Did you?'

'Yes. Oh, yes. Of course.' He nods again and then an admiring smile spreads slowly across his face. 'Wonderful poems. Wonderful, wonderful poems!'

'Really? Did you like them?'

'More than that. I *loved* them.'

Adam cannot help himself: he is absurdly pleased to hear this. It feels as if his poetry has drawn down nothing but embarrassment on him before this moment, until now, at last, there is someone who understands. 'Thank you, Canning,' he says. 'That's good to know.'

Canning: he hears himself slip into the schoolboy appellation. Although half a lifetime has gone past, they are relating to each other like two teenagers.

'Why don't you come for dinner?' Canning says.

'You mean... tonight?'

'Yes, come tonight.'

'Okay. Sure. You'd better tell me where to find you.'

'No, you'll never get there on your own. Let me come and fetch you. Why don't you spend the night with us, Nappy? We're riding back to Port Elizabeth tomorrow, I'll drop you on the way. It'll give us a chance to catch up. What's your address?'

Adam has a moment of shame: he doesn't want Canning to see the run-down house, the back yard full of weeds. On impulse, he gives the address of the house next door, where the blue man lives.

'All right,' Canning says. 'I'll pick you up at seven o'clock. I want you to see our place before the light goes.' He starts walking towards a *bakkie* parked nearby, the back of which is loaded up with some kind of animal carcass – a sheep or a goat. The bloodied tangle of meat wobbles at the feet of an old black man wearing a yellow hat. The old man smiles at Adam, showing two brown stumps of teeth.

Canning has turned back. 'Is it just chance?' he says. 'You know – accident or design? Meeting up like this after so many years, in a parking lot... What do you think?'

'Uh, I don't believe in any big plan, really.'

'Well, you believe what you like, Nappy. But I knew this day would come.' Canning thumps his chest with one fist, smiling broadly. 'Fate,' he says.

When the *bakkie* has disappeared from sight, Adam's high mood frays out into uneasiness. He is going to have dinner that night with somebody he was at school with a long time ago. But the truth is that Canning's name, his face, still mean nothing to Adam. He has no memory of Canning. He doesn't know who he is.

*

He doesn't go home and tackle the weeds after all. Somehow that mission has got sidetracked. Instead he finds himself wandering around the house, staring unseeingly out of the windows. He is thinking about his schooldays.

Adam's childhood is split into two in his mind. There is home, in what was then the Eastern Transvaal. That part of his life is suffused with nostalgia and sentiment. Then there is school, which is something quite separate. School was in Johannesburg: a byzantine complex of sandstone buildings, where he and Gavin had been boarders. That memory is full of rules and punishment and torment. School was not a happy time for him.

The nickname, Nappy, had become attached to him early on. When he'd first arrived at the school, Adam was a frightened, sensitive boy who'd been terrified of this new place he found himself in. For the first few months his body had expressed his anxiety in an involuntary way: he'd wet the bed while he was sleeping. Of course, it was like the end of the world. The other boys had been merciless. Every morning they had gathered around, lifting the sheets, pointing at his sodden pyjamas, hooting and jeering. One of them had said something about him needing a nappy, and the name was close enough to his surname, Napier, to seem witty. So it had stuck, a badge of shame, long after the bed-wetting had stopped.

It is quite possible that most of the other boys have forgotten the original incident. But Adam has never forgotten. It is branded into him with all the heat of humiliation. He has left those days far behind; he is a middle-aged man now. But the moment he heard that name, all the vulnerability and embarrassment returned in an instant. It is astounding how much history can be stored up in two syllables.

He isn't sure any more about going out tonight, about having dinner with Canning. He wishes that he hadn't accepted the invitation so readily. The only reason he'd been such a soft touch was the fact that Canning had read his poems. Not only read them, but loved them. That counts for something with Adam.

He has got himself into a position, though, with the house. It was foolish to have given the wrong address, but now that he has, he must follow through. He's afraid that Canning will arrive early and knock on his neighbour's door. That would be very embarrassing. So he is outside, waiting, wearing his best casual clothes, carrying a bottle of cheap wine, from about a quarter to seven. He stands a little way down, on the street that fronts the blue man's property, close to where he parks his car in the only available piece of shade. Loitering casually there, the neat little house with its immaculate garden behind him, he gives the distinct impression that this is where he lives.

The problem will come, of course, if Canning wants to step inside and have a look. If that happens, he will have to confess. But when Canning arrives, precisely at seven o'clock, he hardly glances at the house; his attention is elsewhere. He is also wearing casual clothes, but with a designer label on them, and they look stiff and unnatural on his body. He is driving a gleaming silver Jeep Grand Cherokee, and he jumps out and opens the passenger door for Adam, then waits to close it behind him. Adam has the unsettling feeling of being courted. The inside of the car smells new, and when Canning gets in behind the wheel all the shiny technology around him gives the same impression as his clothes: of being ill-fitting, expensive and unnatural.

'It's my newest baby,' Canning says, running a plump hand over the upholstery. 'What do you think?'

'Very nice. You bought it recently?'

'Last week, as a matter of fact.'

The sound of the engine is almost inaudible. Through the tinted glass of the windscreen the town looks distant and unreal as they slide silently down the street and up to the main road. They turn right, towards the mountains. As they pass the turn-off to the old road on the right, a garish, painted figure leans into their path. It takes Adam a moment to realize that this is one of the prostitutes he'd heard about, a local woman selling herself at the roadside. She disappears behind them, but the rude colours of her makeup linger somehow in the car.

The town has dropped away now; the ruined-looking countryside spreads around them. Adam thinks: *two hundred million years ago this was a swamp*. He has a shivery sense of the whole landscape looking utterly different, full of sex and death in forms he can hardly imagine. Prehistoric creatures moving through a soupy twilight. Now those animals are a scattering of fossilized bones, and the landscape itself is like a fossil of that time. In all the miles of desolation, the car is a tiny shape, going from nowhere to nowhere.

'Have I changed, Nappy?' Canning says suddenly.

Adam has been planning to ask Canning not to call him Nappy; the name stabs him every time with its sharp point of malice. But the moment passes, and he doesn't speak. Instead he says vaguely, 'Well, we've all got older, Canning.'

'Yes, of course. But do I look the way you'd expect?'

'I don't know. I wasn't expecting anything. I mean, it's a surprise to see you at all.'

Why doesn't he just tell the truth, which is that the man next to him is a stranger? It would make things awkward for a while, but surely they'll get past it? Is it so rude or unusual to forget somebody from long ago? But something in the way Canning relates to him makes Adam hold back; he senses that his admission might matter more than he thinks.

Canning says, 'It's strange, isn't it, Nappy? How years can go by and then you see somebody and it's as if no time has passed? I feel as if we're continuing an old conversation.'

'Yes,' Adam says.

'Now tell me everything. I want to know all about your life.'

'There isn't a lot to tell.' And as he speaks it aloud, he can hear for himself how little there is: two years in the army. Four years of university. Then the same job for twenty years, until the recent upheaval. All of it had felt so rich and elaborate and heavy while he was living through it, but when he looks back, half a lifetime seems very insubstantial.

'And what about you?' he asks when he's finished. 'What've you done since school?'

'Well, I struggled, Nappy. I had a very hard time. I was also in the army, but I was G3K3 – unfit for combat, you know. I was much fatter then, as you remember. Also, I had asthma. So I had an office job up in Pretoria. While I was there I met somebody I went into partnership with. We started up a business, importing and supplying chemicals. My partner left after a while, but I stuck with it. A real battle. I got married along the way, to a girl who worked in the office. Had a child with her. But that's all over now.'

Adam ponders all this. The new car and clothes, Canning's bravura air: it doesn't seem to fit with the image of a chemical salesman. He asks cautiously, 'So are you still in the chemical business...?'

'Oh, no, no!' Canning laughs loudly. 'Everything's changed for me, Nappy. My whole life has turned upside down. You'll see what I mean, in just a little while.'

They have driven much further than Adam expected; the town is far behind them by now. The mountains are very big and close, blocking out the sky. It's like rushing in insulated comfort towards a solid wall. The new pass is visible, high up. As they approach the toll booth at the bottom, Canning slows down. He points to the peculiar little village next to the road that Adam had seen the other day, with its mixture of poverty and pretension, and says, 'I built that.'

'*You* did?'

'Well, not me personally, of course. But I donated the land, I put up the money.'

'Really? But why?'

'To head off a land claim. The people who're living here say they were chased off one of my father's farms. They agreed to drop the claim in exchange for the *Nuwe Hoop* settlement. I gave them the land, I built the houses for nothing.' Canning relates all this off-handedly, as if he's used to carrying out big schemes in a casual way. But then he goes on in a different voice, more confiding and calculating: 'Of course I got the better deal. No more land claim to hassle with. Cheap labour on tap to build the pass. And I'll be using them in my future plans too.'

'Is it your company that built the pass? Liberty Vision?'

'It belongs to a friend of mine, actually.' Canning shoots him a sideways look. 'Do you know Mr Genov? No? A marvellous man. An entrepreneur and a visionary. Don't believe what you've heard about him – he's had a bad press.' He has turned off the main road and is driving on a dirt track past the odd, anomalous shapes of the *Nuwe Hoop* settlement. 'Because of him... and me too, of course... these people have done very well. Partnership between big business and the previously disadvantaged – it's a new South African solution.'

Between the houses, Adam glimpses a low huddle of figures playing some kind of gambling game in the dirt. It is hardly a glorious vision of the future, but he says nothing till they pass the settlement and come to a high fence with a gate and a big sign.

'This is yours? You own a game farm?'

'It was my father's dream,' Canning says, 'not mine.' He has stopped by the gate and he hoots three times, peremptorily. From a concrete building nearby a guard in khaki uniform emerges, wearing a revolver on his hip. There are other khaki figures visible behind him, also armed. The guard hurries to open the gate for them and they bump across a cattle grid and through to the other side. Then they are speeding along a dirt road between *koppies* and termite hills and jumbled boulders, all fired in the copper glow of the late sun. An extraordinary vista opens up around them. It has the look and feel of a rough, unpeopled wilderness, except for a line of telephone poles and a collection of farm buildings that appear to one side. Adam assumes that this must be where Canning lives, but as they get closer he sees that the homestead is abandoned. More than that: the roof has caved in, the walls have been torn down, so that he glimpses the interior rooms through shattered masonry as they sweep past it and on.

'Where is your father, Nappy?' Canning asks him.

Adam is taken by surprise. 'Uh, he's dead, actually. He died a few years ago, not long after my mother.'

'Yes,' Canning says. 'They do die in the end.' His tone is smug and victorious. 'What did he do, your father?'

'He was an engineer.'

'He was good to you?'

'Yes, he was good to everybody. He was a nice man.'

Canning says angrily, 'That's lucky for you.'

They drive on in silence, the dust a taste and texture in Adam's mouth. The road they're on is a good one, in the very lee of the mountains, though other rough roads branch off from it, heading across the plain. After about ten minutes they make a sharp turn, and then everything is different. A cleft opens in the side of the mountains, a long sward of green that glows brilliantly against the dark stone. There is the smell and feel of water. And then the sight of it – a flickering glimpse of a river through trees. The vegetation is vivid and dense, rising in vertical waves. It is shocking, all this verdant profusion, after the epic emptiness they've been driving through. It's like a tropical island that has been towed in from somewhere else and moored incongruously here.

The road climbs into the cool green, the high mountain walls narrowing on either side. They pass through another fence, a gate. Nearby is a labourer's cottage, with chickens and dogs running around. The road veers away, towards a huge building under a thatched roof, bright patterns daubed onto its outside walls. Around it is a cluster of *rondawels*, in the same *faux*-African style. The road fades out into a glimmering lake of lawn, freshly mowed and clipped, studded with trees.

The place is very strange. It is like an old colonial dream of refinement and exclusion, which should have vanished when the dreamer woke up. But here it is, solid and permanent, its windows burning with friendly light – or perhaps the reflection of the lowering sun. It is the very end of the afternoon, pale and pleasant, and through the elongated shadows on the grass a single peacock is carefully stepping.

'Gondwana,' Canning murmurs.

'What?'

'That's what my old man called it, the pretentious old cunt.'

As they walk across the lawn towards the building, the peacock lets out a heart-ripping cry.

*

The first time he sees her: they come around the corner and she is standing on the grass, her back to them. The sun is going down in a spectacular arterial sewage of colour, but she appears indifferent to the display. She seems rapt in some private fantasy, holding a long suede coat closed around her body, despite the heat. She hears them and turns. Under the coat she is wearing a short, shimmery blue dress, and her legs are very long. Although her feet are bare, it's as if she's wearing high heels. Even before he sees the bright paint on her face, Adam has a flash of the woman on the road outside the town, selling herself. She seems to have been transported here, garish and gorgeous and improbable.

Once that first image fades, he sees past it to how beautiful she is. She is like an exotic doll, all her tiny features in immaculate proportion. She's also young; at least ten years younger than Canning – which means ten years younger than Adam too.

'My wife, Baby,' Canning says. 'Baby, this is Nappy.'

She holds out her hand. He can feel her long nails in his palm. The sensation lets something loose in him – distaste mixed with desire. He holds her fingers for a second longer than is necessary.

'I've heard so much about you,' she says. 'My husband has talked about you so many times.'

Her voice is low, husky, a little disinterested. The accent is neutral and rootless, hard to place. Her eyes linger on him for a moment, summing him up, before dismissing him.

'What do you think?' Canning says proudly. 'I told you my wife is amazing.'

'Yes,' Adam murmurs. He doesn't know what else to say. It's true: she is amazing – though perhaps not in the way that Canning means. And what kind of a name is Baby?

'I'm just going to show Nappy around.'

'Yes, do,' she says.

But Canning doesn't move. He stands there, smiling fixedly, appearing almost desperate, staring at his wife as if he's the one who's just met her. She pulls the coat tighter around herself and gives a languid little shrug, before turning around and gazing into the distance. Only then, with a discernible effort, does Canning set himself in motion. Adam follows him the last few steps into the big building, both of them casting a backward glance towards the singular figure, standing alone on the grass.

Now they have walked into a tall, sepulchral space, in which Adam's eyes have to adjust. He sees constituent elements before he sees the whole: slate floors, high conical roof, prints of wildlife paintings on the walls, between signboards with names on them like *reception*, *wellness centre*, *conference rooms*. It feels as if it should be jammed with people, but the place is empty. The sound of their feet quavers coldly around them.

'What is this? A game lodge?'

'There you are. Right first time.'

Other details are coming to him now: animal heads mounted on the wall. A fireplace framed by two gleaming white tusks, a zebra-skin spread out on the floor in front of it.

'But where are the people?'

'Well, we're here, aren't we?'

Canning seems to be enjoying Adam's confusion. He leads his guest down some stairs towards a bar, fully stocked with drinks. Through a set of doors to one side, Adam sees a kitchen in which there is a flurry of menial activity. 'No, no,' Canning says, when Adam holds out the wine he's brought along. 'Put that away. Let me mix you one of my lethal little cocktails. It took me years to get the formula just right.' He concocts a toxic-looking, bright blue mixture and dispenses it into two tall glasses, giving one to Adam. 'Cheers,' he says. 'Here's to old friends!'

'Old friends,' Adam says, and drinks.

'Are you surprised by my wife?' Canning asks abruptly.

'Surprised? No. Why would I be?'

'Well. Because she's black, for one thing.'

'But who cares about that?'

That is, in fact, the least surprising thing about her.

'We're a new South African couple,' Canning says.

Adam feels irritated. There is nothing very new, or even especially unusual, about having a black spouse these days, and it seems gratuitous to be harping on it. Though it's also true that Canning isn't your typical modern South African man. But the surprise is connected to Canning, not Baby, and it's as if he himself recognizes this fact when his tone changes suddenly, from pride to panic:

'I love my wife, Nappy. I love her very badly! I don't want to give her up.'

Afterwards, when Adam remembers this conversation, it is that one word, 'badly', which stands out for him. How can you love somebody *badly*? But he says, in a soothing voice, 'You don't have to give her up, do you?'

Canning is sunk in gloom now, as if the twilight has affected him. But then his mood switches again. 'Come with me,' he says. 'There's something special I want to show you.'

The light is fading as they go back out onto the lawn. Adam looks, but Baby has disappeared. Canning leads him away from the complex, in the direction of the river. They pass in silence through concentric rings of cultivation that radiate outwards, each one a little wilder and more unkempt than the last. There is an orchard, and below that an open field, churned-up and broken, in which nothing has been planted. Then a wall of trees goes up, complex and knotted, lush with the proximity to water. Along the way, Adam sees the greeny-blue, outrageous shapes of peacocks everywhere.

'What is it with the birds?'

'My father had a thing for them. He started out with two, but they kept multiplying.'

'Your father built this place, then?'

Canning doesn't answer. It's almost dark, and Adam doesn't want to go into the forest. But Canning takes him along the edge of the trees, to the top of a high bank, which looks down on a large, sunken pit, enclosed by a wall. An arena of some kind. They stand, looking down into gloomy vegetable growth. A smell rises to them, rank and unfathomable.

'This was going to be the swimming pool,' Canning says. 'But it's been put to another use in the meantime. How about that?'

'What?'

But then he sees it. Or rather: he sees the eyes. They are luminous and yellow, apparently disembodied, as if the undergrowth is gazing at him. He takes a step back.

'Jesus Christ,' he says. 'Is that...?'

Yes, it is. He can see the body now, behind the glowing stare. He has an involuntary urge to run, but he holds himself in place.

Canning says smugly, 'It's a lion. My father's little pet.'

'But why is it here?'

'He wasn't going to keep it here. Not permanently. There was a whole family, a what do you call it, a *pride* of them that were going to be let loose out there.' He gestures at the surrounding dimness. 'This is the last one.'

'What happened to the others?'

'I sold them,' Canning says. 'To hunters and circuses. I'll get rid of this one too, eventually. But it's kind of fun to keep him in the meantime.'

At this moment two workers appear, wearing the same khaki uniforms as the guard at the gate. They are carrying between them a dripping sack, which they drag to the edge of the enclosure. Below them, in the crepuscular blue, the lion has started to pace: back and forth, up and down, a restless power with nowhere to go. The workers look across at Canning. He makes a lazy gesture of assent, like a Roman emperor at a circus. The workers lift their sack and tip it, and into the pit there tumbles a slurry of red meat and bones – the carcass, whatever it is, that Adam saw in the back of the *bakkie* this morning.

The lion doesn't approach immediately. It continues its pacing, stopping every now and then to look balefully up at the two spectators. The workers fold up their sack and leave. It is all inexplicable: Adam is surrounded by a mystery, which seems to centre on the odd man standing next to him, sipping loudly on his blue cocktail. He feels as if he's fallen through a hole into another world.

'I don't understand,' he says.

'What?'

'This. This whole place.' He gestures at what's around them.

'Ah.' Canning takes him literally. 'It's a bit of a geographical freak. Something to do with the mountains, a sort of micro-climate in the *kloof*, volcanic minerals in the soil, an aquifer, condensation…' He breaks off irritably. 'I don't know, Nappy. It's here, isn't that enough?'

'I wasn't talking about the *kloof*.'

'Well, what then?'

He says again, 'The whole place.'

'Ah,' Canning says. 'Right. Well, that's a long story. But I'll try to make it short.'

Adam waits. Below them, the lion has started to eat. There is the sound of tearing, followed by guttural swallowing.

'Basically,' Canning tells him, 'this was my father's big dream. His whole life he worked towards only one thing – his game park. He saved money and bought different farms and patched them together. Forty years, it took him. And just when it all came together – bang! A major coronary.'

'Leaving it to you?'

'My father and I hadn't spoken since I left school. A few decades of silence. So it wasn't his plan to leave it to me, no.

But he hadn't made a will and he had no other heirs. My mother died when she was giving birth to me, as you know. So I was the next one in line. It took them months to track me down. And of course it changed my whole life. My business was folding, I was on the edge of losing everything. Then this. A whole new start. Magic! That was three years ago, and I haven't looked back. My father would rather have torched this place than let me have it, but there you are.' Canning sniggers. 'Typical of him not to plan for the future. He really imagined he would never die.'

'How old was he?'

'Sixty-six. Young, really. But his malice wore him out.'

Adam can't decide whether Canning is speaking ironically or not. Tentatively, he suggests, 'You seem quite bitter about him.'

'Bitter?' Canning snorts and drains his glass. 'That's one way of putting it. Well, you know the history. You remember our big conversation at school.'

Adam says quickly, 'Yes, of course.'

'You loved your father, didn't you, Nappy?'

'Yes, I did,' Adam says. He feels almost guilty: his love is a form of ambivalence, which is weak compared with what he senses in Canning. Hatred is certainty; certainty is strength.

'I thought so. I could hear it in your voice earlier, when you spoke about him. Then you can't understand how I feel.'

'I suppose not.'

Canning stares moodily at his feet for a long moment. Then he says, 'We'd better go back, Nappy. It's getting dark, and my glass is empty.'

*

They are on the front *stoep* of the lodge, watching the old black man in the yellow hat who'd been on the back of the *bakkie* that morning and is now busy making a fire under an oak tree nearby. An old woman, perhaps his wife, carries out cutlery and condiments and bowls of salad to a table that's been set up. But the three of them, on whom all this activity is centred, are idle, hovering in the middle of a beautiful vacuum.

Canning has polished off his third cocktail already and is noticeably unsteady on his feet. But the moment his glass is empty he heads off indoors to replenish it, leaving Adam alone with Baby. She has kept herself a little apart, sitting on the railing, half-twined, half-collapsed against a stone pillar, head tilted sideways, eyes closed. She could be asleep – but she suddenly gives a shudder and her eyes snap open. 'Listen to them,' she says. 'Every night at this time. It makes my skin go cold.'

'What?'

Then he hears it: a scaly clicking and rustling, like something furtive in the sky.

'It's the birds,' she says. 'They sleep on the roof.'

She is staring at him – but really through him – with an expression of horror. He notices something peculiar: she has green eyes, which he's never seen in a black person before. And not only that – one eye is distinctly larger than the other. This tiny imbalance seems to reflect a deeper imbalance in her character, which both draws and disturbs him.

'You don't like them?' he says.

She focuses on his face, but her expression doesn't change. As if she's answering his question, and perhaps she is, she murmurs, 'I hate it here.'

'You're not serious, are you?'

'Of course I am. All this space. All this... wildness. They can cover it in cement as far as I'm concerned.'

'But it's *beautiful*,' he says.

She gives a snorting laugh. 'You look at it once and then what? There's nothing to do here. It's boring. Give me the city –

the city's what I like. Clubs and parties and people, something happening.'

'I moved here to get away from the city.'

She is watching him now with a faint interest. 'What do you do?'

'Me? I'm a poet.'

'Yes,' she says, 'but what do you *do*? What's your job?'

'That *is* my job,' he says, all his self-doubt rising into his throat, making his voice go squeaky.

The interest fades in her face; she glances away. 'That must be why you like it here.'

'This is an incredible place,' he says quietly. Despite himself, he speaks with real feeling, and part of it is an obscure anger towards her. 'It reminds me... this will sound stupid, but it reminds me of being a boy. The area I grew up in was like this. Green and intense, like life that can't be squashed down.'

She gives a little toss of her head, and it's as if she's shrugging him off. 'I also grew up in the countryside,' she says. 'That didn't make me love it.'

He has started actively to dislike her. He doesn't speak for a moment, then he asks, 'Where did you live?'

'Oh... in a lot of places. We moved around.'

'But where? Which part of the country?'

'Small towns. All over.' She sounds half-asleep and thoroughly bored with the conversation. 'I saw enough of nature when I was small. It's just things trying to get bigger, things screwing and eating each other. Don't talk to me about nature.'

Canning suddenly emerges from the house in a loud, illogical flurry. 'Where are you two? Ah, yes, over there. Have you been getting better acquainted? That's good. You're my two favourite people on the planet, I want you to like each other. But come over to the fire, it'll be time to put the meat on soon. Great to have you here, Nappy.'

The old black man has disappeared, and the fire is an enticing point of light and heat. As Adam steps down from the *stoep* behind Canning, he looks back to where Baby is sitting unmoving on the railing, but his eye is caught by a flare of light in the sky. Against the glow, the row of peacocks on the roof is stamped out in strange silhouette.

'Jesus Christ,' he says. 'What is that?'

'What?'

'That light, way up there.'

It wells up again, a spooky yellow blaze, like a god searching through the clouds with a torch.

'Cars going through the pass,' Canning says flatly. To his wife he calls plaintively, 'Why don't you come and join us?'

Her only answer is to slide off the railing and disappear indoors without a backward glance.

'Just leave her,' Canning says to Adam, as if he's the one who had spoken.

They sit in deck-chairs, watching the flames burn down. The conversation leaps around in a fractured, disjointed way, from Canning's father to Adam's poetry to the farm. At only one point does their talk settle down to a steady topic for a while. This is when, after the fifth or sixth cocktail, Canning undergoes an odd transformation. He glares at Adam, then starts to lecture him in a high, nasal voice. 'This is your final warning... six cuts for you next time... no, don't grin at me, boy, I don't want to see your teeth, do I look like a dentist to you?'

Adam is so astounded that it takes him a few seconds to realize that Canning is doing an imitation – a surprisingly good one – of a teacher from long ago.

'Mr Groenewald,' Canning says. 'Do you remember how we used to climb out of the window, one by one, whenever his back was turned...?'

'Yes,' Adam says, the memory coming back with unexpected fullness – it must've been buried in him somewhere.

'And old Mr Joubert, who wanted to ravish Miss Weir, the science teacher with the big boobs. Remember the day her one breast fell out of her dress onto the table, in the middle of an experiment? And Mr Kleynhans, the PT teacher, who used to watch us when we showered? And Bennie Broome, with the red bike that we called the menstrual cycle?'

'Yes,' Adam says. 'I do remember!'

He has always felt disdain for those people who talk endlessly about their schooldays as if they were the fount of innocence and happiness. He mistrusts that kind of sentiment, because he knows too well how wretched he'd felt back then. Yet tonight, for some reason – perhaps the blue cocktails – this loose, nostalgic rambling is comfortable.

He decides to offer a memory of his own. 'What about that special assembly,' he says, 'when the first black student came to the school?'

Canning blinks and frowns. 'What?' he says. 'No, I don't remember that.'

'Yes, yes,' Adam says eagerly. It's one of his strongest impressions from that period. 'We were all called to the hall for a message from the headmaster. He told us it was a momentous day – that the son of a diplomat from Swaziland was coming to the school, that we all had to make him welcome.'

'Are you sure, Nappy?'

'Of course I'm sure.' Even at the time, Adam had been aware of history impinging on his existence. 'Afterwards, when we went back to class, the Afrikaans teacher looked very glum and said something about how this used to be a school he wanted to send his son to, but not any more.'

'Really? It doesn't ring a bell with me at all.' Canning shakes his head and frowns. 'Well, I can tell you, I drove through the school a couple of years ago when I was up there, and it's mostly black kids now.'

'Yes,' Adam says. 'But he was the first one.'

'And did you?' a voice suddenly asks from behind them.

They both turn, startled. Baby has come out quietly and settled herself close by in the shadows; she must have been listening for a while.

'Did we what?'

'Did you make him welcome,' she says, 'the little black boy?' She has an odd, twisted smile on her face and Adam suddenly realizes that it's him she's looking at.

'Uh, yes,' he says, too forcefully. 'Of course I made him welcome!'

But it isn't true. He'd gone past him in the corridor a few times and had noticed the lonely, bemused expression on his face. The black boy had been something exotic and new, something to get used to. But Adam had never spoken a word to him.

*

At the end of the evening, Canning rises on loose legs amongst the rinds and bones, the coals almost burned out, and says, 'Time for bed. We're in this *rondawel*, Nappy, why don't you sleep next door?'

'I'll get the keys,' Baby says. She has been sitting curled up in a chair to one side, her coat wrapped around her, gazing dreamily at the fire. She has hardly spoken a word the whole night. Now she stirs and unfolds her legs and goes off inside.

It's very late by now; there is darkness all around. The stars are smeared thickly overhead. Canning reels closer to Adam. 'This has been an important night for me,' he says. In the red glow of the coals, with his face loosened by drink, his sulky top lip appears a little puffy, almost sensual.

'For me too, Canning.' And he feels this to be true, although he couldn't say why.

Canning throws out his arms to embrace Adam and, as he does so, plants a wet kiss on his mouth. It's a startling moment, and the shock half-clears Adam's head. But by then Canning has gone again, a lopsided figure tacking into the dark.

When Baby emerges from the lodge, keys in hand, Adam follows her to one of the nearby *rondawels*. It's clean and comfortable inside, with the same design as the lodge, the same pretence at ethnic simplicity: smooth mud floors, and the thatch showing between the wooden struts of the roof. But a mosquito net is draped over the double bed, and there is a television discreetly hidden in a cabinet; through the open door of the bathroom he can see the gleam of Italian tiles. This is five-star luxury, with an artful veneer of modesty on top.

She holds the keys out to him; as he takes them, she is already moving away, towards the door.

'Baby,' he says.

It's the first time he's used her name and both of them are a little rigid as she turns around to face him. They hold a cool, steady look between them for a moment.

'Yes?' she says.

'Earlier on, you said he's talked about me many times. What has he told you about me?'

The unbalanced green eyes are full of sympathy or amusement – it's hard to tell which. 'That you were at school with him. That you were his hero.'

'That's all? Nothing else?'

'There was one particular night, he says. When he was about to crack. But you talked to him, and everything changed. His whole future was different, because of you.'

'How? What did I say to him?'

The gesture most natural to her is the shrug. 'You were there,' she says. 'You know better than me.'

The look between them lasts for a moment longer. It's as if they're having another conversation – a conversation completely different to their words – and then she turns and heads for the door again.

He stands there, not moving, for a few minutes after she's gone. He can hear the tiny noises – voices, footsteps, windows opening and closing – of the pair of them getting ready to sleep next door. Then he is suddenly exhausted. He undresses exactly where he's standing and rolls into bed.

6

He wakes into pre-dawn dimness, with no idea of where he is. The mosquito net enshrouds him, like the last skeins of a dream. Then he remembers, and sits up quickly. The movement dislodges a bolt of pain, which shoots from the back of his head and down his neck. He has slept off the buoyancy and crossed the front lines of a hangover: a toxic uneasiness is rising.

He gets out of bed and goes to the window. Something has woken him: a sound, still vibrating under his skin. Then it comes again, a dragging, guttural noise, like a piece of heavy furniture being moved nearby. It's the lion roaring, half a kilometre away, in its enclosure.

He shivers, in primitive, atavistic dread. Through the window he can see the lawn, frosted in moonlight, and the high mountain walls on either side; and the oddness of this little green island comes to him again. What kind of place is this, full of peacock screams in the daytime and these terrible roars in the night?

Now he finds his mind going back to Canning. He thinks he has him sussed out. Canning is a *nouveau riche* type, who had a very bad relationship with his father, but who managed, through sheer luck, to inherit his fortune. Without this place, what is that silly name again – Gondwana – what would Canning be? A chemical salesman from Port Elizabeth, for God's sake – a nothing, a nobody. He would still be married to his first, no doubt dowdy wife, and they would be living in a little house somewhere off the map in well-deserved obscurity. Instead he has fallen into this dreamy prosperity, with a gorgeous black woman hanging on. There is a certain mystery to Baby, a certain haziness to her origins, but it's clear that she is the power in the relationship. The devotion and love between them is a one-way affair. That is obvious. She had barely glanced at her husband the whole evening; hardly spoken a word. It's a marriage that must finally end in shipwreck.

He sees who Canning is. But what he still doesn't know is who Canning *was*. The question has suddenly become important. There must be some image, surely, some spotty schoolboy face he can dredge up? But when he tries to get a fix on it, there is nothing. He has a vague sense of familiarity with Canning, but otherwise there is a blankness, an erasure.

What makes it worse is that, for Canning, Adam is obviously a significant figure. He seems to remember him intensely. A certain feeling radiates from Canning, a kind of infatuation, a juvenile crush; it makes Adam uncomfortable, like sitting too close to a fire. For an unpleasant moment he wonders whether there wasn't some kind of homosexual encounter, which he's pushed aside in his mind. But no – he isn't likely to have forgotten that.

The effort of trying to remember is setting things loose in him. He has the sensation of pushing against a psychic wall, an invisible, elastic barrier, on the other side of which the past is stored up. Unbidden, a picture comes to him of the uniform they'd had to wear at school: grey pants, white shirt, a blue and red blazer. And he has a quick flash of a desk-top with a set of initials, DG, that somebody had carved into it with a pen-knife. Who was DG and why are his initials haunting him now? Why that memory, but not others? Why the top of the desk, but not Canning?

The questions are tiring; he shakes them off. Outside, the moonlight has faded and the sun is coming up. He knows he won't go back to sleep, so he dresses quickly and goes out.

The air is cool. The grass is silvered with dew, in which peacock feet have left cryptic hieroglyphic signs. There is nobody else around as he walks away from the lodge, towards the trees. He has it in mind to go back to the lion enclosure, but when he has passed the orchard he finds himself on the wrong path and he keeps going, wherever it will take him.

In five minutes he's in the woods, with the sound of water nearby. The undergrowth is striped through with early light. A blue and yellow butterfly flits around him, signalling its beauty. The path is following the *kloof*, heading towards its narrowest point. The further he goes, the more tentative the track becomes, till the undergrowth is dragging at his feet. Trees crowd in on both sides, speaking in the voices of insects and birds.

Just when he is considering turning back, the vegetation thins away and he comes out on the bank of the river, at the point where it emerges from the mountains. Dark walls rise on either side like portals; the water jets between boulders, then spreads immediately below into a wide, calm pool. In the first light the surface is almost statuesque and solid, flawlessly reflecting the far bank, the sky.

Only now does it occur to him that this must be the same river that flows through the town. It's unlikely that there are two of them, this size, in this part of the world. The realization jolts him. There is a connection, suddenly, in the form of a living blue vein, between the place where he lives and this inexplicable green paradise.

He goes over to the edge. The transparency of the water shows him a mysterious nether terrain of boulders and logs and splotches of light. He sees a fish suspended, like a hovering bird.

He looks around carefully, to make sure that he's alone, and then sheds his clothes on the bank. He turns his chest to the sun, trying to take its heat into his paleness. Let him open up to the world! The poet in him will sing about moments like these.

He hesitates for a moment before slipping in. The coldness envelops him. He swims out into the middle of the pool, where it's deepest. The current is barely perceptible, a faint tugging on the skin, but he imagines it washing him clean, carrying the past away. It is like baptism, but for that you need to be fully immersed: he ducks his head beneath the surface. The mirror breaks soundlessly, then composes itself around him again – sky, trees, the river-bank leaning in.

His feet find a rock and he perches there, half of his body in suspension, the other half projecting into the world. He is like the still point at the centre of everything. The first man, alone on the very first morning.

And then not.

Because somebody else is there.

First he can feel the eyes. A feeling, that's all – an animal alarm, some vestigial instinct in his cells. He remembers the unearthly roaring in the night as he peers into the trees, making out only light and shadow and the liquid movement of birds. He turns sharply the other way. The far bank is even more inscrutable. He stares and stares – until, quite suddenly, he sees.

It's a horrible moment. His body becomes colder than the water. Centuries of history drop away: the forest itself is staring at him – *into* him – with a dark face, lined and worn and old, marinated in ancient contempt. The face belongs here. Adam is the intruder, alien and unwanted; the single element in the scene that doesn't fit. All his pagan hymns to the landscape depart, unwritten. He is about to vanish without a trace, and the shock jolts him off the rock, into deep water again.

So they look at one another, the black face in the forest and the naked white man, treading water.

Then he sees the hat. A dirty yellow hat, slanted skewly on top of the face. He knows this hat; he saw it yesterday, on the head of that old black guy, who must be as startled as Adam at this encounter. The world becomes ordinary as he enters time again.

'You gave me a fright,' he calls crossly, trying to smile.

But the man has gone again, the leaves vibrating behind him like a slammed door.

Adam splashes around for a while, trying to look nonchalant. But his little pristine moment is over: he feels exposed and vulnerable, out in the open like this. Soon he flounders his way, huffing and puffing, to the bank. He's not primeval and magnificent any more, the original man: he is middle-aged and unemployed, with skinny legs and the start of a paunch, pink flesh gleaming like a target. He can't get dressed fast enough.

Then he is going at a half-jog through the forest, looking back over his shoulder, his clothes sticking to him like a clammy second skin. Only when he comes out into the open again, in the bare field, does he slow down. There are coloured workers in the orchard, all dressed in that ubiquitous khaki uniform, spraying the trees; he catches the sweet, chemical whiff of poison. They greet him with smiles and doffed caps: old-fashioned rural courtesy, full of submission.

Canning is on the lawn, knocking golf balls aimlessly about with a putter. He looks haunted and pale, but he manages a ghastly smile. 'What's your handicap?' he says.

'What?'

'How many over par? Your *handicap*?'

'I have no idea what you're talking about.'

'You *must* play golf, Nappy. Sport of the gods.'

'No,' Adam says crossly. 'I don't. Sorry.' He doesn't want to be having this conversation, in the hot sun, with a headache; he wants to be going home. On the grass at his feet he finds a stray peacock feather, which he picks up and studies, pretending to be absorbed.

'We'll be leaving in a minute, Nappy,' Canning tells him. 'Baby's just getting packed.'

On the way into town, there is hardly any talk; all of them, for different reasons, are quiet today. But they do exchange telephone numbers and Canning makes it clear that they will be back the following weekend. 'You can come around any time,' he says. 'No need to call.'

'All right,' Adam says. But he isn't sure, at this moment, whether he will ever see the two of them again.

Baby speaks for the first time today as he is getting out of the car. She is wearing an enormous pair of dark glasses, which stand out against the rich colours of her makeup like a double bruise stamped into her face. But now she takes them off and stares back through the rear window. Canning has pulled up exactly where Adam had waited last night, in front of the blue man's house, with its ordered garden full of luxuriant flower-beds. But she hardly glances at what, to all appearances, is his home; instead it's at his actual home that she's staring. In horror.

'Who lives *there*?' she says.

'Oh, there,' Adam says quickly. 'I think it's empty.'

'What a terrible old place. It looks haunted.'

'It's an eyesore,' Canning agrees. 'Maybe you should set fire to it by accident.'

'Ha ha,' Adam says.

7

He rings his brother that evening. They talk in a general way for a while, and then Adam brings the conversation around to their schooldays. It's not a topic they often dwell on; under Adam's casual tone, there is a guarded, defensive note.

'Tell me something,' he says. 'Do you remember somebody called Canning?'

'Hmmm. I think I do. He was in your year, not mine.'

'What did he look like?'

'Jeez, Ad, I couldn't tell you. Kind of average and boring. Why?'

'I ran into him up here recently. But I can't really place him. Was he a friend of mine? Did I hang out with him?'

'I don't know. If you don't remember him, why should I? He was sort of a nobody, I think, a bit of a background character.' Gavin yawns. 'So how's it going up there otherwise? Have you tackled the weeds yet?'

The weeds. They seem, somehow, more numerous than before, rustling and hissing, mocking him in a foreign tongue. When he's finished talking to Gavin he goes out onto the back *stoep* and stares at them. What better way to mark a new beginning than by clearing out the weeds?

*

He's up at sunrise the next day. He wants to start early, before the heat builds. With the solid heft of the pick in his hand, he is full of power and purpose. But in five minutes he's gasping and reeling, slippery with sweat. The earth is hard and resilient as iron. The pick bounces off it, making hardly a dent, throwing his own force back at him. The sun is well clear of the horizon by now.

He works a while, rests a while, works again. After an hour he has cleared a tiny space, not much bigger than himself. And he hasn't even managed to dig the weeds out of the ground: all he's done is break off the stems at the base, leaving the roots buried. Despite the gloves, his hands are raw from the thorns and blistered from using the pick. The sun pours down its molten malevolence on him. When he wipes the sweat from his eyes, he sees the yard stretching away.

A voice says, 'No, man, that's not going to work.'

The blue man is leaning on the fence.

'Why not?' Adam says.

'You need to make the ground soft first. You got to run the water over it, let it loosen up. Then you can pull those things out.'

The blue man has a hoarse, soft voice, with a heavy Afrikaans accent; Adam has to lean forward to hear him. From close up, he can see the lines on his face, the teary quality of his blue eyes behind their glasses, the way he has combed a few long hairs sideways over his head to hide the baldness. There are nicotine stains on his fingers and on the fringe of his moustache. He is about sixty years old and – now that Adam and he are squaring up to each other like this – just an ordinary man. He looks avuncular and friendly; a neighbour, like any other.

He says, 'I see your windmill is broken. It's a small problem. I can fix it for you, if you like. Then you can fill up the dam and run water over the ground.'

'Would you? I'd really appreciate that. Thank you.'

They have slipped into conversation so obliquely that it's no big deal. Weeks and weeks of silence; then they are suddenly chatting over the fence. Why didn't they just talk to each other in the first place? Adam decides to introduce himself. By now names are almost incidental, almost unnecessary, but they go through the ritual. The blue man says, 'Blom,' and they shake hands.

Blom. It could be a first name or a surname. Somehow it doesn't matter: one word is enough of a designation, as with Canning. But no; it's not like Canning. The surname has stuck on Canning because it's an echo from schoolboy days. 'Blom' is something else: an extraneous oddity, like a hat.

The blue man lets himself through the strands of wire and comes plodding over to the windmill. He measures and mutters to himself. 'I think I might have a pipe that fits,' he says. He goes off and comes back again with the pipe and a box of tools.

He is there for a few hours, banging and hammering and welding. He'd said it wasn't a big job, but he exudes an intense flurry of toil and concentration. Adam makes tea and carries it out to him, feeling all spare and wifely. While they are standing there, sipping from their mugs, looking out over the brown weeds moving in the wind, Blom says, 'I've seen you over the fence. Many times.'

'Yes. Me too. I saw you see.'

'I also moved here recently. I came here only one or two months before you. So we are like the new boys on the block!' He laughs immoderately.

'Yes,' Adam says. 'It's all a bit strange to me still. I've never lived out in the countryside before.'

'*Ja*, I can see that, *ou maat*. I can see you're a city boy. Don't know up from down. But *moenie* worry *nie*, you'll start to like it. Soon it'll be like you lived here your whole life.'

'I don't know about that,' Adam says, looking uneasily at the metal innards of the windmill, the weeds vibrating in the breeze. 'You can't really change who you are.'

'That isn't true,' Blom says with sudden seriousness. 'Didn't you ever imagine moving to a new place, where nobody knows you, leaving the past behind... Didn't you ever think about that? Starting again from nothing?'

'Well, maybe. Lots of people have done that, to escape from something. But that's just a con, isn't it? You'd just be pretending. You wouldn't really be a different person.'

'Do you believe in God, Adam?'

'No. That is, I don't know.'

'You should believe. If you accept the Lord into your heart, it's like life starting again. Not pretending – for real. The whole past washed away! But I don't judge you. We are all sinners in the eyes of God. Me above all. But I came through that test. My faith is stronger than before.'

'That's good,' Adam says, and sips at his tea.

'I have been reborn. And that's when I decided to start again. A whole new life! I gave up my old ways. All my sins. I became a new man.'

'I can understand that,' Adam says. 'I'm also changing my life.'

'*Ja*? How is that?'

'Oh, just... getting away from things. Taking time out to think.' He leaves it at that. Poetry versus religion: he doubts they'd have a language in common.

Later, at the end of the afternoon, Blom is done. He steps back, hands on hips, to see. From the pipes that lead into the dam there is a clunking and throbbing, and then a rush of brown water. It fades, then comes again. With every rotation of the heavy old blades above, there is a sudden gush down below. The colour of the water changes, becoming clearer.

A headiness goes through Adam, out of proportion to the scene. It feels good, this successful labour with the elements. To have this pure transparency, driven up from under the ground by wind – it is a kind of magic. Although he hasn't done any work himself, he has drawn closer to the world.

Blom comes inside to clean up. In the bathroom, he strips off his shirt before washing at the sink. While getting him a clean towel, Adam notices a bad scar on his back. It doesn't look surgical; more like an accident. He would like to ask about it, but they don't know each other well enough. Scars are a kind of history; they may have been made by stories too personal to be discussed.

Afterwards, in the kitchen, they drink another cup of tea. 'Thank you very much for all your trouble,' Adam says, but Blom only nods. It occurs to Adam that gratitude may not be enough. 'Can I pay you for your time?' he says.

Blom holds up a hand, palm outward, in refusal. 'People must help each other,' he says. 'But if you want to give me something, you can let me have that.'

He is pointing at the peacock feather Adam had picked up at Gondwana. It's been lying on the sideboard since he brought it home; he hasn't looked at it once. 'That? Sure. Take it.'

He can't imagine what Blom might want it for, but he's happy to part with it. There's no real use, in the end, for Beauty. He feels touched all over again to watch the solitary figure of his neighbour plodding away afterwards through the brown weeds, his tool-box in one hand, the long glossy feather in the other.

When he thinks about Canning and his wife, he knows they would never help anybody like this. No, they are city people, with their corruption and complexities – they are, in fact, too much like him. Blom is a rough diamond, a real salt-of-the-earth type. The charity they've exchanged today is as simple and pure as the water still running into his dam. He is learning country ways at last!

That night, when Adam sits out on the steps and sees the blue man smoking a cigarette outside his back door, each wears a name and a face for the other. Adam raises a hand in greeting, and Blom waves back.

*

All night he can hear water running into the dam. He imagines that it might be the same water he swam in a few days before. It's possible that it has travelled across the countryside, then percolated through the ground at the bottom of the river into some subterranean pool, from which the windmill has drawn it up.

In the morning he goes out to stare at the dark disc of the surface. There are strange things floating there, released perhaps from the mud at the bottom. Leaves and feathers. The dead shell of a dragonfly. He turns the tap on the outlet pipe and lets the water run. It pours across the parched ground like an explosion in slow motion. At first the soil is too hard to take it in, but after a few minutes the ground swallows in shock. The earth changes colour, from brown to black. Then the dam is dry. He closes off the pipe, to let it start filling again. He waits for the standing puddles to sink in, to loosen the ground, before he fetches the pick.

This time there is no resistance: the weeds lift out cleanly, roots and all. They are passive and brittle. He starts piling them up, to be burned later. He works quickly; he has a vision of the whole yard being cleared. But after he's gone a short way, the ground is hard and dry again. The water has soaked only a small area at the very top of the yard. He realizes that he will have to do this in stages: dig a channel for the water, flood a new section, then clear it. It will take a long time, maybe months, to get all the weeds out.

But that's all right. Man against the earth: it's an old story, perhaps the oldest one of all. Already – even though the cleared space is small – he feels good. It's the satisfaction of physical work: of honest sweat and broken skin. And the satisfaction of seeing the weeds in retreat, the turned soil taking their place.

8

He has thought about Canning and Baby from time to time during the week, with both irritation and excitement. He's aware, in almost a physical way, of the weekend coming closer, but he doesn't like the pull that they exert on him, he fights against it, so that when he drives out to Gondwana in the late morning on Saturday, the journey happens almost vaguely, as if he's actually headed somewhere else. It's only when he turns in at the gate that a sense of inevitability closes around him, like a soft fist.

He is prepared for a long discussion with the guard. But the man – not the same one as before – grins and tells him, 'Mr Canning, he say you are coming.' Then there is the vast landscape opening around him, with its hot distances, its broken, abandoned farmsteads. And ahead of him, like something dark and secret and forbidden, that green fold in the mountains.

There is another car, a Mercedes, parked under the trees. A visitor. And when he has crossed to the lodge, Adam hears a strange voice speaking. He stops for a moment to listen – not eavesdropping exactly; just getting his bearings.

'As it stands,' the voice is saying, 'the EIA can't be passed. It's too negative. We need a new report, with positive conclusions. Then he'll pass it.'

Canning's voice answers. 'I'm working on it. I'll have a new EIA in a couple of weeks. But I'm not convinced he'll pass it, even then.'

'He's jumpy, it's true. But if you make the donation we talked about, he'll move on it.'

'I'll make the donation. I've got it ready. It's all wrapped up, just waiting to be delivered.'

'Go ahead and deliver it. Then when you submit the EIA, it'll be passed smoothly. I'm guaranteeing it, I spoke to him this morning.'

Adam can't place at first where this exchange is happening. He's in that high, central space, where sounds break and echo. But when he walks a little further, in the big mirror above the reception desk he sees the two of them huddled in chairs in front of the fireplace. They seem knotted together in a parody of conspiracy, and their voices carry the low, private note of collusion.

'I'm anxious,' Canning is saying. 'This is holding everything up. Mr Genov is very keen to move forward.'

'So am I. You know that. I've also got a stake in this, remember.'

'Yes, of course. I'm just saying.'

The visitor is a short, shiny black man, in his early thirties, wearing snappy casual clothes. Even in profile, at a distance, he looks familiar to Adam. He is leaning forward, towards Canning, but he senses the intruder and pulls quickly back.

'Oh,' Canning says, and jumps up. There is a minuscule beat in which he looks uncertain, but then his usual hearty demeanour takes over. 'Come in, come in,' he says. 'This is Sipho Moloi, up from Cape Town for the day. Sipho, this is Nappy.'

Adam smarts under the nickname as they shake hands. But Sipho Moloi wears a gleaming grin. Yes, Adam has seen him before, maybe on television – and he has the eager vacancy of a continuity announcer as he says, with too much sincerity, 'I am so very happy to meet you.' An awkward pause follows on.

Canning says, 'We're just talking business for a second, Nappy. Could I give you to Baby for a while? She's outside, at the room. Why don't you go and chat to her?'

Adam's eyes have adjusted to the dimmer light indoors; as he goes back out onto the lawn he is momentarily dazzled by the sun. He struggles to find the right one in the circle of identical *rondawels* and has to knock on three doors before Baby's voice answers. He can hear at once that she is peevish and fretful.

'Oh, I wasn't expecting a visitor,' she says. 'I haven't got any makeup on.'

Makeup seems to be the least of it: she's still in bed in her nightclothes, her hair hanging loose around her shoulders. Around her, like space-debris encircling a planet, is a litter of old cups, mascara sticks, hair-brushes and dropped clothes. Spread out on the duvet is some kind of card game, apparently abandoned halfway through. All of the mess seems to emanate from Baby; there is no trace of Canning, except for a single jacket hung over a chair.

'How are you?' she says tonelessly. She doesn't look at him as she speaks; her long nails continue to flick through the pages of a fashion magazine.

'I'm fine.' He has to raise his voice to be heard above the simultaneous clamour of the television and a radio blaring from the bathroom. 'What about you? Are you ill?'

'Yes,' she says. 'I am ill – with boredom.' She sweeps the cards onto the floor with a tiny, impatient hand.

'You should come outside. It's a gorgeous day.'

'Outside? What would I do there?'

'You could sit in the sun, or go for a walk.'

'Come in,' she says, by way of answer. 'Sit down.' And once he has entered the room and put himself down in an armchair, her mood seems to lift: she smiles radiantly at him and throws the magazine aside. 'Would you like something to drink?'

He asks for a coffee; there is a coffee machine on the kitchen counter, along with sugar and Cremora. But she doesn't move from the bed; she picks up a telephone next to her and speaks tersely to somebody. While they wait she takes a hand-mirror and various bits of makeup that are scattered around and starts unselfconsciously to paint her face. In a few minutes the old black woman he'd seen last week comes in with a cup. In her age and her air of tattered futility, she is everything Baby is not. But no glance, no acknowledgement, passes between the two women, except in the form of command.

'The coffee is for the master, Grace. Put it down there.'

Adam takes it from her. There is a tiny, involuntary contact between their hands, and he wonders, abstractedly, what it feels like for somebody like Grace to be taking orders from Baby. Just a few years ago they would've both been in the same position: exiled from power, with no prospects, no future. Now everything has changed for Baby, while for Grace it has all stayed the same. He glances at the old lady, but she shows nothing in her face; she doesn't even raise her eyes as she goes out.

With remarkable swiftness, Baby has filled in the blank oval of her face – her lips, eyebrows, cheekbones, have all taken on form. As he watches her daub a lurid green shadow onto her eyelids, Adam has a flash of the same obscure anger she'd stirred up in him last week. Who is she, this vain, vacuous, lovely little doll, to whom all the lush beauty outside is just torment and boredom? Yet his irritation is inseparable from desire, and with a mixture of both he finds himself asking her, 'Where did you guys meet?'

'Me and Kenneth?'

It's part of the strangeness of this whole setup that he doesn't know who she means. Then he realizes: Canning has a first name. 'Yes,' he says. 'You and Kenneth.'

'It was in Johannesburg. A mutual friend introduced us. At a party.'

'And was it love at first sight?'

'Something like that.'

She has finished with her face; she examines the final effect in the mirror before setting it aside. Without pausing, she takes up a vial of nail polish and starts working on the spread fingers of her left hand. She seems not to notice that he's there. His longing and anger more intense, Adam says, 'What're they talking about in there?'

'Kenneth and Sipho? Just business.'

'Well, I'm sorry that I've been forced on you.'

'No, I'm happy to see you.'

But she doesn't look happy; she looks indifferent. He has finished the coffee and is about to make an excuse and leave when she looks directly at him with her brilliant green gaze and says, 'Could you help me for a minute?'

'What do you want me to do?'

'Could you do the nails on my right hand? Do you mind? I always mess it up.'

He crosses uncertainly to the bed. She is holding the hand out to him, coolly. He sits down on the edge of the mattress and goes to work with the brush. The lacquer is green, the same shade as her eyes, and the artificial smell of it stings his nose. At the same time he's conscious of her long, slender fingers in his palm, and the nearness of her breasts under their filmy white cloth. He can feel that she's looking at him, but he doesn't return the gaze.

'You're spilling,' she murmurs.

'Sorry.'

'Your hand is shaking.'

'No, it's not,' he says, but he can feel the tremor himself. He tries to keep his attention on the task. 'I'm interested in your name,' he says fiercely. 'Where does it come from?'

'Baby? It's just a name.'

'Yes, but it's unusual. Who chose it, your mother or your father?'

'I don't know,' she says crossly. 'I wasn't there.' She pulls her hand away sharply. 'Never mind,' she tells him. 'You're messing it up. I'll finish it myself.'

He's about to answer her when he hears Canning's voice outside. In a moment he's on his feet and has moved several steps from the bed. The movement is involuntary; his nearness to Baby feels illicit and dangerous, something he must conceal. But she is calm, blowing on her nails, as her husband blusters in, full of effusion and apology.

'Sorry about that, Nappy, just had to take care of a few things. I hope Baby has looked after you?'

'I've looked after him very well,' she says. Her voice and her eyes are steady. She picks up the brush and starts to paint the last fingernail, carefully and exactly.

*

Adam and Canning and Sipho Moloi sit in the cavernous restaurant of the lodge, the only customers in a thicket of tables and chairs. They are waited on by the old black couple, who lurch in and out through a pair of swinging doors that lead to the unseen kitchen beyond. Adam watches them come and go, but he can't work them out. He says to Canning. 'It's quite unusual, isn't it, to see...'

He becomes aware of Sipho, and doesn't finish.

'Blacks in this part of the world, you mean?' Canning is gnawing on a drumstick, pulling off pieces with his fingers. 'They were my father's most devoted servants, actually. They followed him around from farm to farm, all over the country. They started out in the Orange Free State, went all the way up north, almost to the Limpopo, and ended up here. I remember them from when I was a small boy. Ezekiel must've been a young man then, in his early twenties.' The thought makes him glance reflectively at the old man, who thinks he's being summoned, and comes forward.

'Ja, my Kleinbaas...?'

'No, no, I'm not calling you, Ezekiel. But tell Mr Adam, did you like the *Oubaas*?'

Ezekiel bares his two worn fangs in a smile. *'Ja, ja, die Oubaas, hy was baie goed vir ons...'*

'And for how many years did you work for him, Ezekiel?'

'Meer as veertig jaar, Kleinbaas.'

'And were you happy, Ezekiel?'

'Ja, hy was goed vir ons, die Oubaas...'

'Thank you, Ezekiel. You can bring me some toothpicks, please.'

Through this whole exchange, Sipho Moloi has kept his eyes demurely down, while he chews fastidiously. Adam has another moment like the one in the *rondawel*, where he wonders at what wordless perceptions might be passing between this young, well-heeled black yuppie, and the poor old family retainer. But perhaps he is the only one who notices: the two of them are so far from one another, sitting at such divergent points of history, that they might be in different worlds. Instead it's Adam who's left with an acute awareness of the life that Canning's thoughtless cross-questioning has evoked: the blind economic dependence, the drifting around from one place to another in the wake of the *Oubaas*, the indeterminate destiny ahead...

'He doesn't like me much, actually,' Canning says, as Ezekiel goes to the kitchen. 'He much preferred my father. The old man could speak his language, at least.'

For the first time, Sipho glances up with a flash of genuine interest. 'Really?' he says. 'Your father spoke isiXhosa?'

'Oh, yes. And Zulu too, as a matter of fact. He was the old-style feudal overlord, you know. Could give orders to the serfs in their own language.'

'You didn't ever want to learn yourself?'

'Never thought about it, actually. And now it's too late. The brain has hardened.' He's finished with the chicken bone; his mouth is shiny with grease. 'Don't know what to do about Ezekiel and Grace,' he adds musingly. 'They're pretty useless these days. Not much future there. I'll have to make a plan.'

Sipho has finished his meal; he lays down his knife and fork, wipes his fingers on his napkin. 'I'm going to leave you in a minute, Kenneth,' he says. 'There's a long road in front of me.'

'That's a shame, Sipho. Can't I persuade you to stay the night?'

'No, I've got things to do. But I'll be back soon enough.'

'All right. I'll walk you out, but just wait for me for a minute, I have to go and pee.' When Adam and Sipho are alone, they smile at each other self-consciously, looking for something to say. The buzzing of a fly at the window next to them sounds uncomfortably loud.

'And where do you fit into the picture?' Sipho says at last.

'Me? I, uh, I know Canning from school.'

'Ah. So you know each other very well.'

'You could say so. What about you? Where did you two meet?'

'Nicolai introduced us.' He glances at Adam. 'Mr Genov, I mean. Do you know Mr Genov?'

'I've heard his name. But I don't know him. He doesn't sound… local.'

'Well, he lives here now, of course. But he comes from somewhere else. Russia, I think. Or maybe Bulgaria…? Anyway, it doesn't matter, Eastern Europe somewhere. He's moved around a lot. He's a man of the world. Are you sure you've never met him?'

'No. I mean, yes.'

'So you're not part of the deal.'

'What deal is that?'

He looks away. 'Well, I mean... you and Kenneth aren't in business together.'

'No, no. I'm not a businessman.' Another pause, then Adam says, 'What about you? You're in television, right?'

'Television?' His friendly face looks puzzled. 'I don't follow you.'

Coming up behind Adam, Canning says, 'Where do you get that from? Sipho's involved in government.'

'The government...? Oh, I beg your pardon, I thought...'

'I really have to leave now, Kenneth. It's late already.'

Adam trails behind them to the car. He feels embarrassed by his gaffe, but he has placed Sipho by now: his name, his face appear occasionally in the media. He is a mid-ranking politician, one of the new, young crowd, both known and unknown, in the way of nebulous officials. At least it explains the cheap celebrity veneer. But that's about all it explains.

*

Canning takes him for a drive. They head out of the *kloof*, across the dry plain. There are dirt tracks looping and meandering out there, made for the purpose of game viewing. Their drive consequently has an aimless quality to it, exacerbated by Canning's tendency to speed up or slow down without apparent reason. Along the way they pass more shattered homesteads and Canning explains that his father had had to dynamite any habitable buildings on the various farms he'd bought, so that squatters could not move in. It's as if the land has been emptied out by war.

'I'm sorry if I offended your friend just now,' Adam says, after a silence sets in.

'What? Oh, you mean Sipho...? He's not my friend. He's a wanker.'

Adam is startled. The cosy camaraderie he'd seen in the dining room an hour before seemed natural, unforced. Now Canning dismisses it with a casual wave of his hand.

Not long afterwards, at an arbitrary place in the middle of a flat stretch, Canning pulls over. 'There's something I want to show you,' he says.

Adam follows him out, into heat and white light. A little way off the road, next to a dry watercourse, is a little cave. It's a tiny, dark grotto, nothing special, but he points to a series of paintings along the rock wall.

Adam crouches down. 'Bushman art?' he says. 'Is it real?' The figures in the paintings are stick-like but expressive, the colours still bright. It appears to be a hunting scene: people with bows and arrows, pursuing animals.

'Yes, of course they're real,' Canning says impatiently. 'But forget them, I'm showing you something else.'

It takes Adam a while to make out another engraving altogether. This is a set of intertwined names cut into the rock. *Kenneth/Lindile*. There's a blurred date underneath.

'I don't understand,' Adam says, puzzled.

'My first playmate,' Canning tells him, 'was a little black boy, Lindile. He was the son of Ezekiel and Grace – you know, the old couple at the lodge.'

'You did this?'

'Me and him, yes. Long ago, when we were very young. Before we grew up and realized how complicated the world was. It was an innocent time.' Canning's eyes have actually filmed over with moisture. 'I often think about back then, Nappy. What I wouldn't give to rewind to that time.'

'Where is Lindile now?'

'Oh, I don't know. He's around. But we're not friends any more. Like I said, the world got complicated. My father paid for him to study in Cape Town, but he got all political and turned angry. So my father stopped paying and he disappeared. I haven't seen him in years.' He continues to gaze at the piece of juvenile graffiti, his face softened by sentiment.

There are contradictions in Canning's story that Adam can't work out. On the one hand, he refers to his childhood in slighting, bitter terms; on the other, he lapses into moments like these, where he becomes whimsical and nostalgic. He speaks about his father as a hard, angry man, an old-style feudal overlord, but then mentions casually that he could speak two black languages and paid for the education of his loyal servants' child. It's hard sometimes to know where one's sympathies should lie.

And the contradiction extends to other aspects of Canning too. He speaks about Adam as some kind of childhood hero, but except for a general air of reverence he shows no genuine interest in him. Aside from a few perfunctory questions, he hasn't tried to find out anything about Adam's life in town, or what circumstances had led to him moving up here, or even what he's done the past week since they met. In Canning's company, Adam doesn't feel like a real person so much as a symbol from long ago, whose full significance he doesn't understand.

But then again, unexpectedly, Canning is capable of human, solicitous gestures. On the drive back to the lodge, he suddenly says, 'You know, Nappy, I wanted to say…' He hesitates, looking embarrassed, then goes on: 'It's just that I noticed… you don't seem to have a lot of money at the moment. Your car, I mean, your clothes… what I'm trying to say is, if you ever need money, you just have to drop the word.'

Adam is taken by surprise. 'Well, that's very kind of you, Canning.'

'Not at all. It's just,' he says forcefully, 'I know what it's like to be poor. I battled for a long time myself, in my early years. The whole chemical business, you know. But things are all right now. That's my good luck! But I'd like to share my luck with you, Nappy.'

'Thank you, Canning.'

'Now we won't mention it again, unless you need to.'

They drive on in silence, while Adam struggles with himself. Canning's basic contradiction seems to have infected him too. It's hard not to be touched by the offer of money, however fumblingly it was made. But at the same time his pride bristles: the two of them hardly know each other, after all, and there is something presumptuous and invasive in even discussing it. And what does he mean about his car and his clothes?

Back at the lodge, the evening is a repeat of last week: the fire under the tree, the endless blue cocktails, the drunken talk around the coals. Baby doesn't emerge from the *rondawel* to join them, and neither man mentions her, but for both of them her absence is like a kind of presence.

9

He stays the night again. In the morning, they are going through all the pleasantries of goodbye when Canning suddenly hits his forehead with his palm. 'I almost forgot,' he says. 'I wanted to ask you a little favour. Would you be able to deliver a parcel for me in town? It's just some papers, I'd do it myself, but I'm in a bit of a rush.'

'No problem.'

'Thanks, Nappy. You're saving me a detour. Could you hang on just one moment?'

Adam is standing at the car and he watches a peacock make its stately way across the lawn while he waits. Every few steps it stops and flares its tail magnificently. The display seems to serve no purpose, except as a show of beauty. Adam approves: loveliness for its own sake is a worthy creed, he thinks. Yet he has not written a single poem since he got here.

Canning comes back out with a package. 'The address is written on the front,' he says. 'Would you be able to deliver it tonight? I'll make sure somebody's waiting at, say, eight o'clock.'

'Sure,' Adam says, weighing the parcel in his hands. It's compact but hefty, and it gives off a satisfying crinkling sound. 'I don't recognise this address.'

'It's in the township. Just go over the river and ask anybody for the street. And Adam – it's important. Please look after it.'

'Of course,' Adam says, speaking in a casual tone to cover his anxiety. Making deliveries to the township, even out here in the countryside, isn't in his normal ambit of activity, but he doesn't want to say that to Canning.

'We'll be seeing you next weekend, I hope? Don't wait for Saturday. Come on Friday – stay the weekend. You're part of the family now.'

He thinks about that on the drive home. The family: Canning's little circle. He's beginning to have an inkling of what that might involve. With his black wife and his multiracial business associates, Canning's repeated claims to be a new South African man are starting to look less hollow than before. It's Adam, by contrast, who feels a little outside events, a little superfluous.

He wonders what the parcel might contain. Papers, Canning had said; but papers dealing with what? There is some kind of money-making scheme afoot, that much is clear. He supposes that it has to do with the game farm, with getting it started again, now that Canning's father is dead. That can't be a simple process, Adam imagines, though what it entails he wouldn't know. The world of business, of money and power: it has always been a mystery to him. It's a part of life he's never felt equipped to understand. No, he was made for simpler, leaner things, though he can't quite decide what they are.

At eight that night he drives across the bridge to the other side of the river. Though he sees the township off in the distance every day, this is the first time he's actually been there. Nevertheless, the tiny houses, the burnt-out, scrappy gardens, the pot-holed roads and sputtering streetlamps: it's all known, all familiar. He has thought of it as far milder than the townships in the city; a place without danger. But as he noses slowly along, trying to find a street name, he notices a few groups of carousing drunk men. His car is a minor event; people stare at him as he passes and somebody yells out wordlessly at him. Sunday night in the country, after a weekend of hard revels: this is a task perhaps better left till daylight.

He is on the verge of turning around and heading home, when he passes a woman walking on her own. He stops and asks her the way. Yes, that is Smit street, that one over there, she tells him; and he's no sooner in the street than he finds the house he's looking for. It's a neater, bigger place than the houses nearby, with the start of a good garden around it. He parks outside and hurries in. The door is opened almost immediately to his knock by a youngish man who looks vaguely familiar. They shake hands, and the man says, 'How are you,' in a nervous, friendly way.

'I was asked to bring this to you. Mr Canning, from the game farm...'

'Come inside for a minute.'

He steps into a murky front room. He can see another room beyond, where a woman and a child are watching television. The young man closes the interleading door, then returns expectantly.

'Thank you,' he says, as Adam gives him the parcel. He holds it away from him, with the tips of his fingers, as if it might dirty him. Then they stand in uncomfortable proximity, as though waiting for something meaningful to happen. The atmosphere is not quite hostile, but it isn't relaxed either; there's a tension with no clear cause.

'Well,' Adam says. 'I'd better be off.'

A voice from the television carries metallically through the door. The young man says to him, 'The trees are still there.'

'I beg your pardon...?'

'The three aliens. In your front garden. I noticed the other day, as I went past. They're still there.'

Adam stares at him in astonishment. And suddenly understands. 'Oh, it's *you*,' he says. 'I didn't realize.'

The young man nods, although he also looks surprised. 'Who did you think it was?' he says. 'How is the poetry coming along?'

The short drive back to the other side of town feels inordinately long. Something about the encounter he's just had stays with Adam, perturbing him. It's as if an object at the edge of a room, which he's noticed unconsciously out the corner of his eye, has been removed when his head was turned. A tiny displacement, almost indiscernible, but enough to nag at his mind. The phone is ringing as he comes through the front door and when he picks it up, Canning's voice says immediately, 'Is it done?'

'Yes, I've just come in.'

'Ah, good man, yes, good.' It's only now, when his voice softens, that Adam recognises how peremptory that initial tone had been. 'You're a real friend, Nappy. One in a million.'

'That was the mayor,' he says.

'Um, yes,' Canning says, sounding guarded again. 'So what?'

'Nothing. Just… you hadn't mentioned it was the mayor.'

'Didn't I tell you that? I should've mentioned it. Well, thanks a lot, Nappy, it means a lot to me that you did that. Will we see you on Friday?'

'See you on Friday,' he says.

*

Before Friday comes, he sits down at his desk. What impulse takes him there he doesn't know; he hasn't attempted poetry in weeks. But he has no sooner placed himself than the words begin to fall out of him – words pressured by some nameless internal sensation rising volcanically at his core. In a couple of hours he is looking down at his first complete poem in half a lifetime.

Other poems follow on. Over the next few days the same feeling carries him back to the page. It's as if he is giving voice to unspoken words that have piled up dangerously inside. Sometimes he can experience them almost physically: word stacked on word, like bricks laid in rows, walling off his mouth.

Now that they've been released, these words take on a life of their own. He hears them as a rustling, a seamless susurration at the very edge of things. At first, particular sentences, specific meanings, don't stand out. He thinks of them as the leftover scurf of human talk, everything that has ever been said, moving in endless waves through the universe, unable to die.

In time the words become grafted onto the presence in the house, which still drifts in and out erratically. He senses it most acutely at night, when the world shrinks to the size of a few connected rooms. It has never felt menacing or malicious, this presence, and its occasional nearness is company for him. He still talks to it in a half-real, half-fanciful way. But now its replies take on a tone and volition of their own.

My, my, it says, reading over his shoulder. *Looks like the real thing.*

'Well, I am a poet.'

I was beginning to have my doubts about that.

'Oh, I was collecting myself. You can't just snap into it after such a long break.'

Yes, I see. But I'm surprised. I would never have thought of you as such a hot type.

'Hot?'

Mmm. Such a would-be lover boy.

'I really don't know what you mean.'

But when he reads the poems again, he does understand. He's been so caught up with rediscovering his gift that what the words are saying is almost secondary. But of course they have a subject; of course they have a theme. It wasn't immediately apparent, not even to him, but now that it's been pointed out, he sees it right away.

He's been writing about *her* – about Baby. More specifically, he's been writing about his longing for her. Not as a would-be lover, that part is nonsense, but with a sort of metaphysical yearning. Until now, he's been trying to write poems about the wilderness, a world empty of people, while all the time he's needed a human being to focus on. And here at last she is, intervening between him and the landscape – not an identifiable person, but an emblematic female figure, seen against the backdrop of a primal, primitive garden. All of it is very biblical.

The poems have also broken the mould of his first collection in other ways. Part of what's been hindering him is an obsession with the metre and rhyme – the mechanics of the exercise. Instead, now that he has a real subject, what's poured forth is in free verse, a spontaneous explosion of language in which the technicalities of form are subservient to his passion. This is right and proper and obvious: the way it should be. Yet there is also something wanton and uncontained about it, something abandoned, which makes him slightly ashamed. It would be all right for an adolescent, but he's middle-aged, supposedly past all that looseness of feeling.

After a bit of hesitation, he tells Baby about the poems the next weekend. He doesn't know what he's expecting or wanting from her, but she only stares coolly back at him.

'Poems? About me?'

'Well, not *you* exactly. But somebody like you. Or no – what am I saying? It *is* you, but a heightened aspect of you. A dream-you, if you know what I mean.'

'No,' she says. 'I don't know what you mean.'

They are sitting outside in the shade on a pair of fold-out chairs. It's the Saturday afternoon, and Canning has withdrawn into the lodge to make a conference call. Once again he has asked Adam to occupy himself with Baby, and Adam is happy to oblige.

'You're like a kind of muse,' he tells her now.

'A *what*?'

He starts backing off, feeling oddly hurt by her bemusement. 'Well, it doesn't matter,' he mumbles. 'They're just scribblings.'

'I don't really know about poetry,' she says, looking away.

'It doesn't matter,' he says again.

'Kenneth showed me your other poems. Your book. He read some of them to me. That was some time ago, before I met you. But I didn't understand them.'

'Oh,' he says. 'I don't understand them myself.'

He changes the subject and their talk moves on to other, less dangerous things. But the exchange stays with him, giving him both pleasure and pang when he thinks back on it. He feels a little further away from her, a little colder, but also a little closer and warmer towards her husband. Had Canning really done that – read his words aloud to her when Adam wasn't around?

Nevertheless, he doesn't mention the poems to Canning.

10

The words keep coming. Some of the urgency fades after the initial burst, but at the end of every weekend, after he's visited Gondwana, he sits down at his desk with that familiar inward glow, which outlasts the act of writing: even in his idle times, he feels fired now with conviction and certainty, a sense of powerful purpose. *This* is what he came up here for; *this* is the self that he wanted to discover.

He doesn't return to the weeds. They were always a substitute occupation. He feels no guilt these days when he hears them rattling in the wind out there. Writing poems is like a different kind of purging. Though there is a definite moment of unease when he sits on the back step one morning and notices, in the patch of ground he'd cleared at the top of the yard, that a fresh round of weeds is springing up. He goes closer to see and there's no doubt about it: a fuzz, a soft, green stubble of them, questing out of the soil. As fast as he had taken out the old dead weeds, new ones are suddenly sprouting.

He bends down and tears one of the little plants out. It comes away easily, a translucent filament topped with two bright leaves. It is months away from becoming the tough, thorny adversary he's been dealing with. But it will: the future is encoded in its cells. It's the water that's done it – the same water he'd used to soften the ground. Generations of seeds are lying dormant under the surface, waiting for his labours to release them. The very means of clearing the yard is what will fill it again. He has a melancholy insight into powers that he cannot understand: there are thousands and thousands of weeds, a rising green tide made of numbers and fecundity, and through them an intelligence is at work, larger than each individual plant, replenishing itself through secret strategy.

He's distracted from these metaphysical qualms by the abrupt appearance of his neighbour at the fence. Blom has a way of creeping up soundlessly, then suddenly barking a greeting. 'Morning! I see you've got a problem there.'

Adam jumps. 'Yes, they're growing back.'

'You can get weed killer at the co-op. Only thing that'll sort those buggers out.'

'That means soaking the whole place in poison. I'm not keen on that.'

Blom smirks and shrugs. 'Then dig, my friend. Dig.'

There have been a few of these conversations recently. Since he'd come over to fix the windmill, Blom has lost his distance and inhibition. He has been using a familiar, matey tone with Adam. Their talks have always been brief, usually conducted over the fence, and they centre on some or other point related to the garden. But when the exchange is over, Blom always hangs around a bit longer than necessary. He never looks at Adam directly in these moments, but stares off at a slant, a cigarette glowing at the corner of his mouth like a lit fuse. It appears as if there is something on his mind, something he would like to say. After standing there for a while in his quietly feverish way, he usually turns quickly and goes back inside his house.

But not today. After hanging around for a minute or two, he suddenly tells Adam, 'You know, I was afraid of you the first time I saw you.'

'That first morning?' Adam says. 'When I was sitting out here?'

Blom nods. 'I thought the place was empty. I wasn't expecting anybody. Then I looked up and saw you.'

'It's natural,' Adam says. 'To get a fright.'

Blom's eyes are fixed and wide, looking somewhere else. 'I thought for a second,' he says, with a strangled little laugh, 'that you'd come to kill me.'

Adam blinks. 'But why would I do that?'

'I don't know why.' He laughs again – a high, disturbing sound. 'I just thought it: that man will kill me. I don't know why it came into my mind.'

'I won't kill you,' Adam says. 'What nonsense.' The thought stays with him all day, keeping him unsettled.

What to think about Blom? He is both obvious and mysterious. The two of them haven't had anything like a personal chat and Adam is happy to leave it that way: he likes the neighbourly distance between them. But then one night there is a knock on the kitchen door and when he opens it Blom is on the concrete outside, a bottle of brandy in his hand. He has a vague, unsteady air about him. 'I decided to come and have a *dop* with you, my *pêl*,' he announces.

Adam is dismayed, but he lets him in. A line is definitely being crossed here. He hasn't wanted relations with the blue man to reach this point, with both of them sitting around in his lounge, drinking brandy and Coke, talking about their lives. But as the evening wears on, the alcohol unpicks Adam's reserve, so that he almost enjoys Blom's company.

His story is ordinary – a tale of small-town life, drifting from one place to another in the Karoo. He has held down a variety of manual jobs, as a mechanic and handyman, at one time doing repair work for the railways. He was married, he says, for forty years, but his wife had passed away recently. That had been the impetus for his last move, from Middelburg to here. He had arrived in the town not long before Adam.

'But I tell you, *ou maat*,' he sighs, 'I think that was the last time. A man can't keep jumping around like this! No, it's finished now, I'm going to stay here until I die.'

He has delivered this whole account in a casual, relaxed way. But then, even in his most languid moments, there is something febrile about Blom. He peers anxiously at Adam now, looking apparently for condemnation or approval.

'That's good,' Adam says. 'It's nice to... to be settled somewhere.'

Blom considers this, then his face cracks open in a beaming smile. It's as if he's relieved about something. 'Thank you,' he says. 'You are my only true friend!'

The declaration startles Adam. The two of them hardly know each other, but even if they spent many more hours together, he doubts they would ever be friends. Blom is rural and Afrikaans and working class; Adam is a bourgeois city type. Their proximity here is an accident, an artificial encounter.

Perhaps to bring this home to Blom, Adam starts talking about himself. He tells about his previous job, and about the move up to the town, stressing how passing and temporary it is. He means these details to show how different they are, but the moment he mentions his poems, Blom becomes serious and intense. 'I also make poems,' he says.

'I don't follow you.'

'You come and visit me sometime, I'll show my poems to you.'

'Oh,' Adam says. 'Okay.' This talk baffles him, but he isn't curious to find out what it means. He has had enough enforced friendliness for one evening and he's relieved, not long afterwards, when Blom says that he has to go.

Over the next while there are several more chats over the fence, but Blom doesn't arrive unexpectedly at the door again. He hints that he's expecting a return visit from Adam, but when this doesn't happen, an element of wary reserve creeps back between them. They go back to keeping their distance. They are friendly, but not too close.

*

All of this feels like part of a growing harmony in Adam's life, a settling into his new incarnation. The weekdays in town are only half of it. The other half is the weekends he spends out at Gondwana, with Canning and Baby. The days there are unattached to anything else. Even time seems to pass at a different pace – much faster, slipping over him like wind.

When he thinks back afterwards on these visits, it's as if he's taken part in something heightened and artificial: a drama in a theatre full of rich colours and subtle lighting effects, with a row of roosting peacocks as an audience. The supporting cast is numerous and nameless. Everywhere in the background there are servants dressed in khaki. They are the guards at the gate, the labourers in the fields, the workers repairing fences. They are, he understands, the community of people from *Nuwe Hoop*, at the gate to the farm. Outside the fence they are individual in their poverty, but inside, in their generic pale uniforms, they are like a single entity, a chorus without a voice. Closer to the centre, there is Ezekiel and Grace, for some reason the only two servants allowed to work in the echoing, empty lodge and the surrounding buildings. They have names and a dim past, which trails behind them when they walk, though their lines are few and indistinct. In the middle of the stage there is Canning and his wife, with their cryptic dialogue, their mysterious exits and entrances. They seem to have usurped the main roles by accident, like understudies suddenly thrust into the spotlight.

His own part in this is as yet obscure. At certain moments he thinks of himself as a central character, at others he is merely a spectator. Nor is it entirely obvious yet whether this is tragedy or farce.

On his visits, he always sleeps in the same *rondawel* where he spent the first night, and it's soon so familiar to him that he starts leaving some of his clothes in the cupboard. His weekends there become ordinary and normal so quickly that it's hard to believe he didn't know these people until recently. When Canning talks about what old friends they are, it almost feels true to Adam. In the beginning he had felt like a fraud, a bit of an impostor. But by now he has half-persuaded himself that they do have a meaningful connection going all the way back to childhood. He almost does have a memory of Canning from their schooldays, and in time it's hard to know whether this hazy half-impression is recalled or invented.

He spends most of these weekends in Canning's company, where time shapes itself around a certain routine. There are the fires under the tree at night, the round upon round of blue cocktails. At dusk Canning likes to go down to the lion's enclosure, to watch the feeding. And during the long, hot days, he likes to take Adam on outings into the bush, either in the jeep or on foot.

There is something about these excursions that hearkens back to boyhood, as if they're a pair of adolescents, with no adult cares or responsibilities, tramping off on some loose adventure. Canning likes to pack sandwiches and flasks of tea, which he carries in a rucksack. He has a stick which accompanies him on some of the rougher missions. In his designer outdoor gear, wearing a floppy hat and dark glasses, slathered in sun-cream, Canning resembles nothing so much as a plump, enthusiastic scout on a camp.

Adam is more demure and restrained. He has never been one for dressing up and exploring. But the lush green foliage of the *kloof* has set something free in him, something to do with his early years. He feels fresh and rejuvenated when he's out there, and his energy rises accordingly. He finds himself enjoying these little jaunts, in part for the physical release they bring, in part – he has to admit it eventually – because he starts to quite like Canning's company.

So they head out into the scrub together, to climb some *koppie* that Canning remembers from when he was a boy, or to a swimming-hole he used to frequent with Lindile, his first black playmate. A lot of these expeditions are nostalgic, burrowing down into special sites from Canning's past. Once he takes Adam to a stretch of the river that is famous for its fossils. And they have no sooner arrived than Adam trips, quite literally, over a chunk of rock that on closer inspection shows itself to be a kind of prehistoric mollusc. He is dazzled and amazed, until he searches around and finds other casts and impressions scattered nearby, or sticking out of the crumbly river-bank.

'This is extraordinary,' he says. 'It should be a national heritage site or something.'

'Yes,' Canning says sniffily. 'This was a prehistoric flood-plain, with a lot of silt. Very conducive to fossils. Some of them are two hundred and fifty million years old. Rich pickings here. We did have a team from some or other university digging once. I remember watching them as a boy. But then they upset my father and he chased them off.'

On the way back, they drive along the perimeter fence, close to the main road. Canning stops at one point to investigate a section where the bottom of the fence has been forced up, so that somebody could crawl through. 'Poachers,' he says. 'They were a real problem for a while.' He takes a crowbar from the boot of the car and bashes away at the fence, trying to knock the wire into shape.

'Something I don't understand,' Adam says. 'You talk about poachers, and this is supposed to be a game farm. But where are the animals?'

In all the time he's spent driving or walking around, he has hardly seen anything, except for birds or insects, and once a startled buck.

'Well, my father died just when he'd started stocking the place. There were zebra and kudu and things, but the really big animals weren't installed yet. He was going to have them all, you know, the big five. Then he popped his clogs. It was after that, while they were trying to wind up the estate and look for me and all the rest of it, that the place fell to pieces. That's when the poaching happened, on quite a big scale. We lost a lot of game. When I got here, the farm had pretty much been cleaned out. I signed up the local community, the *Nuwe Hoop* people, to guard the place. But the truth is, they were doing the poaching too. The guards and the thieves were the same people – there's South Africa in a nutshell.'

The cynicism of this last comment takes Adam by surprise; but only because it comes from Canning. He seems so given to flowery declarations of hope and happiness that these little dark asides are shocking. But as time goes by and they get to know each other better, Adam becomes more used to the two warring extremes of Canning's nature. He will hold forth sentimentally on some topic and then, an instant later, the sentiment will turn inside out, becoming abrasive and nasty. His alternating moods of buoyancy and bleakness sometimes follow on so quickly from each other that he seems like two different people joined together.

Almost nothing seems exempt from this withering counterpoint. He frequently goes from rhapsodizing about what a wonderful place the new South Africa is to denouncing it as a den of vice and violence in the next breath. But he is just as equivocal on the subject of people. Many of the visitors to Gondwana are described in glowing terms, then immediately written off as corrupt or inept. Even Baby swings between being amazing and cruel in Canning's emotional vocabulary.

The one subject on which he never shows ambivalence is his father. His feelings there are clean and simple. His father was – and is – a looming, hateful presence, fixed forever in antipathy towards him. It's up to Adam to pick up the contradictions.

'Tell me about this place,' he says to Canning one day. 'You said it was your father's big dream. Why? I mean, what was he trying to do here?'

A heaviness comes over Canning, pressing him down. 'I don't know how to explain,' he says.

'Try.'

'He didn't like other people much, my father. After my mother died, he hated the world even more. Me first and foremost. I think what he wanted was to live in the middle of a huge wilderness, with no people around. Animals, plants, the mountains, the sky – he had this fantasy of himself alone here in nature. He wanted to restore this place to the way it might've looked. You know, before the modern world arrived.'

'Gondwana.'

'Exactly. He did research, he found out what animals and plants used to be here, before people moved through and destroyed it all. He was trying to stock it with those same species, as far as he could. If he had a way to resurrect the dinosaurs, he would've done that too.' Canning mulls on this thought for a while, then his face loosens into familiar sentiment. 'The old bastard,' he says softly, more to himself than anything. But for once, in speaking of his father, there is a discernible trace of longing in his voice.

Now the contradictions in Canning seem to extend backwards, to the shadowy figure of his father behind him. Adam has tried, but he doesn't understand. 'Why did he hate you?' he asks, judging that Canning might be in the mood to talk.

'Because I was fat and useless. Well, you remember how I was. I wasn't the most virile and manly of chaps. He hated weakness, my old man. He couldn't take anything that smelled needy or vulnerable. And I was, as a child. I didn't have a mother, of course.'

'You said she died giving birth to you?'

'Yes. I suppose that's really why he hated me, if you want the truth. He couldn't forgive me for killing her, and then surviving.' He reflects, with emotion that turns into perspicacious calm. 'Actually, he would've probably hated me anyway, whoever I was. That's just the way of it. He loved my mother and when she was gone, there was no love left. Only hate.'

'But this place,' Adam persists. 'It doesn't really fit with his fantasy, does it? He was hardly going to be alone here. He built the lodge, the *rondawels*... he was counting on lots of visitors.'

'Yes. Well. He was a dreamer, but he was also pragmatic. He had to make the dream pay for itself. But he would've kept away.'

'How? He would've been in the thick of it.'

'Not really. You haven't seen his house yet.'

'What do you mean?'

'I'll show you,' Canning says. 'Next weekend.'

And he does. Though Adam doesn't mention it again, on his next visit Canning leads him into the forest behind the lodge. Adam thinks at first that he's being taken to the pool where he swam on the first morning, but they are following a different path, one that comes out at a crooked, crude, tiny house, set at the base of the mountains and made of their same stone, so that it seems to fade into the backdrop. It's like a house in a fairy-tale: a witch's cottage at the heart of the woods.

'There,' Canning says. 'I grew up in that house.'

'But this is incredible. I had no idea it was here.'

'That's how he wanted it. While the game farm ran itself down there, he was going to live up here, out of sight.'

And Adam can see how that might be possible. The mountains, the thick trees: they ring the clearing, closing it off, turning it into an island.

'Who lives here now?'

'Nobody. It's stood empty since he died.'

'Can we go in?'

'Go ahead if you like. It isn't locked. But I'll stay here.'

Canning hangs back with such a palpable air of dread and revulsion that Adam's curiosity feels like betrayal. 'Another time,' he says.

Before they head off into the forest again, Canning looks around at the cleared space. 'My mother's ashes are scattered here,' he says. He tries to speak off-handedly, but his voice catches in his throat; for a second he squeaks like an adolescent.

He does go inside the cottage not long afterwards, but not with Canning. Instead it's Baby who shows him around, like a sardonic guide with a tourist. On almost every weekend that he visits Gondwana, Adam is left alone with Baby at some point. Canning is frequently occupied with business arrangements: there are visitors like Sipho Moloi dropping by, or private telephone calls that have to be made, or letters to be written, or meetings taking place. There are oblique references to contracts and 'understandings', often featuring the mysterious Mr Genov. None of this is properly explained, and Adam assumes all of it is connected with getting the game farm up and running again. Part of the reason he doesn't ask is that his attention is elsewhere: when Canning is occupied like this, he always palms Adam off on Baby.

On the first few occasions they just sit around talking, her boredom infecting them both. But over time he persuades her to go on little strolls into the woods with him. He takes this as a small victory over her cynical disregard for Beauty. On their third or fourth walk they land up, half by accident, at the crooked cottage at the foot of the cliff.

'I really want to go inside,' he tells her.

'So go. There's nothing to see, I've been in already.'

'Come on. Please come with me.'

'Ooh, are you scared?' she teases him, but then she leads the way. Four rooms with small windows, low ceilings. They pass without speaking through a kitchen, a bathroom, in which there is no gentleness, no trace of decoration. There isn't a living-room; this is the house of a man who didn't believe in sitting about. It's all very bare, very basic. There is also no electricity; half-liquefied candles stand petrified in saucers. Unexplained marks stain the walls, like maps to unknown continents, and an indefinable smell hangs heavy on the air. The place feels distinctly haunted, though that might just be the human relics lying around: a pair of leather boots waits expectantly in the passage, still shaped to the feet which wore them, and a thick coat hangs behind the door, like the outline of a body. There are hats and cups on hooks, and a hunting rifle fixed to the wall.

Adam shivers; the house is creepy. It's as if the *Oubaas*, Canning's father, has just stepped outside for a moment and will be returning soon. The air of watchfulness is deepened by multiple glass eyes, all set into the heads of dead and stuffed animals – the surplus, Adam supposes, of the others back at the lodge. There are birds and buck and baboons and even a stray warthog, all mounted on islands of wood in rigid perpetuity. A thronging bestiary, like the menagerie on the ark.

'He liked to kill things, this guy,' Adam says.

'Mmmm.'

'Did you ever meet him – your father-in-law?'

'He was already gone when I arrived on the scene. But from what Kenneth says, he'd have shot and stuffed me as well.'

He laughs uneasily at the image of her, preserved amongst the animals.

'Look at this,' she says. 'Kenneth used to sleep here.'

He takes her word for it, though there is nothing to indicate this was a child's room. A bed, a desk and a cupboard, all empty. The window looks out almost directly onto the cliff, which seals off the view in a blank pane of stone. It is easy to imagine the schoolboy Canning here, at home for the holidays – though it is just as easy to imagine him *not* here, the room cleaned out and used for other things. No, Canning has left no trace; more powerful ghosts are in residence.

And nowhere more so than in the last room. An old double bed with brass rails. The mattress is bare. Almost no other furniture, except for a chest-of-drawers. And on the wall above the bed – very bizarre – the snarling head of a leopard.

'Imagine,' she says. 'Kenneth was made on that bed.'

She has spoken with irony, but the image stays with him. Forty three years ago, the *Oubaas* toiling to his climax between the thighs of his wife. Exactly here, in this spot – the starburst of possible Cannings, only one of which had found its mark.

'Enough,' he says, wanting to escape both the mental picture and the place. 'Let's get out of here.'

On the walk back to the lodge, neither of them talks. Adam finds himself oddly moved by Canning's past, which even now he doesn't fully comprehend. The powerful, raging father; the softer, loving mother – they are like mythical figures, both gone now, between whom the frightened form of the long-ago Canning takes shape. Adam's mood stays heavy until – just as they emerge from the trees – she puts a hand on his shoulder.

'Are you all right?' she says softly.

'Me? Yes... Yes, I'm fine.' He smiles at her, a little too brightly.

They have a curious familiarity, the two of them, which springs up only when they're alone together. Ever since that day when she had asked him to paint her fingernails, there has been an unspoken awareness between them, made – on Adam's side – from yearning and frustration. What Baby feels isn't clear, but she is certainly conscious of the effect that she has on him. She will often engineer some kind of physical contact, asking him to massage her shoulders or brush her hair, and these moments stir danger and desire in him. But she will just as quickly lapse into peevishness, treating him like an unwanted intrusion. He has the sense of a game being played out between them, in which both of them are involved, though only she knows the rules.

But then at other moments – like now – she becomes somebody else again: a tender, gentle person, without guile. Something in him opens and turns to her at times like these. But the moment passes; her hand falls away; they hurry on to the lodge.

Canning is waiting for them, pacing up and down on the *stoep*. 'There you are,' he cries when he sees them. 'I was just starting to get worried.'

Canning often worries when they go off on their walks, but his insecurity has nothing to do with jealousy. Rather, he seems to have an irrational fear that his wife will disappear without a trace when he isn't looking. 'It's crazy, I know,' he confesses to Adam a little later, when they're alone together, 'but it feels like something will take her away if I don't keep watch.'

'You're afraid of losing her. But she's not about to leave you, Canning.'

'You don't think so? Oh, thank you for saying that!'

Adam stares at Canning. His new-old friend is a complex and sometimes interesting man, and though certain aspects of him are irritating, there are also deeper reaches of his character, shading off into torment and heartbreak, which draw sympathy.

'She arrived so suddenly in my life,' he says. 'What's to stop her disappearing just as quickly?'

'Why would she? She's happy with you.'

'Yes, of course she is,' Canning says musingly, but his face is full of doubt. Then his expression changes. 'I'm glad you've had a chance to get to know her a bit, Nappy. I'm glad you two like each other.'

'Yes, she's lovely. I've enjoyed spending time with her.'

He nods solemnly, his eyes shining. 'You two are the people who matter most to me in the world,' he says. 'I want you to be friends!'

Baby is the centre and point of Canning's new life: that much is clear. He talks about her obsessively, usually in exalted, overwrought terms, while a febrile emotion rises in him, like religious fervour. But the dark element to his emotions shows itself too. Often, just after he has spoken about how 'amazing' Baby is, or how she has transformed his life, Canning will lapse into brooding introspection, and then start muttering about how unfeeling she is.

Once he tells Adam: 'I don't think she notices me at all.'

'I'm sure that's not true.'

'No, it is true, Nappy. Believe me. Whole days go by sometimes when she doesn't even speak to me.'

'Well, she does seem very cut off. From everybody.'

'But I'm her husband! I'm married to her!' Canning's face fills up with anguish. 'I had a wife and daughter, you know. I destroyed a happy home to be with her. Look here.' He fumbles for his wallet and takes out a well-handled photograph of a brown-haired woman holding a little girl. She seems, to Adam's eyes, like the wife he would have imagined for Canning: plump like him, a little plain and weary. 'Adele,' he announces. 'And my little girl, Celeste.'

'Where are they now?'

'They're in Johannesburg. But I don't see them any more. Adele has custody and she won't let me near. I'm afraid I didn't behave very well. I caused a lot of pain.'

Adam hands the photograph back. Canning looks at it for a moment, an indefinable expression on his face, before he puts it away. He says, neutrally, 'I gave up a lot to be with Baby.' But a moment later, he relents; he takes Adam by the arm. 'I hope you don't mind me talking like this, Nappy. Please understand – I adore her. I would never give her up.'

'I do understand.'

'I know you do. You're my best friend, Nappy. You're the only person I can talk to like this.'

Adam feels both pity and distaste at these moments; he isn't good with lugubrious confession. But at the same time, he is eager to hear about Baby. The questions he has put to her about herself, her past, have mostly gone unanswered. It seems to be a perverse part of the game between them that she keeps herself mysterious. So he has to rely on whatever Canning tells him to learn anything about her.

As time goes by and their ambiguous connection grows, Canning lets slip a few painful truths. There is the admission one evening, while they're watching the lion eating a fresh carcass in its enclosure, that he and Baby no longer sleep together. In the beginning, he tells Adam, there was quite a lot of passion, but after they got married, Baby didn't want to touch him any more. There were a few stray encounters, but one night she had pushed him away definitively, and it had just never happened again.

'Why not?' Adam says. 'What are her reasons? What does she say?'

'We don't discuss it.'

'You never bring it up?'

'No. It's too painful, Nappy.' Some of that pain is evident in Canning's eyes now; he blinks rapidly to get rid of tears. 'I do try my luck still sometimes,' he adds sadly, 'but it never works.'

Despite himself, Adam is touched both by sympathy and a treacherous stab of joy, quickly concealed. And Canning himself is afraid he's revealed too much. On the walk back to the lodge from the lion's enclosure, he suddenly says, 'Nappy... what I told you just now. It stays between us, okay?'

'Of course, Canning. That goes without saying.'

'Thank you.' He puts a hand on Adam's shoulder, and the heat of his palm is like the secret brand of friendship. 'I haven't shared that with anybody else, Nappy. Not anybody in the whole world!'

'I'm glad you feel you can confide in me, Canning.'

'I do, Nappy. I trust you completely.'

Which must be true, because other revelations follow on, just a week later. This time the honesty is fuelled by alcohol. The two of them are sitting around the fire under the oak tree, after their usual Saturday night meal. Baby has disappeared, into the lodge or back to the *rondawel*. Canning throws another log onto the coals, and the flames jump up, throwing shadows, gigantic and distorted, across the grass. From the roof, the silent peacocks observe. After a long silence he tells Adam, 'You know, her name isn't really Baby.'

This announcement has been offered up freely, leading on from nothing that went before. Adam freezes, afraid to move in case it stops Canning from unburdening himself.

'She chose that name because of a character on television. A soap opera, I think. She liked the character because... oh, I don't remember. All of it,' he says, his voice rising suddenly to a pitch of pain, 'all of it is a big, rotten lie!'

Adam has never seen such raw emotion in him before. A pause follows, in which Canning's breathing calms down, and his body seems somehow to shrink. Then he says quietly, 'I'm part of it too. I cover for her. I keep up the pretence.'

Adam finally stirs himself, unsticking his dry lips from each other. It seems safe by now to speak. 'But what's the pretence?'

A shiver goes through Canning, but the truth is pouring forth easily now, almost without effort. 'When I first met her,' he says, 'she was working as a call-girl in Jo'burg. That story of hers, about how we met socially, through a mutual friend – it isn't true. Or it's only true in a certain way. A *euphemistic* way.'

'Really?' Adam says. His attempt at quiet neutrality fails him; he can hear the shock in his own voice.

Canning must hear it too, because he glances worriedly at Adam and immediately starts to retreat. 'Please understand, Nappy, she wasn't a common street whore. No, she worked for an escort service. Quite a high-class place.'

'I'm not... I'm not passing judgement.'

'And she had things to overcome. I promise you, Nappy, her early life was terrible. I could tell you stories that would make you cry. She comes from a hard place. She had a bad, tough start. She's travelled a long way in her life.'

'I believe you,' Adam says, and he does. All kinds of unexplained details are falling into place – the way she speaks, that held, controlled, fabricated voice of no fixed abode. Or the occasional flash of an underlying hardness in her face, little splashes of vulgarity now and then. But more than anything else, it's the secrecy that makes sense: her need to conceal everything about the past.

'Please, please,' Canning says, very concerned now, 'don't think less of her. Don't let this change the way you see her.'

'It won't.' But of course it changes everything; he will never see her in the same way again.

'Because she really is remarkable, Nappy. If you only knew everything... my wife is amazing.'

'I know she is.'

And, for the first time, it seems true. Adam doesn't feel alienated from her: on the contrary, a kinship between them has been strengthened. He is not the only one whose connection to Canning is built on lies; he is not the only impostor. But the burning curiosity he had felt about her has suddenly faded; he's not sure he wants to know all the tacky details of her life. He can imagine only too well what such a story might involve: the upward struggle out of poverty, the ruthless reliance on her beauty to create opportunities for herself, the sordid rooms and squalid situations she would have passed through... No, it is better not to hear all that. It is possible, he thinks, to spoil everything. It is possible to know too much.

For some reason, there is only one question that still seems urgently important. 'Tell me,' he says, leaning forward to put a hand on Canning's arm, 'what is her real name?'

Canning looks at him and opens his mouth to answer, but at this moment Baby emerges from the lodge and comes walking towards them. She passes across one of the lights on the front *stoep*, and for an instant her body is a dark mass in silhouette, impossible to measure; then she is just a woman again, diminutive and gorgeous and angry. She throws herself down into a chair.

'What are you two talking about?' she says.

'Nothing,' Canning says.

And it's as if they have, in fact, been talking about nothing.

11

Summer waxes to its height. The daylight seems perpetually fixed at noon. On the hills outside town a fire breaks out and it burns for days, casting a pall of smoke across the sun, glowing red at night like a weird galaxy hanging low in the firmament. The end of the year comes, and the coloured lights, left hanging on the streetlamps from the previous season, are switched on. There's a great deal of public drunkenness. Fanie Prinsloo's hotel advertises a gut-buster Christmas platter. The staff at the supermarket in town wear festive paper hats and some of the windows in the main street are garnished with glitter and cheap ornaments. But these little pockets of enforced jollity only emphasize the sun-stricken emptiness of the dirt roads beyond, and the melancholy distances spreading away to the horizon.

A few days before Christmas there is a knock on the back door. It's the first time since his unexpected visit that the blue man has approached so directly, but he's not coming to stay. Instead, with an air of coy embarrassment, he works his way up to asking whether Adam might be free on Christmas Day. 'Because I've got this big turkey I'm going to cook, and I thought you might like...'

'Oh, I can't, I'm sorry,' Adam says quickly. 'I'm going to be with my friends.'

'*Ja, ja,* I thought so... I know you're away every weekend... but I just took a chance.'

'Thank you very much. I would've liked that.'

'*Ja*, well. Another time.' Blom glares at him with sorrowful accusation. 'You still haven't come to see my poems.'

'Your poems?'

'You remember, I told you...'

'Yes, I do remember. I'll come over soon, I promise. I've just been very busy.' He does have a vague recollection, somewhere in a previous conversation, of this enigmatic talk about poems, but he has no desire to pay his neighbour a visit. He experiences an odd flash of anger towards this old man, advertising his loneliness so awkwardly at the back door. But as the blue figure plods away, he looks so solitary and vulnerable that Adam feels guilty. Blom sitting by himself, eating his turkey: it's an image to wring the heart.

Adam has been invited to spend a few days out at Gondwana, from Christmas to New Year. He has been looking forward to it as a quiet, private idyll, away from the false festivity in the town. But when the time comes, it turns out to be raucous, with a great deal of alcohol flowing. Sipho Moloi is there with his wife, and another couple, Enoch and Ruth Nandi. There is a lot of laughter and back-slapping, a lot of blue cocktails being passed around. For the first time Baby seems actually to enjoy herself; she becomes voluble and animated, but Adam is subdued. He even considers going back to town.

By the time New Year rolls around, some of the revelry has thinned out. Sipho and his wife have departed; only the Nandis are left. On the stroke of midnight Canning asks everybody to raise their glasses to the great year that lies ahead, and all of them look at each other with a significance through which the promise of future prosperity runs like a lode of silver.

All except Adam. He doesn't understand the endless arcane whispers about business, none of which appear to manifest in any obvious progress. Quite the opposite: everything around him seems stalled and suspended, waiting for release.

The party breaks up at about two in the morning. On the way to bed, Adam stops to look at the occasional flare of headlamps in the sky, a surreal sight which never fails to mesmerize him. A moment or two later Canning slaps a limp arm around his shoulders and Adam catches a familiar whiff of that strong personal smell – sweat and aftershave.

'Ah, Nappy,' he says. 'My old friend. It feels so right that you're around to watch all of this come together.'

'What's been holding you up?'

'How do you mean?'

'Well, the game farm is set and ready. It just needs to be re-stocked, as far as I can see. Why all the scheming and plotting?'

'The game farm? I don't follow you.' Canning blinks and then his expression changes, becoming shifty and shrewd. 'But I'm not making a game farm.'

'You're not? But I thought...'

'No. I have big plans, Nappy. But not in that direction.'

'Well, what then?'

'I can't tell you yet. But I will, very soon. We're just waiting for a few bureaucratic gears to shift. Land to be rezoned and so forth.'

'Rezoned as what?'

For a second, Canning hesitates. His expression strains in the direction of confession, then snaps back into place. 'I can't tell you,' he says again. 'Not yet.'

But very soon afterwards, he does.

*

Canning has mentioned several times that he wants to take Adam on a special walk, to the source of the river. This will mean a difficult hike into the mountains, through water a lot of the way. The idea of it is intimidating, and they have kept putting it off. But one weekend towards the end of January, Canning is fired up with the notion of tackling the river. It's not clear why the prospect has taken such firm hold all of a sudden, but Adam agrees that Saturday will be a good day.

They are up just before dawn, heading into the *kloof*. The departure point is the pool where Adam swam the first morning. It had seemed to him then that the river arrived fully formed, but once they have crossed the first barrier of stones, they find themselves following a blue road between high grey walls. There are places where they can step on rocks, but in between they must wade or swim. Sometimes the water is shallow, sometimes it is chest deep. It is cold and powerful, and the effect of so much noise and force, rushing relentlessly against them, is both exhilarating and terrifying. It seems possible that anything might happen: the earth could close on them, or a giant wave could roll down the gorge.

Although they are constantly toiling uphill, the mountains climb higher and higher around them, till eventually they are in a narrow channel, with the sky a shining strip far above. The current is so strong that Adam fears he might lose his footing and be carried back all the way to where he started. But they emerge at last, over a stone lip, into a wide, dark pool, almost a lake, which lies very still in a basin of rock, like a huge eye staring up at the sun. It isn't possible to go further. The mountain walls have come together; they are at the very top of the *kloof*.

'But where does the water come from?' Adam says.

'In there.' Canning points to the far edge of the pool. There is an overhang in the cliff, and underneath it the water and the shadow close into one. From this cave the river wells up, without appearing to move.

Adam shivers. He had expected something different: a bubbling fountain bursting out of the ground, something clear and harmless. But this place is somehow sinister. He can imagine too vividly the dark subterranean tunnels, winding deeper and deeper under the mountains, towards some echoing, ultimate womb.

It has been their plan to picnic here, but there is nowhere pleasant or friendly to sit. They cast around among the dripping stones, till Canning looks up and spies a ledge, halfway up the side of the rock wall. 'What about there?' he says.

They have to climb. It's not as sheer as it looks, and there are crevices and footholds along the way, but a fall would be potentially fatal. Adam is fitter and more agile than Canning, and he arrives at the ledge a full couple of minutes in the lead. It's been worth the effort: there is sun up here, and a spectacular view, and he settles himself to wait.

As Canning comes up, wheezing and panting, it happens. His foot slips, he loses his grip, his eyes widen in fear. He is actually in the act of falling. The drop underneath him at this point is smooth and deep, with jagged rocks at the bottom. For an instant, time stands still. Then Adam's hand shoots out and grabs hold of Canning's hand; he pulls him up to safety.

It takes a few moments for Canning to speak. Then all he can say is, 'Thank you.'

Adam nods. They are behaving calmly, with small words and gestures, but they both have a sense of an utterly different future flashing past them and away. In this other branch of fate, Canning falls, and everything that follows on is different. But the moment passes, marked by the smallest of exchanges.

'I think you might have saved my life there,' Canning says.

'I think I might.'

Then they are sitting side by side on the ledge, two middle-aged men drying off in the sun. They are both wearing shorts and running shoes; their T-shirts have been put away in a small backpack that Canning carries. Adam casts a furtive sideways look at his companion, to compare. Canning's body is flabby and pale, a little endomorphic and sexless, his big belly overhanging his shorts. Next to him, Adam feels lean and thin; he feels almost desirable.

'Isn't this something?' Canning says.

They have a view not only down into the stony hollow in the mountains, but over the top of a ridge to the simmering plains in the distance. The world is both rising and falling around them.

'How did you find this place?'

'I came here with Lindile,' Canning says. 'You know, my first – '

'Your first black friend, yes.' Adam is irritated by these constant references to a halcyon, unfallen time.

Canning doesn't seem to notice. But perhaps he is more aware than he shows. After they have settled themselves properly, and unpacked their picnic lunch from the backpack and have sunk into a contented midday reverie, he suddenly says, 'Enjoy this while you can. It's not going to last much longer.'

'What do you mean?'

'There are big changes coming here, Nappy. It's about to happen at last.'

'What is?'

Canning is halfway through eating a sandwich; he puts it down and wipes his mouth, but there are still stray crumbs clinging to his lips. 'I'm turning this place into a golf course,' he says.

'Excuse me?'

But the only answer is a nod: solemn and determined.

Adam laughs. It's a hollow sound, reverberating in the rocky basin. But as the resonances die away, he understands how unfunny this proposal is. His mind is going backwards, through the preceding months, making sense of little unexplained moments and details. He has assumed that all of it – the business talk, the secret letters and visits from people like Sipho Moloi – is about getting the game farm up and running again, but now he realizes: it's about replacing the game farm with something else.

'Canning,' he says. 'You can't.'

'Why not?'

'This place… the farm… it'll be completely ruined.'

'Yes.'

'But why would you want to do that?'

'Revenge,' Canning says.

'Revenge on who?'

'You know who, Nappy. You know better than anybody.' Canning leans towards him, and for a second Adam sees his own image, dually reflected in the other man's eyes. 'Remember what you told me,' he says.

For a nauseating instant the truth wells up in Adam's mouth, ready to be disgorged. *No*, he wants to say, *I don't remember what I told you, I don't remember any of it, not even who you were*. But he doesn't speak and Canning prattles on, oblivious.

'Of course it's not just revenge. I have healthy capitalist instincts too, I'll make a lot of money out of the deal.' Almost by reflex, he touches his pockets when he says the word 'money', but he's carrying no small change today. 'I love this place too, in my own way. You know that – you've seen it. But in the end, it still belongs to my father. It's his big dream, not mine.' His voice drops, taking on a dreamy quality of its own. 'You know,' he says, 'I sometimes imagine my old man, looking down at me. I know that's not possible, but I imagine it anyway. I like to think of how helpless and furious he feels when he sees my black wife. I like to think of his rage and despair when he sees this place in my hands. And I go to sleep happy at night when I think of how I'll dismantle his dream. Bit by bit, piece by piece. I'm going to savour every second of it.'

This has been spoken so simply that it cancels out any reply. And as revenge, it can hardly be bettered. The vision of a primitive, barbaric landscape will be completely wiped out. In its place there will be a sculpted, artificial fantasy of fairways and bunkers and putting greens, planted with little flags. Desolation flowers briefly in Adam. The emptiness, the spiritual vapidity, are hard to express; the word that comes to him is *desecration.*

But he doesn't say that. Instead he mutters, 'It's the wrong terrain, surely...? Too dry and hot.'

'They played golf on the moon, Nappy, you know that? They play golf in the snow, with red balls. You can play golf just about anywhere. You need grass for the tees and the greens, but otherwise you can use almost any terrain. And here the plan is to make the semi-desert conditions a *feature* of the course.' Canning warms to his theme; there's no stopping him now. 'Look, you need about a hundred and thirty hectares to make a twenty-seven hole course. We've easily got that in land that fronts the river. So the course will be designed near to the water. Oh, and guess who's designing it for us?' He speaks a name triumphantly that means nothing to Adam. When he gets no reaction, he says, 'He's very famous, Nappy. One of the best-known golfers in the world.'

'I told you, Canning. I know nothing about golf.'

'Well, all right. But you've got to appreciate the beauty of the scheme. Just listen to this.'

And he's off again, animated and ardent, laying out his plans. Adam tries to listen, but his mind can only catch at fragments. How the lodge will become a luxury hotel. How half of the current land will be sold off to raise funds to construct another two hundred and fifty *rondawels* of varying sizes. How the most important principle will be exclusivity. Membership will be very expensive and limited and the only people allowed to play will be members and their guests, or hotel guests. No stay, no play.

How they will exploit the interest in fossils by building a dinosaur theme park.

How they will put up an equestrian centre and riding trails. How they plan a small zoo, with whatever animals are left on the farm.

How they are looking at building a casino.

How the khaki-clad workers from *Nuwe Hoop* will be right there, on tap, to work as caddies and groundskeepers and general staff at the hotel. The satellite village has been *very* conveniently placed, at a distance but also close enough. It's a win-win situation for everybody.

How the new road, the pass over the mountains, is projected to bring six times the current amount of traffic through here in just two years.

How membership – has he said this already? – will be very limited. Three hundred places only. Hence the name of the course. Ingadi three hundred.

Ingadi means 'garden' in Zulu.

'Personally,' Canning says, 'I wanted a Xhosa name. This was never a Zulu area, of course. Eluhlangeni – isn't that a beautiful word? – means 'in the place of creation' or some such shit in Xhosa. That's the name I'd use. Ingadi just doesn't have the same ring. Not much poetry to it, I'm sure you'll agree. But Enoch Nandi is our black empowerment partner, and he's a Zulu, and he wants a Zulu name. So Ingadi it is. Who am I to argue, I'm only the dumb whitey who's put up the land. So, hey, cool, whatever.'

When Canning stops talking at last, the silence is profound. Adam looks out over the nearby ridge to the sun-baked plains, but now the vista has altered. He can only see what will come.

'What are you thinking?' Canning says at last.

'Just that... all of this is going to end.'

'Yes. I suppose it is.' He slaps Adam on the back. 'But don't worry, Nappy. We'll stay in touch. I'm planning to move down to Cape Town very soon, and we'll see a lot of each other. You won't be stuck out here for ever, will you? Well, I'm glad I told you. It's been weighing on me. It's going to be public knowledge very soon, so I wanted to let you know first.' He dusts bits of bread off his lap and starts packing the picnic away. 'We'd better think about heading back.'

Adam hates Canning all the way down the *kloof*. He stares at that chunky pink back in front of him, and keeps replaying that moment in his mind, when Canning had almost fallen and he, Adam, had put a hand out to save him. In his fantasies now, he doesn't extend a hand.

Canning is whistling an inane melody, the same three or four bars, over and over, and the tall enclosing walls echo and amplify it. By the time they emerge into Gondwana again, the sun is going down, and the sky is a bloodbath of violent colour overhead. As they go through the woods toward the lodge, Canning falls back into step with Adam. 'By the way. I wanted to say... I would encourage you to buy in, I would make a plan to get you membership. But the fact is, it's not a good idea.' He puts an arm conspiratorially over Adam's shoulders and draws him in. 'This is just between ourselves, Nappy. Not a word to anybody. But Mr Genov – he's my partner in this, you know – wants to *lose* money with this scheme. Not right now, but in a couple of years. I don't know the details, I don't *want* to know... but when the time is right, it's all going to turn belly-up. For tax reasons, or maybe he just needs to move money around... I don't ask. I'll be long gone by then.'

This is too much. The travesty that Canning is cooking up is made of greed and absurdity, with a big moral hollowness at the core. An infantile desire is rising in Adam, to throw himself on the ground and wail and beat with his fists, but he does nothing, he just keeps on walking passively under Canning's sheltering arm. It's only when they have come to where Baby is waiting outside the lodge, and Canning has clapped his hands together and suggested he mix a round of cocktails for everybody, that Adam's moment of rebellion takes place. In a small, strangled voice he says, 'I wish you wouldn't call me Nappy.'

'Sorry...?'

'My name is Adam. I wish you'd call me by my name.'

The note of anguish has been fetched up from deep inside, all the way from his childhood, and it silences both of them. They are staring at him, stupefied, as he goes on half-heartedly:

'I hate being called Nappy. It's a cruel, stupid name... I've always hated it.'

'Adam,' Canning says at last, 'I'm sorry.'

He is immediately overcome by shame and self-consciousness. He is making a big scene about nothing. 'It doesn't matter. Forget it.'

'No. No. I didn't realize – '

'Leave it, Canning. I shouldn't have spoken – '

'Of course you should. I apologize. How insensitive I've been, please forgive me...'

They make up clumsily in the twilight. Adam just wants this moment to pass, but as Canning embraces him, patting his back and murmuring into his ear, he gazes over his shoulder and into Baby's eyes. A certain look goes between them.

*

Things are awkward for a while. It's all *Adam* this and *Adam* that, his name being pointedly wielded. They get through their evening around the fire and then he makes an excuse and heads for bed, but he can't sleep. His mind is full of the devastation that is to come. Twisting and turning, he sees people in checked pants, driving little carts, carrying striped umbrellas, tramping all over the landscape. It feels like betrayal, but of what exactly he isn't sure.

It takes a few hours before it strikes him that the betrayal is personal. He's the one who's been stabbed in the back. There is no reason for it, but he has come to feel that this extraordinary green oasis belongs to him; it reminds him, on an almost cellular level, of the landscape of his childhood. His visits out here have been like a return to a lost, forgotten part of his life. He has been thinking that it will never come to an end. But now he knows that it *will* end, and probably soon. And the person responsible is sleeping next door, perhaps ten feet away: Canning's snores carry through the darkness – leisurely, unconscious, the snores of a drunk man. Adam has to sit up and block his ears.

Canning. Even now, it is hard to conjure up his face. He is a powerful blandness that came sidling in from out of frame, and now occupies the whole picture. He seemed so nebulous, so trustworthy – but he cannot be trusted. All of the talk about how important Adam is, what an old dear friend he is; yet now he is to be sidelined again, exiled from the garden, back to where he came from. Canning wanted Adam as a witness, nothing more.

But as a witness to *what*, exactly? The word 'revenge' has been mentioned, there have been cryptic allusions to an important conversation between them, yet Adam is no clearer now than he was at the beginning. Canning's father is dead, and you cannot take revenge on the dead. What's happening is being played out, on some useless symbolic level, for the benefit of an audience. Well, Adam doesn't want to be part of the audience any more. It comes to him now that he should pack his things and leave this place and never, never come back. It was a mistake to think that he could fit in, however tangentially, with these people; they are too different from him, too caught up in their avarice and ambition. He has nothing in common with them.

The snoring from next door is more powerful than ever. There is no chance now that he will be able to fall asleep, and no point, in any case, in waiting for morning. Better to leave in the dark, without goodbye; that way, the departure will certainly be final.

Having made up his mind, he moves into action. He switches on the lamp next to the bed. He has no idea what the time is, but it feels like the dead hollow after midnight. He gets dressed and moves around the room, packing up all the clothes and other bits and pieces he's left here over the last while. In a few minutes the room is bare and functional again: an ordinary hotel room, ready for the next guest.

When he steps out the door, onto the grass, another figure is standing there, dressed in a luminous white robe. He gets such a fright that he drops his bag, but even before it hits the ground he recognizes her.

'I heard you moving around,' she says.

'Yes, I, uh… I just stepped out for some air.'

They both look down at his bag, but by unspoken resolve neither of them mentions it. They move a few steps towards each other, then stop again.

'The snoring is terrible,' she says. 'Did it wake you too?'

'Actually, I've been awake for a while.'

There is silence between them after that. He moves closer to her, but stops again, unsure of himself. He can feel the heat coming off the front of her body; he can hear the sound of her breathing. 'I want…' he says, 'I would like…' but his nerve fails him. It is easier, somehow, to act: he walks the last few steps towards her and then they are grabbing at each other, blundering and fumbling in the dark. Their mouths miss, then realign and collide. He has an instant of clarity: this is what they've been moving towards, since the first time he saw her in almost this very spot.

Fusion, and then confusion: both of them hear a break in the snoring from the *rondawel* behind them. Canning makes a mumbling, glottal sound in his throat; he is rising towards the surface. They pull away from each other, though they stay half-embraced. Their moment is tapering to a close.

She puts a hand up against his chest and speaks smoothly, efficiently. 'He has an important phone call tomorrow afternoon,' she says. 'It'll take a long time. We'll go for a walk together to the cottage – his father's place.'

He shakes his head slowly. 'No,' he says. 'Not there.'

'It's the one place he'll never come to.'

Part of his mind considers this, admiring the cunning of its logic, even as he watches her let go of him and walk swiftly away, back inside the dark room. He himself doesn't move, standing there in the deep blue shadows, waiting for something, he's not sure what, to show him which direction to go in. He could continue with his exit, pick up his bag, head on towards the car and the road to town. The other way is indistinct, though he understands too well what she's proposed. But he *can't* – can he? – go through with it. To betray Canning like that. In his childhood home.

He'll never know.

'But *I* will.'

Bear it, then.

'He doesn't deserve it. A shabby betrayal.'

His whole life is a betrayal too.

'Of what?'

But he knows what. He pictures the landscape again, plundered and deformed, sold out for money and revenge. And this image leads him now to a deeper sadness in himself: he has moved here, to the countryside, because he wanted to speak with childlike simplicity about nature, but he finally understands he's been deserted by that voice. A great complexity has sprung up between him and the world. His childhood – the time when things could be simple and beautiful – has gone for ever, corrupted and covered over by all the accretions of his life, till it has disappeared from sight. He can no longer look at a river, a branch, a stone, and see it for what it is. Instead he sees his own history, written in metaphors. He has lost his innocence, and in this moment Canning is responsible.

He picks up his bag, he goes back inside.

12

There is something in a secret that wants to be told. The guilt doesn't touch Adam until later, when he's back at home. Then what happened, what he did, begins to eat at him.

That was dirty. The wife of your oldest friend.

'He's not my oldest friend! I don't even remember him from back then.'

Does that make it better? He trusts you.

'But he can't be trusted himself.'

What has he ever done to you? He's looked after you, invited you in, fed you… and now this.

'It happened, all right? It wasn't planned, it just happened.'

Not true. Of course it was planned.

'I couldn't just walk away.'

Why not?

He needs a human listener, somebody fallible who understands. Of course, he doesn't explain it to himself like this. He doesn't tell himself: *I have a guilty conscience, I have nobody to talk to, therefore I am seeking out my neighbour, who is a man I barely know*. But these are the reasons, when Blom is in his workshop one night, that Adam stands thinking for a long moment before crossing through the fence. Lifting the wire strands and stepping through is easy, but he feels he has done something forbidden.

He approaches the shed cautiously. The metallic shrieking is loud and he can see the radiant rain of sparks. But he's not prepared for the weirdness of what he encounters when he gets to the doorway. In his blue overalls and goggles, in the glare of the blowtorch, Blom is an apparition from another planet. He is bent over a twisted piece of metal, with metal all around him, and fire in his hand. He is so much a part of what he's doing that he doesn't see Adam there, until he hears his name.

Then Blom gets a terrible fright. He goes berserk, screaming and flailing and trying to run, the blowtorch scorching a wild signature on the air. It is comical as well as terrifying, but eventually he goes quiet and stands very still, breathing.

'I'm sorry,' Adam says.

'I thought...' Blom says, '... I thought...'

I thought you'd come to kill me.

Fear has a stink, indistinguishable from the smell of burned metal. But almost immediately the mood turns: the blue man is delighted to see him. A smile breaks out on his old leather face. 'You came to visit me in the end,' he says. 'Let me get the brandy to celebrate!'

Adam waits in the shed, while Blom hurries off to the house. There is only one chair, small and lopsided, which he perches on carefully, looking around. The shed is a low, cramped place, lit by a gas-lamp hung up in the corner. The effect is stark, with the metal walls and the tools and the pieces of scrap, all bleached of colour against their own shadows, like a photographic negative. When Blom comes back, he too looks unnaturally pale, drained of colour and blood by the light. He pours brandy and Coke into enamel mugs for both of them, then crouches down close to Adam, leaning against the wall. 'You want to see my poems?' he says.

'All right. Show me.'

Adam has imagined some kind of conversation between them, however stilted and uneven, from which his confession might evolve. He hasn't banked on this childlike excitement from his neighbour, who is rummaging amongst the burglar bars and security gates, all in various stages of construction, picking out from between the straight lines and right angles a series of other, less evident shapes. Adam has been aware of them, till now, as small, inexplicable knots at the edge of his consciousness, but he hasn't looked directly at them until Blom starts setting them down in front of him. Even then he has to stare hard before he can make them out.

'My poems!'

The blue man is full of pride. And it does occur to Adam that these imitations of the natural world – animals and insects and trees and stars – are what he himself is aspiring to, in words. But the metal sculptures are obvious and sentimental images, the kind of African kitsch that tourists might buy at the side of the road.

That judgement must show in his face, because Blom slumps visibly, becoming downcast. 'Not poems like yours,' he mutters. 'Just my little hobby.'

'No, no,' Adam says quickly. 'They're very nice.'

'Just passing the time. Nothing important.' With the tip of his toe, the blue man knocks one of his creations on its side.

'No, Blom… *Mr* Blom… I like them. It's just that I never expected something like this from you.'

And it is truly surprising – that such tough, tobacco stained hands should have given rise to anything imaginary. Blom is a little mollified, but a silence has opened between them now, full of distance and nearness, in which the only sound is an occasional slurp of brandy. This hasn't worked out as Adam wanted; he hasn't voiced any of his guilt. Instead it's his neighbour who seems on the verge of some urgent revelation.

'You really like them?' he says eventually.

'Yes, I do. They're very pretty.'

He stares at Adam for a moment, as if weighing him up. Then he says suddenly, 'I made one for you.' He goes to the corner of the shed and takes out one final sculpture; he gives it carefully to Adam, as if it might break.

And this one is different. It is indisputably *real*. Not pretty at all – full of spikes and power, there's something unwholesome about it, though it's hard to say what, because there's no discernible outline or shape. Adam is silenced by it, not least because of one particular element that Blom has worked in.

'I used the peacock feather you gave me.'

'Yes, I see that.'

'Are you angry?'

'Why would I be angry?'

But he does, in fact, feel somehow angry. There is a glowing eye-shape in the plumage, which seems to stare directly at him. The sense of accusation is profound. Neither of them speaks for a long time and then Adam gets quickly to his feet.

'Well, thank you for everything,' he says. 'I'd better be going.'

The whole encounter has been off-key, and he doesn't try to conceal his distaste for the horrible metal gift. He has to fight a desire to hurl it away – into the weeds and darkness – as he crosses back to his side of the fence. No, it has been a very unsatisfactory visit.

And it becomes even more so in his mind, every time he goes past the sculpture. He has set it down, for want of a better place, on top of his notebook. Whenever he walks through the room he sees it there – or it, somehow, sees him. Sometimes he stops and glowers at it. The guilt of what's happened with Baby is somehow embodied in it, inseparable from the taste of cheap brandy. Around the gorgeous colours of the peacock feather, the contorted shape is eloquent with its torque and twist; it disturbs him in a deep, wordless way. But however much he stares, the metal never softens into meaning. In the end, he always walks away.

*

His affair with Baby – if that's what it is – changes everything. He continues to go out to Gondwana for his weekly visits, ostensibly to see Canning. But his real motive now is the occasional hour or two that he spends at the cottage with Baby. There is obvious secrecy and danger to these assignations, but they become easier to arrange as Canning is drawn further into plans and preparations for his golf course. His mind is increasingly abstracted, he must deal with more and more meetings and phone calls. At these times he throws Adam and Baby together. 'Will you two look after each other?' he might say. 'Why don't you go for a walk?' It's almost as if he's complicit in what they've set up between them.

So the opportunities come freely and seemingly naturally, till it's possible almost to feel relaxed about it. Nevertheless, Baby keeps up a cool, convincing front of detachment from Adam while they're in public. And she often insists that he goes ahead of her to wait, so that they're not seen arriving at the cottage together.

Sometimes the wait is a long one and on a couple of occasions she has failed to turn up at all. He comes to know the drab, stark interior of the place very well. Everything in it is there for a purpose. The materials are what must have been immediately to hand, from the thatch of the roof to the stone walls to the floors made of mud and dung – polished, so Baby has told him, with ox blood. The one possible concession to aesthetic taste is the assortment of dead animals, standing or hanging around in dubious decoration.

Adam thinks he has, by extension, a sense of the man who lived here too. Beauty and violence together: it would be easy to hate the old man. But Adam has a sneaking fascination with him. It's his guilty secret that he suspects they might have been alike; that they might have understood one another far too well. The house resembles, in its roughness and simplicity, the one where Adam lives in town. But the affinity runs deeper than that. He can painfully imagine the hours and hours of loneliness here, generating who knows what spectres as company. And Adam can also embrace, with a whole heart, the fantasy of being at the middle of a huge wilderness, with its amoral Beauty. The poems he could write here! Canning's father liked to shoot animals, of course, which is a pity; but it could've been his way of fixing that essential Beauty in place. Perhaps not so different to a poem, when you came down to it: just another kind of shooting.

For Baby, the house has no history, no shadows; it's just a backdrop to her meetings with Adam. They meet in order to fuck (no other word for it), always in the *Oubaas*'s bed, where – he keeps remembering – Canning was probably conceived. He notices, after that first time, that the place has been swept out and linen has been spread on the mattress. A pragmatic arrangement. And of course, when he is lying on the bed, under the stuffed yellow snarl of the leopard on the wall, the world shrinks to a small zone of significance for him too. But he cannot shake off – even in these most intimate moments – the idea of a connection between Canning's father and himself that passes through his black lover, using her as a medium.

He looks forward to their sessions with a kind of primal excitement. There is an intensity to their joinings that borders on violence. Often he discovers marks and bruises on himself afterwards, made perhaps by her nails, her teeth. He can never remember receiving these tiny injuries; when he's in bed with her, the clamour of consciousness draws in on a point of white heat, where past and future converge. He becomes somebody else, a creature he doesn't know: this stranger-self is a powerful, goatish, reckless figure, who fornicates without restraint and talks dirty and doesn't care what damage he's doing.

It isn't love; it's something else. At certain moments it feels closer to hate. Or rapture, maybe – or just a kind of furious narcissism. He is throwing off all the restraints and inhibitions that have shackled and deformed him his whole life. It's strong and scary, like catching fire. Afterwards he comes back slowly, to the world and to himself. These returns are painful, with words taking shape in him, and everything that attaches to the words.

Later, they lapse into murmurous conversations on the bed while they lie twined together. A genuine tenderness does enter things here, deepened by its absence elsewhere. This kind of languid indulgence is cued into him by the past; by previous involvements he's had. But even in her most unguarded moments, she is never entirely disarmed. He wonders how many other beds she has lain on like this, with how many other men; and he doesn't quite believe anything she says.

When he'd first met her, he had wanted to know about her life. But since Canning has told him too much, he doesn't want to know more. His curiosity has frozen on the edge of a deep drop, and she notices the change. Once she says to him:

'Why don't you ask questions any more? You used to bother me all the time. 'Where do you come from?' 'Who chose your name?' You asked about everything. And now nothing.'

'What I really wanted,' he says, 'was this. What we're doing.' He lifts a strand of her hair, winds it around his finger, tugs gently. 'What does anything else matter?'

'It might matter a lot,' she says. 'Ask me something.'

'What?'

'Anything. Ask me any question you like, and I'll tell you the truth. But just one question.'

In this moment he believes her sincerity. There is something hard and pointed in her stare, like two nails pushing into his flesh. Under the challenge he senses in her a reckless desire to tell the truth, to reveal herself, and he draws back from it.

'Why did you marry Canning?' he asks.

She goes very still and after a second she sits up. 'Why do you call him that?' she says. 'Why don't you use his first name?'

'First name, surname, what does it matter?'

'It's childish. You do it nastily. You don't like him.'

'I do like him,' he says, and hears the complicated idiocy of his position. Nevertheless, in spite of everything, it's true: he *does* like Canning. At least in part.

She rolls off the bed and starts to gather up her scattered clothing. After she's dressed she will touch up her makeup. He knows this single-minded routine; he has watched it numerous times; he's fascinated and a little scared at how instantly she leaves him behind.

'I asked my one question,' he says. 'You didn't answer.'

'Any *other* question.'

'No. That's the one.'

Without looking at him, her voice blank, she says, 'Because I fell in love with him.'

'That isn't true.'

She laughs at him – a gutsy sound with the rattle of cruelty in it. She's halfway through putting on her lipstick and there's a bright red smear across her teeth. 'Are you jealous?' she says. 'You poor baby. He's my husband.'

'Come on, you don't even notice him. You hardly touch him.'

'Not in public. But we have our moments.'

'That's not what he says. He told me you never fuck any more.' The word splats rudely onto the floor between them; he has spoken on impulse, from a sudden upwelling of envy. He is almost instantly sorry, but she only laughs again.

'Do you believe that?' she says.

'Why would he lie about it?'

'Kenneth is very dramatic. He exaggerates everything, in a good or a bad way. Haven't you noticed that?'

'There's no sexy spark between the two of you,' he says. 'You can't fool me, it's obvious. You're more like brother and sister.'

She considers this seriously, before telling him: 'There's a lot of love possible between a brother and a sister. I owe Kenneth a lot. I won't forget what he's done for me.'

'What has he done for you?'

'I've got a good life now, Adam. It didn't used to be like this.'

'How did it used to be?'

He has asked too urgently; her face seals against him. They have come full circle by now. 'Always questioning,' she says coldly. 'Always digging. Can't you just be happy with what you've got right now?'

'No. I want a future as well.'

'What kind of future can you offer me?'

The question silences him, with its thin edge of sarcasm and its underlying truth. He can offer her nothing. His bank account has dwindled to four figures now; his back yard is still full of weeds. Yet he burns with an adolescent rage to be driving with her on an open road somewhere, the rejected past behind them, an unknown destiny ahead.

'Is it so important?' he says at last. 'To have money? To have... *things*?'

'It's everything,' she answers simply.

'Not for me,' he says. 'To hell with that.'

He is angry, and he means it. To hell with the pair of them, and their brother-sister love; to hell with their money and their golf course!

'You talk about the future,' he tells her, 'as if I mean something to you. But all along, you and he have been planning to sell this place, after you've finished wrecking it. I'm just a diversion for you, a pastime. I don't matter to you.'

'You do matter,' she says. 'But of course this won't last. What did you think? It's childish to believe the world stands still, when all the time it's turning and turning.'

'Leave him,' he says suddenly, surprised by his own intensity. 'Leave him and come live with me.'

She freezes in the act of putting on a shoe and looks at him with interest for a moment. 'Don't be crazy,' she says quietly. 'I'll never do that. Don't start dreaming things that can't happen.'

'They *can* happen,' he says. 'If you want them to. We have a pretty explosive time in here. It could be like this every day, for the rest of our lives.'

As he says the words, he hears how raw and callow they are. What is he going on about? He doesn't *want* to be with her for the rest of their lives; he doesn't even want to be with her for a few hours. What happens between them is powerful precisely because it is hurried and secret. Living in drab semi-poverty together, one day following on another, he suspects they would start to loathe each other very quickly. They can only conduct this business in little sequestered interludes, where they seem to strike each other at angles, generating fire.

She has both shoes on now. She bends to kiss him on the forehead, a chaste, ironic contact. 'See you in the real world,' she says. He watches her peer through the crack of the door, one way, then the other way, before slipping out. After which he lies naked on the bed for a long time, while the room goes cool.

He remembers this as one seamless event. But in fact it's made of little pieces from various afternoons.

*

The next time he'll see her is when he's back at the lodge, in his clothes and in his other role, as Canning's friend and confidant. Then he and Baby are formal and distant with each other again; there is no frivolity and flirting. He has tried to push the limits, tried to catch her eye, or in other ways endorse their private intimacy. But she doesn't respond and in time he has learned to play his part completely. His life, it sometimes seems, has become arranged in a series of compartments. None of his various incarnations feels like the real, the true Adam; yet each of them is true in its own way.

He is surprised at how easily all this comes to him. He has a gift for duplicity. The mystery isn't in how hard betrayal is, but how simple. It requires no special skills. Betrayal is natural, like an extension of his character – which, disturbingly, perhaps it is.

And it only gets easier. Everything becomes a habit. Habit is what you do without thinking, and nothing is exempt from deadening repetition. Even murder, he realizes, could become a habit. The first time might be difficult, but after that you were just repeating something you'd already done. Each subsequent occasion would be easier, until you could stand among piles of corpses and dream up lines of poetry.

Yet he does feel guilt. It still comes over him in a nauseating rush sometimes when he's alone in town. Then he looks back on his other selves with a mixture of horror and amazement. *That was me*, he thinks. *I spoke that word, I made that gesture*. He is tormented by what he remembers and frequently resolves to break it off – never go back there, never see the pair of them again. And the resolution is very clear, very final, until the weekend comes. Then the self-disgust turns inside out, and becomes that heady mix of dread and desire again, bolstered by all sorts of petty rationalizations; and before he knows it, he is driving down that familiar road.

He longs to tell somebody about it. There is no point in telling, yet the yearning is strong. But there is nobody he can talk to. His brother would only scoff or judge, and he has tried the blue man next door, without success. He has no other friends left. Except for one.

It is a symptom of the impasse his life has reached that Canning is perhaps the only person he could really turn to. And there have been a couple of extreme moments when confession has been just there, like an inedible shape in his mouth, wanting to come out. It would be so easy to speak the words. A simple sentence would do it – truth, then all the ugliness to follow. But even the ugliness would be freedom and release; from them, and more especially from himself. All of it over and done, no going back.

It occurs to him that Canning might know already. Adam studies him carefully, but his innocence seems unfeigned. Though there are some unnerving moments. Once Canning asks him, with aggressive cheerfulness, whether he has anybody in his life.

'You mean a romantic involvement? No, nothing like that.'

'Why not? Don't you get lonely?'

'Sure. But I'm not really cut out for that sort of thing.'

'I used to feel like that, even when I was married. The first time, I mean. But when Baby came along, everything changed. It was like finding the missing half of me.'

Adam only nods; he can't bring himself to speak. And his discomfort verges on torture when Canning shifts closer and adds confidingly:

'I want you to be happy like I am. I want you to have somebody like Baby to keep you company too.'

He looks sharply at Canning, but his moon-face is full of tender solicitude.

13

The earth is tilting into winter; the days are shorter, lopped off at each end, and a hard, cold quality has come into the light. At night he sleeps with the windows closed and sometimes he wakes to a pale furring of frost on the ground.

The poems have frozen in him too. At first it had seemed like a natural caesura, on the far side of which the words would simply resume. His attention, in any case, is elsewhere, so that months go by before the obvious truth becomes apparent: he has not written a single line since his affair with Baby began.

The moment he's aware of it, the knowledge starts to hurt him, like the tip of a blade broken off in his flesh. It makes perfect sense, of course, that longing would give rise to poetry; as soon as longing is satisfied, the poems will die. How to go back to where he was? Especially when every instinct, every animal appetite in him, is wanting to press forward, towards some unattainable ideal. In his clearer moments he knows he should drop this thing, he should leave this place and her; yet he also knows that such retreat is beyond him.

It'll end anyway. Better to do it yourself now.

'Why will it end? Why can't it go on like this?'

Don't be such a schoolboy. She's already bored with you, can't you see it?

'What do you know? You're not even real.'

Oh, you're so cruel.

To quell the inner voice, to lay the poems to rest, he takes up his battle with the weeds again. It's been months since he's gone out there, and the green strip at the top of the yard is now as high as his waist. But the plants are soft and pulpy, and when he wets the ground it gives up its grip without a fight. After only a day he has cleared the new weeds out and then he is back with the brown battalions behind.

It becomes – during the week – his single, obsessive preoccupation. Each day he goes a little further, pushing back the frontier another few steps. He uncovers all sorts of objects, lost or abandoned in the weeds. A plastic doll, a tattered parasol. Bits and pieces of an engine. He piles them up near the house, like old artefacts recovered from the sea-bed. He keeps at it – this lonely, self-appointed labour – even though there is nobody to judge or praise him, and there will be no reward when he's done.

*

He asks Baby one day, 'What would Canning do if he found out?'

'About us?' She thinks for a moment. 'I don't know. Collapse and cry, probably.'

'He wouldn't shoot us or something?'

'I don't think so. He's too weak for that. He might shoot himself, I suppose.'

They are lying on the bed in the cottage with a blanket over them. Although it is the middle of the day, a blue-green twilight presses on the window; that morning the first rain of winter has fallen. He has become so used to the aridity and dryness that this change of season is like a change of locale: he feels alone with her in some remote northern fastness, with arctic bleakness encircling the house. It's from this sense of false solitude, and the shared warmth between them, that he slides in behind her, taking hold of one of her breasts in an idle, possessive way, while he murmurs into her ear, 'If he shot himself, we'd be able to do this every day. For the rest of our lives.' He feels her tense against him and adds quickly, in a different voice, 'I don't want him to do it, of course.'

'Sometimes I do.'

He raises himself on one elbow to look at her. There is a long silence between them, and a sudden contraction, a clarity. 'You don't mean that.'

'Yes, I do. He's a nobody.' When he starts to shake his head, she goes on: 'It's the truth. What would he be if his daddy hadn't left him the farm?'

'He's not a bad person.'

'No. He's just a nothing. Which is worse.'

His protest is really a form of agreement; he's excited by the dark scenario he's drawing out of her. 'That's his luck,' he says.

'Luck? Or chance?'

'I don't see the difference.'

'Oh, they're different. Of course they are.' She pulls away from him a little in the encircling hold of his arms and he pulls her back. 'It's just chance, isn't it?' she says. 'That he's in his place, you're in yours. It could just as easily be different.'

'I don't know what you mean.'

'Yes, you do. It could've been you in Kenneth's place. Just think.'

'Right now,' he says smugly, 'I *am* in Kenneth's place.'

And it's true. But then he considers what she actually means. She means the farm, the golf course, the money, the potential that all these open up. To truly be in Canning's place, he has to own Canning's future.

'You know what I think sometimes?' she whispers, her lips grazing his ear. 'It's like a fantasy I have. I imagine if something had to happen to Kenneth. Like an accident. Chance, accident, it's the same thing, really. Accidents happen all the time.'

'What are you saying?'

'Well, you know. A rock fall. A car crash. Somebody goes missing in the mountains. It could easily happen. The farm is a wild place. I think how it would be if Kenneth had to die suddenly. By chance. How different everything would be afterwards.' She giggles suddenly, pressing her face into his neck. 'I'm terrible, aren't I?'

He can't answer. It's as if something has been offered to him, something glistening and beautiful and dangerous, which he has only to reach out and accept. This is his moment; she has told him, without quite saying the words, that she wants to spend her life with him, if he will just do one little thing to make it possible. But he shifts away from her on the bed, and a gust of cold air comes under the blanket.

'Of course,' she says, her tone becoming brusque, 'I don't wish anything bad on my husband.'

He keeps coming back to this conversation afterwards, alone at home. Did she mean what he thought she did? But of course she meant it; of course she wished something bad on her husband. Even to consider it raises the temperature in his brain. He's not weighing it up – not seriously. He's not capable of murder. But what he might be capable of is inaction; of standing by and letting fate takes its course.

To cool his head he goes out into the yard and hacks viciously at the weeds. But sweat and blisters and a pounding pulse don't calm him down today. The memory that keeps coming to him is of Canning on the rock face that afternoon above the river – the moment when he'd slipped and he, Adam, had put out a hand to save him. But what if he *hadn't* put out his hand? What then? Even at the time, Adam had had a vivid sense of a dreamlike other future branching off. If Canning had fallen and died, he would have left behind a blank place, an absence, into which Adam could have stepped.

When Baby had spoken about that possibility, she'd tried to entice him with the notion of wealth. He would have the land, the development, the great prosperity ahead. But none of that matters to him. What he wants is Baby herself – to have her and keep her. He wants her with a painful, restless longing that churns in him. And why not? It isn't fair, it isn't just: that she should be married to a man like Canning – a small, sad sketch of a man, who is in his position not through hard work or brilliance, but through an arbitrary turn of fate. Baby's right; everything is chance. Accident, luck, random collisions. One thing makes another, forming ultimately into a design that seems inevitable. But if a single event in the chain happens differently, or doesn't happen at all, what follows on will be different too.

And yet – his mind does touch on the idea now, but tentatively, fearfully – the future can be changed. Fate can be moulded by the will. A slip, an accident, a misstep on the rock face, and Canning will be gone. And then the immutable design will alter.

Such a small thing. So tiny. One little death in a dusty corner of the world. People are slaughtered in their thousands, all over the planet, every day; the history of the human race is a history of carnage. Murder, not progress, is the great enduring truth, and we shrink from it not in virtue, but in weakness. If we were stronger, if we were *honest*, we would look that truth in the eye. So much blood, a river of it, endlessly flowing: what are a few drops more? What does another death matter?

He recoils from his own mind in alarm. The voice that has been playing in his head is not his own; it belongs to the serpent in the garden. But it continues to whisper, a soft echo at the edge of his brain, even after he throws down the pick and goes back indoors to clean up.

Kind of tempting, isn't it?

'Not at all. What do you take me for?'

A lover. Don't poets kill for love?

'No, you stupid bastard, they *die* for love. Not the same thing at all.'

Still, it's on your mind. I'm surprised at you, I must admit. And impressed. I didn't think you had it in you.

'It's not like that,' he says hotly. 'I'm reflecting on things. Philosophically.'

Ah. Philosophically.

'I could never actually...'

And is that weakness or strength?

'Leave me alone! Go away.'

Laughter, a low, hissing sound, maybe only the wind coming under the door.

But on his next visit to Gondwana, fate presents him with a chance. He's with Canning down at the lion enclosure for the evening feeding session. The carcass has been tipped over the wall; the khaki-coloured workers have withdrawn; the yellow eyes are pacing back and forth in the gloom. But something isn't right – a chunk of bloody meat has got stuck on the way down, hooked to a bush on the bank. Canning makes an exclamation of irritation and hands his blue cocktail to Adam. 'Hold onto this a moment, won't you,' he says.

Then Adam is watching the soles of Canning's shoes as he leans over the top of the enclosure, struggling with a branch to get the piece of meat loose. He makes little grunting sounds of effort and frustration. He is like a precarious weight tilting back and forth on a fulcrum; just one slight misjudgement and he will slide the wrong way, down to the hungry mouth below. And Adam behind him, a glass in each hand like the scales of justice, weighs up a balance of his own.

Go on. It's so easy. Been handed to you on a plate.

'No.'

Just a little push. That's all you have to do. One little push and the rest of your life will be different.

'I can't.'

What're you afraid of? Nobody will ever know. A tragic accident, not your fault at all.

'No, I said! Go away!'

'I can't reach it,' Canning says, sliding back this way, his face suffused with blood. 'What were you saying to me? I couldn't hear properly.'

'Nothing. I'm just talking to myself.'

'Are you all right? Your voice sounds funny.'

'Yes, I'm okay. Just feeling a bit light-headed.'

'Let's go up to the house, shall we? It's getting too dark to see.'

On the way back, a violent trembling thrums through Adam; he drops the glass on the lawn. It doesn't break, but it's as if something inside him has shattered, leaking out its contents, all bright and blue and toxic, onto the grass.

The next day, when he's alone with her at the cottage, he tells her, 'I can't do it. What we talked about last time. I've thought about it, but it's just not possible for me.'

'I don't know what you mean,' she says coldly.

'I can't do anything to Canning. I'm sorry, but I just can't.'

'I didn't ask you to do anything. It was just talk, nothing serious. A little game.'

'Yes,' he says miserably, 'a little game.' But the mood that has opened between them has nothing playful in it; they are both grim and sober and intent. Not long afterwards she makes an excuse and leaves, though they have – for the first time – gone nowhere near the bed.

14

On that same Sunday evening Canning says to him, 'What are you doing next weekend?'

'Uh, coming to visit you, probably.'

'No, you can't, because we won't be here. We'll be in Cape Town, for the launch party.'

'The launch of what?' he asks, though of course he knows.

'Ingadi 300, obviously. What else would we be launching? There's going to be an official announcement.'

'That's great,' Adam says, while his insides clench up.

'Yes,' Canning says, 'it's actually happening.' There's a pause before he adds, 'I'd like you to come along.'

'Where to?'

'To the party. It's going to be at Mr Genov's house. By invitation only. It would mean a lot to me to have you there.'

He thinks about it for a long moment. The idea of the city again, for the first time in more than half a year, fills him with dread. But it's almost outweighed by the prospect of seeing Baby at the party. Maybe there will be a way to be alone with her somewhere.

'All right,' he says. 'I'll come.'

Almost immediately, he doubts his choice. Depression drops on him like a cold, grey lid. The golf course is nearly upon them; he should be finding ways to disentangle himself from these people, to put distance between him and them, rather than making the knots more complicated. But he isn't ready yet to be free and alone again.

*

On the day that follows, Blom has a visitor. Adam is in the yard, digging up weeds, when he notices a nondescript white car pull up at his neighbour's door. The man who gets out is tall, with a heavy build and a big grey moustache. He's dressed in city clothes – dark pants with a white shirt, a jacket slung over his shoulder. The glance that he throws towards Adam is edged with hostility, though he calls out a genial greeting.

Adam watches covertly as the blue man meets his visitor at the door. The two of them clearly know each other, but this is no happy reunion. Rather, there is something formal in the way that they shake hands before passing inside, closing the door behind them. And it's only now, when somebody has at last come to call, that the absence of any other visitors in Blom's life becomes overwhelmingly apparent.

The newcomer is there for a while. It's after a good couple of hours that he emerges again, and then there is a repeat of the handshake, the curt nod of the head, before the car disappears down the hill, going towards the road out of town.

Blom doesn't go back in immediately. He hangs around the back door, pretending to be interested in something on the ground. It's been a few weeks since he and Adam have spoken; since their last peculiar encounter, they've kept away from each other. But after a long, uncomfortable silence he calls out, 'That was an old friend of mine.'

'Oh,' Adam says. 'Nice.' He doesn't know what other response to offer. Blom gives the unhappy impression that he's defending himself, though he hasn't been accused of anything, and after another minute he finally goes indoors.

But that same night there's a knock on the back door and when Adam answers the blue man is on the concrete outside, that familiar bottle in his hand. The level of brandy is low and Blom is swaying slightly on his feet. He smiles apologetically at Adam and says, 'Can I speak to you about something?'

Adam hesitates, looking for an excuse. He doesn't want a repeat of their strained amity; he doesn't want Blom to get too close. But in the end he steps aside and gestures to his neighbour to pass.

Blom seats himself in the lounge, the bottle on the table next to him. There is something defiant in the splay-legged way he occupies the chair, then casts around him for a moment before sniffing and wiping his nose on his sleeve. 'I see my baby over there,' he says abruptly.

'Baby?' Adam is jolted into guilt by the name, but then he realizes Blom means the twisted wire sculpture, crouched with tensile intelligence on top of his notebook. 'Oh, yes, that,' he says.

'You don't like it.'

'Of course I do.' There is a pause before he says, 'Well, no, to be completely honest, I don't like it. I find it quite ugly.'

If he'd expected Blom to be offended, he gets no reaction. His neighbour's dark eyes regard him steadily, and he says, 'Sometimes the truth is ugly.'

'Maybe so.'

'Have you got some glasses?' He indicates the bottle on the table.

Adam is suddenly resentful; he feels invaded by this nervous, knotted man, who's already half-drunk and appears to be settling in. At the same time it occurs to him that, like his neighbour, he has never had any visitor here except Blom: despite numerous promises, his brother hasn't come back to see him, nor have Canning and Baby dropped by. Nobody has sat down with him, made small talk and clinked glasses, the way they might do now. His life used to be made of convivialities like these; now it consists mostly of silences and time.

Nevertheless, he wants the blue man out. 'Mr Blom,' he says, 'you wanted to talk about something. I'm busy working at the moment, I haven't got time to socialize. What is it you wanted to say?'

'Oh, it's like that,' Blom says. 'You think somebody's your friend...' He gets up suddenly and begins striding around the room, giving vent to a big psychic discharge of anxiety. Then he disappears into the kitchen and returns with a glass, which he plonks down on the table. He pours himself a stiff drink, throws himself into the chair and lights a cigarette. As the smoke curls out in blue coils around his head, he glares mournfully at Adam and says, 'They're going to kill me.'

'Who is? What are you talking about?'

'That man who came today isn't my friend. I was lying about that. He came to give me a message.' Changing tack abruptly, Blom says, 'Why don't you sit?'

Adam has stayed on his feet in the hope of keeping the conversation short, but now he sighs and sinks down on the couch in resignation. 'I don't understand,' he says.

'Do you remember that first day when I came here? How I talked about having a new life, being a new person?'

'Yes, I remember.'

'My name isn't Blom.'

'Oh,' Adam says, 'what is it then?' He feels exasperated; along with the smoke, bafflement and confusion are swirling around the room.

'I can't tell you that.'

They stare at each other with genuine enmity. This is fast becoming the oddest conversation of Adam's life and he resolves that he will not speak again before Blom does. But the silence goes on and on, until Adam says quietly, 'You'd better explain what you mean.'

This appears to be the cue that Blom is waiting for. He immediately pulls his chair up close to Adam, so that they are sitting in intimate proximity, and plants a hand on his knee. For a horrible second it seems that Blom might kiss him, but then he bows his head, showing the combed, thin strands of hair, heavy with Brylcreem, across the top of his pate, and their closeness takes on a different quality: this is confession, with Adam in the role of priest.

When Blom starts to speak, his voice is very low; he clears his throat and begins again, and this time the narrative is clearer, though the words still unwind in a colourless monotone. Adam's eyes slide downward, to Blom's hand, still splayed out on his knee. He is listening, every word goes through him, but it's as if what he's hearing takes on form. He has never noticed the physical qualities of Blom's hand before: the thick, square tips of the fingers with their yellow stains, the whorl of grey hair on the back of the first joint. The nails, with a half-moon of dirt under their ragged ends. The vein pulsing thickly in the wrist. The edge of an old tattoo, somebody's name perhaps, showing from under the sleeve. And while Blom tells him who he is and what he's done, Adam thinks: *with that hand. You did it all with that hand.*

In the end, it's more to break free of the hand than the words that Adam moves away. He stands up quickly and the blue man does too, his confession breaking off in mid-flow, both of them taking a few steps back and staring wildly at each other, as if seeing one another for the first time. Which perhaps they are.

'Why are you telling me this?' Adam says.

Blom rocks his weight from foot to foot; he has the shambling, cowed quality of a captive bear. His gaze drops down to the floor and he mumbles something indistinct.

'What's that? I can't hear you.'

'Because you're my friend.'

'No,' Adam says, very clearly. 'I'm not your friend. I don't want to know these things about you. I can't help you.' Despite himself, he feels a pang go through him when he sees the stricken look on the other man's face. In a lower, gentler voice, he says, 'I won't tell anybody, I promise you that. But I'm sorry, Blom, I don't want to hear about it.'

'My name isn't Blom.'

'Whatever your name is.'

The blue man nods slowly and raises his head; the look that passes between them is fraught with shame and anger on both sides. Then he drains his glass and throws it sideways against the wall. It smashes in a tinkling detonation that makes Adam flinch. Almost instantly, all the menace drains out of his neighbour; he seems to shrink a little inside his blue overalls as he heads to the door. Before he goes out he turns and speaks softly, at an angle, not quite facing the room:

'Everything I did, I did for you. And other people like you.'

Then he is gone, seeming to fall out of the room, back into the wind and darkness he emerged from. A storm is beginning outside and the door swings to and fro, letting in the first slanting rattle of rain onto the floor. The emptiness of the house is somehow amplified and it takes Adam a while to move. But even after he's locked the door he feels uneasy and restless and he keeps walking around, checking and rechecking that all the windows are closed. He has the unsettling sensation of expecting a visitor, somebody unwelcome, who anyway doesn't come.

A little later, his eye falls on the sculpture that the blue man had given him, and suddenly he understands it. There's nothing very complicated, after all, in what it's expressing. He doesn't want it here, anywhere close to him, and he picks it up and goes to the back door. With all the force of his arm he hurls the thing away from him, into the rainy dark. He hears the dull thud as it lands.

*

Although he's promised he will not repeat Blom's secret, and he meant the promise when he made it, he finds himself telling everything to Gavin an hour later. He has called his brother to discuss his visit to Cape Town this coming weekend. But while they are talking a pressure rises in him and he finds himself saying, 'You won't believe what just happened to me.'

'What?'

'The man next door here, the neighbour – he's in hiding. He's got a fake name, a fake identity. He's on the witness protection programme. Somebody came today to tell him he has to go up to Jo'burg soon to give testimony in a big trial.'

Gavin whistles through his teeth. 'Why's that?'

Adam tries to repeat what Blom has told him, but his recollection starts to falter. In making his confession, Blom's voice had taken on a flat and formless quality, so that no particular detail stood out. Instead it was the fact of deception that had overwhelmed Adam, and which rises again in him now. That a man so apparently ordinary, who looked like somebody's friendly uncle, should have a past like that...! Adam had taken him at his word – about his name, about his life, about everything – and he has to reconcile this false version of Blom with what he's learned today. Of course, he knows about such people; there's been a lot about them recently in the newspapers and on the television. But they were always, somehow, somewhere else, living, as it were, in another country – not in the house next door, digging in the garden, doing metalwork in their spare time. That the dark and dirty past of South Africa should have taken on form and come to visit Adam at home, wanting absolution... well, it's too much. He stutters and stumbles in his account of it. Gavin grunts a few times to show that he's listening, but before his brother can finish he breaks in to say, '*Ja*, well, there's a lot of these guys around.'

'I've never met anybody like him.'

'How do you know? They don't usually talk about it. I could tell you a few stories about Angola, some incidents I saw up there. Ordinary guys, just like you or me...'

This is a favourite theme of Gavin's. He'd been up on the border for military service and had seen a bit of action. He liked to talk about how the country was full of apparently normal white men, many of whom had committed rape and murder and cut off SWAPO ears; these people were upstanding members of society now, their darkness buried under the surface.

'But that's different,' Adam says, interrupting him. 'We were conscripted, we *had* to go. This is somebody who *chose* to do this stuff for a living. He tortured and killed and kidnapped for the government. I mean, he's a *bad* person.'

'Oh, don't be so naïve, big brother. There was a war on, that was the situation. That's what happens in a war. You think the other side didn't do the same? At those ANC camps in Tanzania, there was also torture and murder going on. Those guys planted bombs in shopping centres, they blew up women and children – '

'It's different,' Adam says, dismayed. 'They were on the right side.'

'There's no right side in a war, there's just your side and the other side. I don't disrespect this guy for what he did back then – it's what he's doing now that's shabby.'

'What are you saying, he should cover up for his bosses? You can't just forget about the past, Gavin. It's got to be opened up, so the whole country can move on.'

'He's turning against his buddies. Jeez, come on, that's low. I've got no respect for a traitor. No wonder he's afraid. I hope they do come and get him before he sings. And you'd better pray they find the right house – they might shoot you by mistake.' This strikes Gavin as hilarious; he roars with laughter down the phone.

'Let's not talk about it any more.' Adam is disturbed and upset; he doesn't know what he was looking for, sharing this story with his brother. He changes the subject to arrangements for the coming weekend and soon afterwards brings the conversation to an end.

But the talk has stirred up an element of human sympathy for the blue man, which he cannot quite subdue. He keeps remembering, for some reason, the vulnerable glimpse of Blom's skull that he'd had while he made his confession: he is just a man, after all, with a man's fear of death. Adam wonders what his name, his real name, might be, but he tries to put the question out of his mind. A name is everything; a name is nothing. No point in thinking about it.

He sees his neighbour a few times over the coming days when he goes out to attack the weeds. Although winter is in full swing now, with low grey skies and the river running full and throaty through the town, they enter into a period of unseasonal balmy weather, which Adam takes advantage of to try to reach the bottom of the yard. Next door, Blom is also out in his garden, wearing a floppy sun-hat, digging furrows to his fruit trees. Although they are sometimes very near to each other, it's as if the fence between them is a wall; they have rewound to the very beginning, when they studiously ignored one another.

He doesn't quite finish with the weeds – there is a last remaining strip of them at the bottom – but on the day before he has to leave for the city he finds the sculpture again. It's buried among the brown stalks, where it must've landed the night he threw it away. He's pulled so much detritus out of the yard that at first he thinks it's just another piece of junk, an abandoned bit of an engine. Then he realizes what he's holding. It's an odd moment of recognition, turning the ugly thing around in his hands. He has a curious feeling of revulsion and indulgence towards it, which is connected to something else completely. He's about to hurl it away again, over the fence into the next-door garden, but something holds him back. He puts it down on the ground behind him instead. And when he's finished working he picks it up and carries it inside, and sets it down on top of his notebook.

15

Gavin is a little fatter, a little more heavy lidded. He watches Adam's discomfiture through a lens of mild malice. 'How's the poetry coming along, Ad?'

'Fine, fine.'

'That's good. I'm glad you're not wasting your time up there. And how're the weeds?'

'Almost finished clearing them. Another day or two and they'll be gone.'

'Oh, that's great,' his brother says, opening a packet of pretzels and pouring them into a bowl. 'Now you can plant something decent there.'

They are sitting in Gavin's lounge, drinking beer. The room is fronted with glass, and the view of Robben Island, surrounded by sea, is like a picture frozen and framed for their enjoyment.

'By the way,' Gavin says, 'that arrived for you by registered mail. I signed for it, I'm sorry, when I saw the surname. I only noticed it was yours afterwards.'

The envelope is big and brown – official looking. It's the first correspondence he's had from the outside world since his old life collapsed. He is almost excited, until he opens it: a summons to court, the date long past, for the traffic fine he'd got eight months ago. When he'd passed the spot this morning – the turn-off, with its one tree – on his way down to Cape Town, it had been the first time he'd thought of the incident in half a year. All of it feels very long ago; his sense of moral outrage seems almost antiquated.

'What am I supposed to do now?' he says. 'You should've forwarded it to me.'

'I meant to. But I didn't get around to it.'

'It says here they'll issue a warrant for my arrest if I miss the court date. Are they going to arrest me?'

'*Ag*, are you crazy? Don't worry, just tear it up. That's what I do with all my tickets. Nobody bothers about that sort of stuff these days.'

Adam doesn't say more, but he's troubled by guilt. He remembers how fired up he'd been at the time, how resolved he was to fight the issue, but he'd got distracted by other things, and now it's too late. He turns his attention to Charmaine, who's next to him on the couch, cross-legged and barefoot. Her hair hangs down loosely, curtaining her enormous eyes. 'How *are* you?' she whispers.

'I'm doing all right, thanks.'

'Your aura is clearer than before. Though there's still some movement. Maybe too much. A lot of fire and turmoil, but it's better than it was.'

Gavin takes a pretzel from the bowl on the table and crunches it with his mouth open. 'I don't mind telling you,' he says, 'that I think you look terrible.'

'Gavin.'

'Well, he does. He's thin and dirty. He needs a haircut. He looks like a refugee.' To Adam he says, 'I've made a booking at a steak-house tonight. I'm going to fatten you up.'

'No,' Adam says. 'I've got this party to go to.' When his brother looks uncomprehending, he goes on: 'I told you about it. It's the reason I've come down here. We talked about it.'

'Oh, *ja*,' Gavin says vaguely. 'Remind me again.'

As Adam runs through the details, Gavin takes on a bored, distracted expression. But he must be listening, because later, as Adam is about to leave, he suddenly announces, 'It'll never fly. This golf course thing of yours.'

'It's not mine, for God's sake. It has nothing to do with me.'

'Out there in the sticks. Who's going to drive out there to play golf?'

'It's on a major new road,' Adam says defensively. 'And the landscape is part of the design.'

'If you've got money in this thing, take it out. I'm telling you – sell your shares. Don't get burnt.'

'Shares?' Adam says. 'What are you talking about? I've got no money for groceries. How would I buy shares?'

The invitation to the party is lying on the kitchen dresser; Gavin picks it up and looks at it. 'Genov,' he says musingly. 'That rings a bell.'

Adam takes the invitation back before another lecture can begin. 'I'd better go,' he says. 'I'm late already.'

*

He doesn't own a suit these days; he's had to borrow one from Gavin. But the jacket is too big, so that the sleeves hang over his hands. Underneath it, his one good shirt is too tight for him, and it smells of mothballs. He feels flagrantly conspicuous, as if he's dressed like a clown, though none of it is too obvious when he looks in the mirror. Nevertheless, he almost balks: it's not just his clothes, but the whole evening ahead, that doesn't fit him any more. Only the prospect of seeing Baby keeps him moving forward.

The house is in a wealthy suburb Adam doesn't know. He has been driving slowly along leafy back roads for half an hour, map in hand, when the blaze of light and the blare of revelry tell him that he's arrived. A liveried flunkey at the gate inspects his invitation, then tells him he will have to park out in the street, there is no place left inside.

The driveway is a long winding approach through trees, with fancy cars parked all along its length. Off to the side he glimpses tennis courts, a swimming pool, a paddock with horses. Only at the top of the drive does he emerge into the full spectacular vulgarity of what awaits him. A castle, all turrets and balustrades and battlements. Everything, from the stone to the architecture, appears to have been brought in from elsewhere. The effect is of an incoherent oddity, like some fantastic spaceship that's crash-landed on top of this hill, with the survivors swarming over the wreckage. There are a lot of people. He can see them through the windows; they overflow the front stairs. He has a moment of wanting to turn around and run. He doesn't belong and he's sure everyone can see it.

Once his invitation has been inspected again, he's allowed through the door. The impression of an accident continues inside, the roar of voices like the moment of impact, infinitely stretched in time. There is an air of crisis, without focus or centre; dance and talk and flirtation are going on everywhere, splintered and amplified by mirrors. But even here, Adam stays outside the frenzy, like a deaf man watching an orchestra. He feels very alone amongst the flesh and festivity. He sees the rooms without the people as cold, tiled space, broken by tasteless statues and expensive paintings, and himself pacing through all this desertion, his footsteps quavering outward in echoing concentric rings.

In a passage, next to a huge Chinese vase, he is confronted by a tall, grinning man with craggy good looks and dark hair combed back. His teeth are numerous and dazzling. Adam has seen the teeth before, on aerosol cans in the supermarket. Which is how he comes to recognize the famous golfer, who has designed the course for Canning. He has long since retired from the game and is more famous these days for his own brand of deodorant. 'Whose friend are *you*?' the golfer shouts, pumping Adam's hand.

'Canning's. I'm looking for him, actually – have you seen him?'

'Who's that?'

'Canning, Kenneth Canning.'

'Never heard of him, old buddy. You look like you could use a drink!'

'Never heard of him? But this whole thing is his idea.'

'Must be some mistake, old buddy. This is Nicolai's baby. Here, have some wine.' He plucks a glass from the tray of a passing waiter and gives it to Adam. 'Nicolai's own label, from his wine estate. Enjoy!' Then the famous golfer is gone, shaking the hand of somebody else in the crowd.

Adam downs the wine as he moves on. It's dry and fragrant, an expensive taste – part of the costly waste that surrounds Canning. But although he can sense his friend close by, somewhere among these people, he can never quite find him. His panic is tempered by the many other faces in the heaving mass that he almost knows, faces on the edge of being familiar, like acquaintances from long ago: small local celebrities, television stars and sports stars, a notorious revolutionary who'd been in jail for fifteen years, socialites and politicians, even a well-known charismatic preacher. Though he has the impulse to greet these people, their names, their connection to him, stay out of reach; he hurries on from them, looking always for Canning, because close to him will be the one person he does want to see. As he enters each room, he feels hopeful and expectant, but as he pushes through the crowd, his eyes deflecting off the face of each new stranger, he becomes more and more despondent, until he gets to the next doorway. There is something dreamlike in the progression and futility, the hovering sense of quest.

Somewhere in the crush he meets Sipho Moloi, who greets him with bright uncertainty, before asking after the health of the minister.

'No, no,' Adam says, 'I met you at Canning's place.'

'Whose place?'

'Canning, Kenneth Canning. You know, where the golf course…'

'Ah!' His face lights up with recognition, then clouds over again. They both smile tightly at each other, anxious to escape.

'I'm looking for him, actually – Canning, I mean. Have you seen him? Or Baby?'

'Yes… I think I saw him… through there. But it was some time ago.'

Adam pushes through into a big courtyard, open to the sky. A live band is playing jazzily in the corner and people are dancing around a fountain that cascades into a stone pool in the middle. There is a roped-off platform to one side, supporting a bizarrely distinctive shape: a mock-up of a putting green, a bunker next to it, and a flag on a pole planted in the centre. Bunting and balloons hang overhead, and the wall is covered with a massive, blown-up backdrop of mountains and green *kloof* and desert stretching away.

Then he does see Baby. She's dressed entirely in white – white dress, white shoes, white blossoms in her hair – and she looks radiant and virginal, as if she's getting married. She's talking to an older man standing against the wall, who has the air and the functional clothes of an impersonal attendant, a butler of some kind.

Having searched for her for so long, he doesn't approach right away, but watches her for a while across the courtyard. She is laughing and animated, full of a vitality he hasn't seen in her before. The dancing, the music, the crowd: now that he's found her, none of these exist for him. But she seems to have drawn power from the swirling colour around her; she looks like one of the gilded, gifted company, with a future of possibility at her feet. As he starts towards her, a pang goes through him, like the blow of an axe; he feels he is looking at a memory, something already lost. Even when he's right in front of her, she doesn't notice him for a moment. Then her eyes fix on him, and for a second he has an impression again of the imbalance in her gaze.

'What are *you* doing here?' she says. Her displeased expression is almost instantly covered with a dazzling smile.

'Canning gave me an invitation, of course.'

'But how sweet.'

'I've been looking for you,' he tells her.

'Have you? Where?'

'Everywhere. Room after room.' He is close to her, so close that their bodies are in contact each time they lean in to speak. He can smell her perfume and feel the heat of her arm. He has a desperate impulse to act recklessly: press her into the wall, kiss her lingeringly in full view of all these people – claim her in some way. But at the same time he knows that it's only because of the crowd that they can be intimate in public like this. He must get her away from here, to somewhere secluded and safe, where they can renew the bond between them. 'Do we have to stay here?' he says hoarsely. 'Isn't there somewhere we can go?'

She pulls back from him. 'Are you mad?' she whispers angrily. 'This is the middle of a party. And I'm busy right now. Go and talk to Kenneth.'

'Where is he?'

She gestures with a flick of her fingernails to where her husband is standing by himself at the back of the courtyard, a lonely figure, sunk in alcohol and shadow. Nobody is near him.

'I saw a swimming pool in the garden as I came in,' Adam tells her. 'It looked quiet out there.'

Her eyes study him with amused disdain. She starts to shake her head, but at that moment a flurry starts up on the platform in the corner. A microphone is being tuned; lights are turning on; people are readying themselves for speeches.

This is the perfect moment to slip away, with the crowd distracted, but she has taken a step back from him. 'I have to go,' she says. 'I'll speak to you later.'

'I came here for you,' he says again.

'Well, you shouldn't have.' For a second her hand touches his arm, and his heart lifts. But her fingers tweak dismissively at his sleeve. 'Your jacket doesn't fit you,' she says, and then she's moving away.

He has a stunned moment of incomprehension: something has passed him by. Hadn't he been clear? Why hadn't she understood? They are two of a kind; neither of them belongs here, in this frivolous city crowd. But she is another person tonight, somebody he doesn't know. The real Baby, the one that he wants to see, is still out there somewhere, in Gondwana, or in his poems.

He goes in the other direction, against the flow of people. Everybody is pressing in towards the corner where the lights are coming up. On the opposite side of the courtyard, in another universe entirely, Canning slouches against the wall; he gives the impression that he is propping up the building. Adam sees something in him that is both touching and repellent: he is the sort of person it would be easy to hurt and forget. But he beams delightedly when he sees Adam. 'I thought you'd changed your mind,' he says. 'I thought you hadn't come after all.'

'I shouldn't have,' Adam says miserably. 'I should have stayed at home.'

'Isn't it awful? I hate all this too.' He looks around. 'Come on. Let's get out of here.'

Adam follows Canning out of the courtyard. The irony isn't lost on him, that he came here hoping to sneak off with Baby, and has ended up leaving with her husband instead. Canning takes him to a passageway with a closed door, on the other side of which is a darkened staircase; at the top of the stairs they are in another carpeted passage, edged by a railing on one side, from which they can look down on the courtyard below.

'There,' Canning says. 'Now we can see without being trampled. Drink?' He holds out a bottle of wine, which he's gripping by the neck; when Adam refuses, he swigs from it himself. His face is flushed and sweaty, his tie and top button are undone. 'Look at this lot,' he says. 'All the beautiful and powerful gathered together. How I'd love to fire-bomb this place.'

Adam scans the heads and foreshortened bodies down below, looking for Baby, but it's hard to recognize anybody. From this perspective the whole scene has altered shape. A few minutes ago they were down there, in the throng; now they are like pigeons or gods, not part of the world they're watching. His attention takes a few seconds to focus on the warm circle of light, with its brighter green circle of fake lawn and flag. A few figures are on the platform. The man in front, who is speaking through the microphone, is the famous golfer. He seems to belong up there, among the camera flashes and synthetic colours; his gleaming grin is like part of the set. He is making a joke, something about an Irishman and a caddy, and the answering laughter and applause rise buoyantly to the hidden watchers like a warm gas.

Then the golfer turns serious. His voice becomes low and confiding. 'Ladies and gentlemen, friends and colleagues... How often in a lifetime can we say that the Good Lord gives us the chance to do something we've dreamed of since we were six years old? Yet that's the sort of chance I've been given. To design my own golf course, to see it take shape in front of my eyes – well, it's more than a sinner like me could hope for... but now it's time,' he goes modestly on, 'for me to hand over to the man who's *given* me this chance, the head honcho himself, the mover and shaker, *Mister* Liberty National, our friend and host tonight... Nicolai Genov.'

'*Oh*,' Adam says. The exclamation is involuntary: he is startled to recognise the older man Baby was speaking to earlier, the one he'd thought was a butler. And Mr Genov doesn't entirely lose the self-effacing reserve, even under the hot lights. He is clearly used to making speeches, but he would obviously prefer, at the same time, to be elsewhere, in the background; and he brings something of the background with him, nebulous and indistinct, to the microphone.

'My friends... I am not going to speak for long... This is a party, after all, and we shouldn't let business get in the way of a good time...'

The accent is hard to place: partly Eastern Europe, but overlaid with other inflections. It is an international accent – the voice of a man who has lived in many different places. He seems to set each word down deliberately, like ornaments arranged on a windowsill.

'... I want to say, if you look around you tonight... is it not good to see so many different people in one room – all different colours, different cultures, everybody mixed... this really is a new South African party!'

The banal phrase sounds like one of Canning's. There's a spatter of appreciative applause – people congratulating themselves – and from his vantage point Adam is briefly caught up in the picture: saris and business suits mingling with African fabrics and Arabic robes. Accents and languages twine companionably together; skins and beads rub agreeably against silk. Even the waiters, in their neutral tuxedos, are a harmonious mixture of black and white and brown. It really is like an advertisement for the new country.

'As all of you know, just a few years ago this would not have been possible... but I'm proud to be part of it, my new mother country that has been so very good to me...'

More clapping, a whistle or two. Despite himself, a warm feeling expands in Adam; the impulse to belong is very strong. But at the same time he remains outside; he knows he's here on sufferance, and there is something unreal about this gathering. It's what's absent, what *isn't* here in this house, that Adam feels truly part of, and which makes him afraid.

'... and this whole venture, our golf estate, is a reflection of this new, multi-cultural spirit...our partners are a mix of colours and backgrounds, like the faces in this room...'

At this moment, Adam sees Baby. He has been looking for her in the wrong place, among the crowd, when she is actually up on the platform, off to one side, half in the spotlight. The tension in her body is keyed up, in a different register to her normal state. He wonders what she is doing there, as if she's about to make a speech, and that thought leads him, by association, to the man standing next to him.

'What about you?' he whispers to Canning. 'Don't you have to speak?'

'Me? No, of course not.'

'But why not? Isn't this your project?'

Canning shrugs impatiently. 'For God's sake,' he says. Down below, Mr Genov is handing over to somebody else, the dapper black man, Enoch Nandi, whom Adam had met at Gondwana over Christmas. On that occasion Canning had been deferential and polite towards him, but now he murmurs snidely, 'There's the black empowerment camouflage.'

'I thought you liked him.'

'Where'd you get that idea? No, I despise him. I despise all of them. It's just a game – a game you have to play.'

Fronts and public faces: power hiding in the shadows. And something comes to Adam in this moment: for the first time he understands that it is exactly the quality in Canning which evokes pity and contempt – the blurred, smudged quality, the invisibility – that most defines him, and is his greatest strength. In his oblique way, he is the moving force that set this whole thing ticking; it's because of him that all these people are in this courtyard tonight, yet almost nobody here knows his name or recognizes his face.

Adam turns his head to look, almost wonderingly, at his friend, but at this moment Canning is staring downward with an expression of sadness and spite and longing. He seems to be focused on the crowd, but then he says, in a small voice, 'See that. In front of everybody. She doesn't care who knows.'

'Knows what?'

Canning says dispiritedly, 'That man has been her lover for the past six months.'

'Who?'

But then he sees. It's Baby that they're both looking at, as she leans toward Nicolai Genov with the same air of heightened excitement that she's worn all evening, whispering something to him behind her hand, and in the tilt of their bodies towards each other, the casually possessive way he is holding onto her elbow, it is blindingly obvious. In some way, Adam realizes, he's known it since the first moment he saw her tonight, and yet the shock is like something new and freshly minted, opening out under his rib-cage. The numbness that follows, the hollow absence of emotion, is like a kind of feeling in itself. He does the calculation: six months – more or less when he'd first met her.

'That dirty Eastern European scumbag,' Canning says, then glances at Adam with a rueful smile. 'There. Now you really know all our secrets.'

The formal part of the evening is breaking up below. Enoch Nandi has finished his speech; the applause has faded; the lights are going down. But it's as if the glow is still on the little party down there – her and the old butler-satyr, and the attentive acolytes around them. Adam and Canning are stranded meanwhile on the cold, dark edge of the arena, both holding onto the railing as if it will keep them from falling.

'Fun's over,' Canning says. 'Now we can really get drunk.' He notices Adam's expression and puts a slack arm over his shoulders. 'Don't take it so badly,' he says. 'It's nothing serious, just a little affair. That's how she is. I don't mind too much. As long as I don't lose her.'

'Maybe you don't mind,' Adam says. 'But I do. Very much.'

'Oh, Adam. Still my loyal friend and protector, after all these years.'

A cold voice behind them says, 'Sir.'

They turn. The man is elegantly dressed. He looks like another guest at the party, but a coarseness in his broad, flat face signals something else. A real butler, maybe – but what kind of butler wears a gun? Adam can see the holster under the man's jacket as he says, 'This is a private area. You shouldn't be up here.'

'It's all right,' Canning says. 'I know Mr Genov very well.'

'And you are...?'

'My name is Canning. Kenneth Canning.'

The man's eyes are dark and depthless, like two pebbles pressed into putty. He shakes his head contemptuously. 'Never heard of you,' he says. 'You'd better go back downstairs.'

*

When Adam gets back to the flat, he's full of a leaden desire to sleep. The last thing he wants is more talk, but Gavin has waited up. He's in front of the television, watching reruns of sports highlights, but he switches it off when Adam comes in. 'How was your party?' he says.

'It was all right,' he says, hovering near the door.

'I checked up on your friend,' Gavin tells him balefully. 'Your Nicolai Genov. I thought his name sounded familiar.'

'I don't want to speak about him.'

'He's only a big player in organised crime. Internationally, mind you. Nothing to be concerned about.'

'I'm not concerned. I don't even know him.'

'He ran from prison in Europe about ten years ago. Jumped bail in a big Mafia trial and came here. He made friends in the old white government, spread a lot of money around. He changed his name, got his citizenship sorted. Now he's in with the new crowd. He's riding high these days, but he can't travel to a lot of countries in case he gets arrested. A very dangerous customer.'

Adam has taken in too much tonight; he has no room for amazement. 'Why are you telling me this?' he says.

'You don't think you should be worried? You're in with a bad bunch. Genov owns a lot of stuff – hotels, casinos, a wine farm or two. But my contacts tell me he's still connected with his old pals in Europe. The business stuff is a front. There's a lot going on, Ad. Money laundering, drug smuggling, maybe human trafficking. You don't want to get involved.'

'You're right, I don't,' Adam says, but then he remembers something Canning told him. 'He's had a bad press,' he says, moving towards the door. 'I've got to sleep, Gavin. I'm leaving early in the morning.'

'Well, don't say I didn't warn you.'

'I won't. Good-night.'

'Good-night,' Gavin says, his voice shot through with outrage. But when he comes to the door of Adam's room a minute later, his tone has changed again; now he sounds plaintive. 'You can't get me in with these guys, can you?' he says.

16

He doesn't get the early start that he wanted, and it's close to midnight when he descends at last into the valley. His house, unlit, obscured by trees, looks like a place where nobody has lived for a very long time. Yet when he steps in through the front door, it's into a warmth and a slight staleness, as if the rooms are inhabited.

Ah, the prodigal returns.

Lying in bed with the light off, the form of his interlocutor shows in sharp silhouette against the glow of the streetlamp outside. Sitting at the window, head tilted at a curious angle. It doesn't help to know that it's his own clothes he's seeing, piled up suggestively on the back of a chair.

Don't take it so hard. You knew it couldn't last.

'I trusted her.'

Trust is an unfortunate word. Under the circumstances.

'But she wanted me. It was her idea that I… that we… get rid of him.'

She might've done the same to you afterwards.

'I don't believe that. I know who she is!'

Maybe not, my friend. You might be better off like this.

'How can I be better off? I'm suffering, can't you see?'

And it's startling, in fact, how much it does hurt. It's been years since he's felt this, the pain of dispossession, a blade cutting into the root. When he wakes in the morning, it comes over him again; he sits on the edge of the bed and weeps like a child. Loss connected to every other loss before, reaching back to some elementary core.

When he pulls himself together he goes out into the yard with his gloves and his pick. Better to subdue this thing through toil. The day is brilliant and clear and cold, and he throws himself into the labour with single-minded intensity. There's been a lot of rain recently and the ground is soaked and soft. By nightfall he's done. Standing at the bottom fence, with the view open at last all the way to the house, the ultimate brown enemy hanging starkly in his hand, he feels no sense of triumph or achievement. All he can see – though their growth is slow because of the winter temperature – is the fresh round of green shoots starting to poke their heads above the surface.

He piles the dead weeds on top of the others in a heap behind the house. He has to make several trips back and forth, and on one of these return journeys he sees his neighbour, the blue man, lurking near his work-shed. Before he can think about it, Adam raises his hand. 'How's it going?' he calls. But Blom looks sharply away and turns his back: another gap, another silence. Adam is alone.

*

He doesn't go out to Gondwana that weekend. It's the very first time since he met up with Canning that he's stayed away. He imagines that his absence will resound – that it will matter terribly. But the days pass without the phone ringing once.

He must keep moving now, he cannot become idle. There is danger for him in stopping. Perhaps he should write – for the first time in weeks, poetry seems possible again. A sense of loss and bereavement: isn't that what sets the music free? But when he sits down at his desk, the page outstares him every time.

He takes to walking, striding up and down the streets of the town, or following the line of the swollen river up the valley. But the backdrop of bare trees and low skies and cold-hardened ground reflects his own condition back at him. He knows he must leave this place soon; he must return to the city.

It's on one of these walks, when he's going aimlessly up and down the main road, that the cavalcade goes past. There are seven of them: massive flat-bed trucks, loaded up with earth-moving equipment. They are strung out in a line, evenly spaced, like peculiar animals travelling in migration. The whole procession bypasses the town with monumental indifference, grinding slowly towards the mountains.

The local people who live along the road have come out of their houses to gawk. Adam overhears one woman saying to her friend, 'I wonder where that lot's heading.'

But he knows exactly where.

*

He goes out there the next day. He knows that it's a mistake, but he cannot help himself: he wants to see this monstrous progress in action. And before he's even through the gate there is evidence of the work happening inside: one of the trucks that he'd seen passing, the bulldozer off-loaded from the back, is parked at the *Nuwe Hoop* settlement. There is a small crowd of people gathered nearby, listening to a foreman reading something from a piece of paper. As Adam watches, the crowd breaks up and starts to climb onto the back of the truck.

The truck is in front of him as he passes through the gate, and then again on the dirt road on the other side. Through the shuddering clouds of dust that its wheels throw up, he can see the indistinct shapes of men and women holding on, all wearing their khaki uniforms. Casual labour, he presumes, for the massive job in hand, and now he understands clearly what Canning meant when he said he'd be using them in the future. An anger starts rising in Adam: a delayed anger, an anger put on hold, with a paralysing helplessness at its heart.

Just before the turn-off into the *kloof*, the truck heads off on a road in the other direction, across the plain towards where a hazy column of dust is rising, like a stain on the sky. Adam follows, but after he has lurched and jolted down the track for a kilometre or two, the scene that confronts him is unexpectedly aimless. The trucks, the equipment, the workers stand about on the intact earth; the dust is being raised by movement, but the digging hasn't begun yet.

Adam has been here before, to this very spot, on a day when he and Canning were the only human figures in sight. Just down there is the little cave where Canning and his first friend – his black playmate from childhood – had carved their initials into the rock. And when he looks in that direction, he notices Canning himself at the overhang, hands in his pockets, shoulders slumped. He seems to be sunk in melancholic reverie, and even here, at the centre of his grand design, he is still an invisible outsider.

Adam parks and walks down there. But even after his name has been spoken aloud, it takes a full minute for Canning to register. He is staring at the weathered initials in the rock, a vexed frown on his face, as if he's trying to decipher some arcane code, but eventually he shakes himself and looks around. 'Oh, hello,' he says. 'I didn't expect you here.' There is no surprise or pleasure at the sight of Adam today.

'I didn't plan to come. But I saw this whole entourage go past…'

'Yes, it's quite a circus, isn't it?' He glances around at the flurry and commotion. 'It's happening,' he says. 'It's actually happening at last.'

He has spoken in a flat voice, quietly, without heat, more to himself than Adam. But there is somehow a deep feeling in his tonelessness. It would be hard to say what the feeling is: not pleasure, or triumph, or satisfaction. It seems closer to sadness, though that is surely unlikely.

Adam points at the rock art, with its ancient figures fixed in their panoramic hunt. 'What about this?' he says. 'You're surely not going to just bulldoze it...?'

'I thought of removing the whole boulder,' Canning says. 'But it's quite a job.'

'It would be worth it, Canning. This is an important record.'

'Only to me. Who else cares? Let them plough it under. The past should stay past, especially mine.'

At first Adam doesn't understand. Then he does: Canning is talking about his own childhood signature, not the San art. The cryptic, colourful figures don't even exist for him.

'Want to go on a helicopter ride?' Canning says now, his tone brightening. 'Come along, there's somebody I want to introduce you to.'

This somebody turns out to be the famous golfer. He is still craggy and toothy and fatuous, just as he was at the party, with no memory whatever of having seen Adam before. 'How are you, old buddy,' he yells, shaking hands. 'Good to meet you!' And he treats Canning – the man whose name he didn't know – with the same bluff, enthusiastic indifference. They are all his buddies, and tomorrow he won't remember any of them.

They ascend into the sky with him. The helicopter is behind a low ridge, away from the main area of activity. The pilot is the famous golfer himself, who appears to power the engine with his own self-regard. Adam has never flown in a helicopter before and the unfamiliar motion, right from the moment of lift-off, unnerves and frightens him. He's not used to the peculiar angles of flight, the way it stops and tilts in mid-air. It's a tiny machine and the metal base, topped by its enclosing transparent bubble, is like nothing so much as a soup plate, skidding around the sky.

The purpose of the flight, it rapidly becomes clear, is to survey the proposed layout of the course from the air. Everything looks different from up there. Adam can see the meandering blue line of the river, with its narrow contiguous band of green. He can see the hills and rocks and trees, reduced at this height to a series of formations and patterns. And when Canning and the golfer, both sitting up front with scrolls of plans spread out on their laps, shout to each other above the thudding of the engine about this dog-leg here, or that fairway there, it's as if they are discussing something conceptual and abstract too. Nothing real. From far up above, the land ceases to be the subject of poetry: it becomes something else, a series of formulations, a mathematical problem to be worked out. And with the army of labourers and the battery of machines down below – also looking toy-like and diminished – the problem will certainly be solved.

He has a moment of such detachment himself. At one point, after they have flown up the length of the river to the place where it emerges from the *kloof* and starts its long journey across the plain, he looks out the window and sees the lodge. He sees Canning's father's cottage behind it, up against the base of the mountains. There are human figures moving down there, neutered and nameless; one of them might be Baby. And for a few seconds, the height from which he views this picture becomes his own. This is how it must be for a god to look at the earth: no connection, no conflict, no yearning for things to be otherwise. No emotional confusion to cloud the mind. For just that moment he is an empty eye; a perfect witness.

It comes to him that time is the great, distorting lens. Up close, human life is a catalogue of pain and power, but when enough time has gone past, everything ceases to matter. Nothing that people do to each other will carry any moral charge eventually. History is just like the ground down there: something neutral and observable, a pattern, a shape. Murder and rape and pillage – in the end, they are just colourful details in a story.

*

Afterwards he drives behind the two of them up to the lodge. Baby is there and for a brief moment, when she catches sight of Adam, her face tightens. Canning's attention is elsewhere, he doesn't notice, and she is almost instantly her polite and distant self again, though she disappears soon afterwards, going outside to the *rondawel*.

The three men eat in the restaurant, a lunch filled mostly with the gassy chatter of the golfer. Canning has barely put down his fork when he's on his feet again, wiping his mouth on his wrist. 'I'm going back down to the site,' he tells Adam. 'They're about to start work. I want to be there for the big moment. You coming along?'

'Uh, no, I don't think so. I'm going to take a walk around here, take a last look at everything.'

'Yes, do. Say goodbye to all of it. It's not going to stay like this much longer.'

Then Canning and his famous guest are gone. Adam is left behind, at the centre of a sudden quietness. He sits at the table for a long time, looking out of the window and thinking. He shouldn't be here and it's not too late to escape. He even pretends that he might, though he knows that he won't or can't, as he gets up and goes to the door.

There is a hint of warmth in the air, the first trace perhaps of returning summer, as he walks across the grass. The door of the *rondawel* is ajar and he slips through without knocking, pushing it closed behind him. She has just emerged from the bathroom and is sitting on the edge of the bed, wearing only a robe, drying her wet hair with a towel. She has her back to him and she doesn't turn at the click of the door, but she says, 'It's so nice to see you again.'

This is a voice he hasn't heard; she is speaking to him out of the newfound distance between them, as if they don't know each other. But the sociable remoteness is at odds with the intimate setting and her half-exposed body. He walks through that clutter of personal debris, the cups and magazines and clothes, to where she is. His hand takes the towel from hers and runs it over her hair. There's a hint of roughness in the motion; something in him wants to hurt her, though it's with genuine tenderness that he pulls the robe off her shoulders. A single drop of water on her backbone seems to hold, in crystalline fragility, everything that's happened between them. He bends down and drinks it off her skin.

'You know this can't go on,' she says. She's speaking quietly now, the distance between them closed up. 'They're starting to build here, this whole place will be full of workers any day now.'

'One last time,' he says.

She hesitates, then with a movement like a shrug she lets the robe drop. He undresses slowly too, letting each garment fall to the floor, till he's completely naked. Along with the *rondawel*, this is something new for them; usually they are half-clothed, ready to conceal themselves at the first sign of interruption. But today they are in another zone, leisurely and sad, playing at husband and wife. The circular dark room is circled in turn by a halo of silence, from beyond which the noises of the forest leak in. He wonders whether they would hear the sound of Canning's car if it returned and whether, at this point, it would matter.

The sex itself takes on the same melancholic quality. The shape of her, the bones and blood and warm flesh, throws him back almost entirely into himself, so that he is caught up in the labyrinthine complexity of his own loneliness. The room falls away; he loses himself, his sense of time and place; he is nowhere. It's not ecstasy, not even pleasure – more like blankness. Then the world draws in upon an infinitely tiny point, through which he eventually falls and flows.

*

Reality reassembles by degrees. First the sensations at the outer reaches of his body, and then everything beyond: the bed with its tangled sheets. The woman lying beneath him. The ochre floor, splotched with sunlight that comes in through the shutters. And something else. A tiny sound, slowly encroaching. He can't place it, can't work it out. A faintly rushing noise, like wind or blood. An angel, dragging huge wings on the ground.

He raises himself on his elbows to look at her. The expression on her face is one he hasn't seen before. He's used to the prepared masks, one after the other, but now he's looking through time at a little girl in her: frightened and helpless and without a plan.

The sound is right outside the door.

Fear has shrunk him inside her. Then they are unjoined and clawing for their clothes. The great timeless unity of love-making has flown apart into its constituent elements of bodily fluid, and terror, and one missing sock.

When the door opens, they freeze. But it's not an angel, or even Canning. It's the old black woman, Ezekiel's wife, he can't remember her name, in a ragged dress, trailing a broom in one hand – the sound they've been hearing. She is so ubiquitous, so everyday and familiar, that they hadn't considered her. Till now.

She has also stopped, quite still, in amazement, at the centre of the irrevocable moment. He has a curious, dissociated image through her eyes: the madam and the master's friend, undressed on the bed, electrified, afraid. Their vulnerability is rude and primal. Then the frieze breaks. The old lady's hand flies up to her mouth, her eyes are wide. In the same instant, Baby is off the bed, covering herself, screeching. She is wild, cracked-open, out of control. The language that spews out of her is raw and dirty – a torrent of abuse from the street, its well-spring in the gutter, not in these fake, elegant surroundings – but afterwards, it is the *sound* that Adam will remember, rather than the clotted words flying with the consistency of fists.

As she backs out of the room, the old lady's fear has a bumbling, cartoonish quality. She is wearing bright red lipstick crayoned onto her mouth and outsized tennis shoes on her feet. Adam sees these details, he knows they are evidence of poverty, but his hysteria finds them funny. When the door slams closed on her at last, he starts to giggle uncontrollably.

He remembers her name. Her name is Grace.

Baby is breathing hard. 'What are you laughing at?' she says.

He wipes his eyes. 'Where did you learn to *talk* like that?'

She turns her stare on him now, and the look on her face is frightening. Not a little girl any more; she is somebody else completely. '*Shut up*,' she tells him, and he does. Instantly.

After a moment he says, 'What are we going to do now?'

'I'll take care of it.'

'How?'

'Leave it to me.'

'Should I offer her money...?'

'No,' she says, her voice as cold as her eyes. 'I told you, I'll take care of it. But you'd better go now. You'd better get dressed and go.'

17

When he thinks of her now, it's with a slow after-burn of grief. His last memory of her – the cold, hard look on her face – can't be separated from the turmoil that stirs in him when he imagines the bulldozers, the havoc they are wreaking out there. He has to turn away from all that, the disturbing prelude to the future. Instead he sits down to read through his poems. There, he thinks, he will find some lasting trace of her, or of how he used to feel about her, before everything went wrong.

There are about twenty poems in all, a nice little stack. He has thought of them as a good start towards a new collection, built around the themes of love and nature. But almost as soon as he begins to read, a deep gloom comes over him. It's not just that the emotion which runs through the poems embarrasses him; it's that the poems themselves are *bad*. The free-flowing language clangs on his inner ear as strained and uncontrolled; what he'd thought of as high, pure feeling has come out on the page as mawkish sentiment, full of rhetoric and cliché.

It's only now that the full extent of his folly is clear to him. His melancholy is like lucidity: he has been a fool, coming to live out here, chasing after the past. He isn't – he never was – a poet; except briefly and badly, as a young man long ago. He has been dabbling in a fantasy version of himself, which he must put away for ever. The whole saga has been a case of mistaken identity.

On a murderous impulse he carries the poems outside. It is painfully obvious to him now that the last half a year has had the illusion of momentum and purpose because of his dealings with the Cannings. That's what has filled up the time. Without the pair of them, his life would be like an old skin with no bones or meat to give it dimension. Well, the moment has come to move on, to purge himself of illusions. And no better way to begin a purge than with a symbolic act.

He finds a clear spot, sheltered from the wind, on the trampled expanse of mud at one corner of the yard. As he strikes the match, his eye falls on the ugly heap of dead weeds he's piled up nearby. And yes, why not? Get rid of all the dross at one go, turn it into ash.

In minutes the bonfire is huge, much bigger than he'd imagined. It's been a couple of weeks since the last rain, so the weeds have had time to dry out; the brown stalks roar, sprouting new leaves of flame. In the yellow conflagration, everything becomes one: no way to tell the difference between poetry and parasite. The hot heart of destruction lets exaltation loose in him; he has a primitive urge to dance, and does in fact caper a bit. But then becomes uneasy at the burning fragments that whirl away in spirals – the thatched roof is very close.

In the end he hurries off to get a bucket and is carrying it out, slopping water over his feet, when a figure emerges from the smoke. He takes a second to recognize his visitor, because his smarting eyes are blinking away tears.

The mayor tells him severely, 'This is against municipal regulations. No fires in a hundred metres of any residence.'

'Yes, I was trying to put it out.'

'I just happened to be driving past when I saw. This is a hazard, you shouldn't have lit it in the first place. I could slap a big fine on you.'

Adam throws the water, unleashing a hissing cloud of steam. But the flames still grope and flicker, and he has to go inside to fill the bucket again. Only then does the circle of heat die down. His moment of triumphant release has become an inconsequential smouldering, which he keeps stubbing and stamping with his feet. A crisped scrap of paper, still with his words inscribed on it, goes drifting past his face.

'I'm sorry,' he tells the mayor. 'I didn't realize it was against the rules.'

'And the three aliens are still there. You could be fined for that as well.'

'I forgot all about them. I'll cut them down later.'

His visitor continues to linger, arms folded in disapproval. It seems he wants personally to oversee the chopping down of the foreign trees, but abruptly his whole demeanour changes. He catches at Adam's sleeve; he whispers, 'Don't tell anybody.'

'Excuse me?'

'It's all right, forget the trees, forget the fire. I won't fine you. But you mustn't say anything to anybody.'

'About what?'

'You know what about!' This whole exchange has taken place in low voices, as if they're meeting furtively in the middle of a crowd. But now, as the steam begins to thin out, the mayor straightens up. In a clearer, braver voice, he says, 'I'm talking about the payment.'

Adam stares at him. 'I don't know what you mean.'

His confusion is genuine, but the mayor smiles broadly in approval. 'That's the way,' he says. 'I like your thinking.' He gives Adam a slow, oily wink, then drops his voice confidingly again. 'It wasn't for me anyway,' he whispers. 'I hope you believe me. Every cent of it was for the party. I did it for my country.'

*

He drives back out to Gondwana. Part of his mind watches himself through the wrong end of a telescope: seeing Adam

Napier heading out on that same lonely stretch of road, going back to that same place again. He's made this journey so often by now that it's like entering a zone of dead time; he's almost not present, and he only comes to himself again when he reaches the gate and the guard won't let him through. He's a man Adam's seen many times before, but he's wearing a new attitude of aloofness today, staring at a point somewhere above the car. No, he says, nobody can go in. Absolutely nobody. Mr Canning's orders.

'But I'm an old friend of his. You know me. I've been here plenty of times.'

'No visitors today.'

'Can't you check with him? I'm sure he doesn't mean me.'

The man shakes his head. He touches casually at the shiny holster on his belt. Adam senses the futility of this dialogue and he turns the car and drives back towards town. But when he's out of sight of the guard and the gate, he slows down. He remembers the day, driving around the farm with Canning, when they'd found evidence of poachers forcing their way in. He too is about to cross a line, one inscribed on the earth and also inside himself.

When he comes to a rest area on the far side of the road, he pulls over. There is a place to leave the car, near a concrete table and seat. He opens the boot, takes out the metal crowbar used to crank up the jack. Then he crosses the tar, to the other side.

The fence is tall and strong, cutting up the view into a grid of lozenges. He is a novice at infiltration, but he sees that the bottom of the fence, in certain places, doesn't connect properly with the ground. He crouches down and goes to work on the wire. When the sound of an engine approaches, he flattens himself into the scrub, but nobody even slows down. His adrenaline is high and he is almost thrilled, in a panic-stricken way, at the skills he's acquiring, the instincts he's discovering in himself.

It doesn't take long to get through. He emerges on the other side as a dirty new-born on his knees, freshly minted from mud. Adam the intruder. Adam the thief. Then he sets off at a trot towards the tall smudge of dust in the sky, perhaps a kilometre distant.

By the time he arrives, he is hot and gasping, basted in sweat. The scene has entirely transformed. On the last occasion he'd stood here, the earth had been whole and complete, but it has since been ripped open and all its innards have come spilling out. Huge piles of rubble rise in grotesque brown cones. The exposed soil is raw and primitive, showing the layers and striations beneath the surface. Men in khaki uniforms are swarming everywhere, appearing and disappearing in the endless fug of dust. Under the lowering sun, this angry, oblivious industry takes on an infernal glow.

He stands staring in amazement. The violent energy of the spectacle is unreal, like something he's cooked up in his brain; and there is something dreamlike, too, in how irrelevant his tiny troubles have become. Nobody pays him any mind; he is one more meaningless observer. But when he spots Canning's diminutive figure, standing on top of a low hill nearby, his resolve returns to him and he climbs determinedly up.

He knew Canning would be here: while this labour is in progress, he will be close by every day, watching. He has set the frenzy in motion and is now more than ever the invisible spectator, separate, apart. And despite the policy at the gate, he shows no surprise at Adam's arrival; he seems absorbed in the furious panorama spread out below. 'Oh, it's you, hello,' he says despondently.

Adam can't speak at first; he's breathing too hard from the climb. When he recovers, he says, 'You lied to me.'

Canning blinks in astonishment. 'How do you mean?'

'That parcel I took to the mayor. It was money. You were bribing him.'

'Oh. Right. Yes.' He looks away again, his dejection like boredom. 'Well, of course it was money.'

'But you told me it was just papers.'

'Yes. Well. I said what you wanted to hear. But you knew it was money. What else would it be?'

'How could you *do* that to me?'

'It's business, Adam. It's the way things work. If everybody just plays their part, it's no big deal.' His bland, oval face is passionless as he explains: 'It's like nature, you see. Strong animals eat the weaker animals. You have to do anything, use any tactic, to survive. I thought you'd understand, Adam, you of all people – I mean, that's what your poems are about. The natural world. Where only the powerful will win.'

'That's *not* what my poems are about.'

'Maybe not. Maybe I didn't understand them. I'm not a creative person, of course. I'm just a businessman.' He seems to deflate a little, like a plastic man with a puncture. When he speaks again, he sounds on the verge of tears. 'Oh, this is terrible,' he says in a small voice. 'This isn't what I wanted at all.'

'What did you want?'

'I wanted you to be part of it. That's why I got you to take the money. Of course I could've done it another way, I could even have paid him myself. But I wanted you involved somehow. It was just a symbolic thing. Nothing serious.'

'I don't understand.'

Canning turns his stricken face towards him. 'You were my hero, Adam. My whole life, since school, you've been my big hero. You're the cause of this, don't you see? All this,' and he gestures at the breaking and building of the landscape below, 'all this is because of you.'

'You keep saying that, but I didn't want this to happen.'

'You know what's funny?' Canning says sadly. 'Now that it's started, I don't want it to happen either. But it's too late now. There's no way to stop it.'

A long silence follows. 'You pulled me in,' Adam says at last, 'you made me an accomplice. But I didn't know what I was doing. We've been playing a game, Canning – a big, ugly game. But the game's over now. It's time to tell the truth. I want you to know something. I'm not going to cover for you. If they ask me, I'm going to tell them everything I know. What I saw, what I heard, what you got me to do. I'll even tell about this conversation we're having now.'

'I understand.' Canning is almost whispering. 'But that isn't very wise.'

'How so?'

'Because you'll make Mr Genov very upset.'

'Well, I'm sorry about that.' He turns and starts down the slope.

Canning's voice carries behind him. 'Wait a minute... Does this mean we're not friends any more? This isn't how I wanted it... I apologize for everything, Nappy.' After a moment, a faint correction comes: 'Sorry, I mean Adam!'

The whole way back to his car, Adam wonders whether that last slip was intentional.

18

The knock comes in the middle of the day. A tentative sound, a light rapping on the front door. It's been a few weeks since the last request for work or money; word must've got around that he has nothing to give, and when he opens the door and sees the two of them, he launches into his usual apologetic refusal. But after a few sentences he trails off.

The faces outside are both strange and familiar, like people in a dream. Old, tired black faces, uncertain and afraid. A man and a woman, wearing dirty, ragged clothes. But what has silenced Adam is the yellow hat, being twisted and untwisted in the old man's hands.

'Ezekiel!' he says. 'Grace!' He has thought of them – though in truth he hasn't thought of them – as gone, erased, disappeared. But now they have found their way to his door.

'*Ja*,' Ezekiel says. He looks as stunned as Adam, but he smiles, showing the brown stumps of teeth.

'What are you doing here?'

'No, we are looking for work, mister Adam. We are trying all the houses here. Because we are hungry. The madam, she told us we must go, but we have no place to go. So we are looking.'

'She told you to go? But why?' As he asks the question, his eyes flick guiltily towards Grace, but she is staring at the ground.

'No, I don't know, mister Adam. She is saying we did something wrong, but we did nothing.'

The silence that follows is filled to the brim.

'Come in,' he says at last. 'Come and sit down.'

As they go obediently past him, he catches the smell of them: an unwashed, sweaty stink. The old man is carrying two plastic bags, and it occurs to Adam that everything they own must be in there. They stand in the middle of the lounge, awkward and out of place, until he gestures to them to sit. Even then they perch on the very edge of the sofa, as if they want to leave no impression on the room.

'Where have you been staying?' he asks them.

'Outside.' The old man flaps his hand in a loose gesture.

'Outside? You mean you've been sleeping rough? But you must have friends, surely, somewhere around here...?'

'We have no friends.' He shakes his head.

Adam remembers what Canning had told him: about how his father had taken the two of them with him, from farm to farm, wherever he went. It had sounded like a tale of mutual loyalty, but now he sees where this story will end. The *Oubaas* is gone; they are alone; they have nobody to help them.

His heart is wrung: he is part of this, part of what has happened to them. His voice trembles slightly as he says, 'What are we going to do with you now?'

Ezekiel says, 'No, I don't know,' and gazes down at his broken boot.

Grace looks up at Adam and a glance goes between them, electrified with a peculiar voltage. He jumps to his feet. He must *do* something; he must act. 'Right,' he says. 'Let's have a word with Canning.'

In a rush of principle and conviction, he goes to the phone. Having something, anything, to do is a relief. But when he tries Canning's mobile number it rings for a while, then goes to voice-mail. He calls the lodge instead and Baby picks up. 'I'm coming out there,' he tells her. 'Please instruct the guard at the gate to let me through.'

'What's this about?'

'I'll explain when I get there.'

He puts the phone down before she can answer and he isn't sure whether she'll do what he's asked. But he'd spoken very insistently and when he gets to the gate, the guard lets him through without a word. On the other side, he drives down that familiar dirt road again, with Ezekiel and Grace sitting beside and behind him like a cargo of silent accusation, and it occurs to him that this may be, after all, a more fitting end to the story: to restore these two old people to their rightful place, before he himself disappears into the background.

As they pull up under the trees outside the house, he sees a small convocation happening on the lawn. Canning and two others, drawn together in feverish deliberation. They stare at his car in alarm and astonishment, giving off a vibration of crisis. Suddenly he is unsure about having the two old people with him. They had felt like a moral ballast, weighting him securely, but now he thinks it was a mistake to bring them along. He should be having this conversation on his own.

'Wait here,' he tells them. They look only too relieved to stay behind.

When he gets out of the car he sees that one of the people on the lawn is Sipho Moloi, who turns away sharply from his approach. Canning breaks with the little group and hurries over to meet him. 'Adam,' he says, smiling glassily, 'this isn't the best moment. We're facing some little challenges right now. Got to sort it all out.'

'I'm not here for a sociable visit. It's just... I thought I might persuade you to reconsider. It isn't fair, Canning. It's not their fault.'

'Fault?' The word hangs in the air between them, then fades away with his smile. 'I don't follow you.'

Only when Adam gestures behind him, at the two stolid shapes in the car, does Canning understand.

'Oh,' he says. '*Them*. Yes. Well, they're not my problem, Adam.' A tightness and impatience have come into his face;

he is visibly straining backwards, to get away. 'They did it to themselves, actually. Baby caught them stealing from the kitchen. And it wasn't the first time.'

'That isn't true.'

'What?'

'They weren't stealing. That's not why. It was something else.'

'Whatever,' Canning says, his face pink. 'I really have to go now, Adam, I'm sorry.'

Baby approaches at this moment. She has, in fact, been watching them from the front veranda for a while; he'd seen her over Canning's shoulder. 'What's the matter?' she says sweetly. 'What's wrong?' But her eyes carry some of the cold quality he saw in them last time, and as Canning hurries away, out of earshot, her whole tone changes. 'Are you mad?' she hisses at him. 'What are you trying to do, bringing them here?'

'Look at them,' he says. 'They have no future.'

'Why is that my problem?'

He is astonished. 'Because you did it to them. You sent them away.'

'You know why. I had to. I told you I'd take care of it. It was the best thing to do. Under the circumstances.'

'The best thing for who?' he says. 'For you?'

'And for you.'

The truth of this stings him into silence. He can only say, 'But I didn't want this.'

'Adam. Adam. They were past their time anyway. They can't stay on – all of this is changing. There's no place for them here any more.'

It comes to him again: what he has been complicit in, what he has not refused. His fury is like a blind dropping down in his head. He wants to grab and shake her; he wants to do violence.

'Fuck the poor,' he says, 'is that it?'

Something flashes across her face, which she seals away. Then, carefully, she says, 'Yes. It's true. I don't care about them. Why should I?'

'Because… that could have been your life.'

'But it isn't,' she says. 'Is it?'

Both of them are conscious of Canning and his associates nearby, of what must be hidden from them. Without that watchful audience, they would be attacking one another right now, using teeth and nails and fists. But they speak instead.

'I know who you are,' he tells her.

She has a tight, brittle smile on her face, and her whisper is like a thin, tiny needle of hatred. 'No, you don't. You don't know anything about me. Not anything. If you did, you wouldn't speak like this. You don't know how I've fought, the things I had to do to get to where I am. If I'm over here and they're over there, that's because I'm stronger. And part of being strong is doing what you have to do. Do you think I'm going to give up my life, give up all *this*, for them? Are you crazy? You can keep your pity and your sentiment, you can keep your white man's weakness. You've never been desperate, not for one day in your life.'

Over her shoulder he sees a peacock, pecking at some insect on the ground. Even here, at the heart of so much finery, there is the brutal appetite, reaching out with its hard little beak to stab, stab, stab. Who could write a poem about a peacock?

He walks away from her, back to the car. The eyes of the two old people show no surprise or disappointment; they hadn't expected anything else.

*

The next time he speaks is when he pulls up at the house in town. 'I have to do something with you,' he says to his passengers. 'I have to make a plan. Do you have any ideas?'

They shake their heads, they look down.

'There must be somebody else you can go to.' Then he remembers. 'What about your son?'

The son – Canning's playmate. Where is Lindile now?

'He is in Cape Town. He is living there.' The first time the old lady speaks.

'And can you contact him there? Do you have a telephone number?'

She fishes around in her plastic bag, comes up with a dirty scrap of paper. The number on it is faintly written in pencil. But it is the one possible solution.

They crowd behind him into the passage as he calls. It rings for a long time before a woman answers. Her English isn't good, and the line crackles, but he understands her to say that Lindile is out, that he'll be back in a few hours. He leaves a message, asking him to call back.

'It's about his parents,' he says. 'His mother and father. They're in trouble and I'm trying to help them.'

The connection hisses, then goes dead. But he feels better afterwards: something has been set in motion, steps have been taken. It's only much later that it occurs to him to wonder what the relationship might be between Lindile and his parents. If they had wanted help from their son, would they not have called him already? Is he meddling in something that he doesn't understand?

Meanwhile he makes tea and sandwiches for his visitors. It is poor food – what he eats these days too – but they consume it quickly, hungrily. Then he herds them into the bathroom. 'Clean yourselves up,' he says, 'it'll make you feel better.' While he runs the bath he goes through his cupboard to look for clothes that might fit them. The old man is about his size, they're almost a match. He takes out trousers, a shirt, a pair of shoes. For Grace he has nothing suitable, except a jersey and a scarf.

While they're washing, he sits in the lounge next door, listening. There is the sound of water splashing, an occasional murmur between them. Is it him that they're discussing? Do they find his hospitality a joke, do they see through it to the shame underneath?

When they come out again, it's not quite a transformation. But they do look cleaner than before. His clothes hang a little loosely on Ezekiel, the shirt sleeves overflow his hands. The shoes slide around on his feet. Grace is wearing the jersey and a set, opaque expression. They come back into the lounge and sit down on the couch again, this time without being invited.

When he goes into the bathroom a little later, there is a ring of black dirt around the tub. While he busies himself scrubbing it away, he reflects on the change in their positions. They are, by a twist of fate, his guests, and he has somehow become the servant. But he embraces the new role, he fits himself to it eagerly. A small measure of humiliation might lessen his crimes, in his own eyes if not in theirs.

At that moment the telephone rings. The voice on the other side is low, flat, almost inaudible. 'This is Lindile,' it says. 'I have a message to call you.'

'Yes! Lindile! This is Adam Napier. I have your parents here with me.' He explains what has happened, without going into detail. He tells nothing that incriminates himself. He has rescued the two old people from the roadside; he has taken it on himself to look after them. No doubt his mother will give a fuller story to Lindile in due course, but by then, Adam hopes, they will be far away.

When he finishes, there is a long silence before Lindile sighs. 'What do you want me to do?' he says.

'Well, I don't know. Are you in a position to help them? Give them a place to stay? There's nothing for them up here.'

'No,' Lindile says. It's unclear whether he's refusing or agreeing.

'They're your parents,' Adam says desperately. 'They have a big problem. Don't you want to help them?'

'Who are you?' Lindile says unexpectedly.

'Me? I'm... I'm a friend of Canning's. I mean, Kenneth's. I used to visit the farm.'

Another sigh. The low voice says, 'I cannot come tomorrow. The earliest I can be there is the weekend. Saturday.'

The weekend is still a couple of days away. While he gives his address, Adam is already thinking ahead, to how he must look after these two. He can't put them out to sleep in the open again. But to have them sleeping in the house, under the same roof, is more than he'd bargained for.

He wishes he had money. With money, a great deal would be possible. He could pay for them to sleep at the hotel; he could give them a proper meal at a restaurant. Better yet, he could give them a big cash donation and send them on their way, his conscience eased. With money, he could put a gap between him and them; he could wash his hands of them completely.

But he doesn't have a lot of money left. In fact, without the help of his brother, his position wouldn't be too different from theirs. So he has no choice but to fall back on the comforts he can offer, which are practical and immediate. He can share what he has: another meal of bread and cheese and tea, and a bed for the night.

Which throws up another problem. There is only one bed in the house, the one that he uses. But he's troubled by the idea of letting them sleep on the floor: there are two of them, and they're old – old enough to be his parents.

That image, of his mother and father without a place to sleep, decides him. 'Take my bed,' he tells them, and they accept without any argument. He has a faint prickle of resentment, instantly replaced by guilt: it's because of him, after all, that they are here. Let him sleep on the ground for a few nights – it's hardly a fair exchange.

*

Over the next few days, they don't leave the house. They are always there, sitting in the lounge, looking sad and enigmatic. Occasionally a few words pass between them, but otherwise they seem to generate a fraught silence, against which even the tiniest sounds take on resonance. The creak of the couch. The window-pane vibrating in the wind. The squeaking of Grace's shoes as she walks aimlessly about.

Like him, they are waiting. But their old life has ended; they are leaving their old life behind. While he is waiting to go on with his life, to pick up where he left off. At the same time he suspects that his life won't be the same; something – but what exactly? – has changed.

Sometimes it's too much. Sometimes he can't bear to sit here for another second, hemmed in by these two. They're like a pair of dark attendant angels, familiar spirits, here only to keep a watchful eye on him, toting up the moral score in a ledger. At these moments he jumps up. 'I'm going to the shop,' he tells them. 'Will you be all right till I come back?'

There are always errands he can think up to keep him busy. But often he goes out without an aim, taking one of his walks through the town, no destination in mind, just passing the time. On one of these missions, going past the municipal office, he sees a small crowd of protesters on the lawn outside: the people from the township, he thinks, still angry about the lack of housing and services. But then he notices that this is a different group, with different placards and a different mood. Fanie Prinsloo, the ex-Springbok rugby player, is in front, shouting something through a megaphone.

He's carrying a placard that says, SOLD DOWN THE RIVER.

The story comes to him in bits and pieces as he moves among the bystanders. And some of it arrives later, in the form of a photocopied pamphlet dropped into his letter-box. There is hysteria and anger about the impact of the golf course on the natural environment, especially the river. There are figures showing that the golf course is likely to consume three million litres of water a day, which means that the river will dry up. The future of the town itself is under threat.

Adam is troubled by all of this, in a personal way. And his unease grows deeper when he gets a call from his brother later in the day. '*Ja*,' Gavin tells him triumphantly. 'Looks like the shit's hitting the fan.'

'What are you talking about?'

'With your friend from school, the golf course guy. And Genov, that old crook. It's all over the papers this afternoon. Front page news. Listen to this.'

Gavin reads him the article, but what he's hearing doesn't get through to Adam. His head is swimming and he has only the most general impression afterwards – of land being rezoned through improper procedures, allegations of nepotism, and a suspect tender process. The whole golf course deal seems to be imploding.

He cuts his brother short. 'I don't get it,' he says. 'What's actually going on?'

'Haven't you been listening? It's unravelling, that's what's going on. What started it is this government character, what's his name again, somebody Moloi, giving the construction contract to a company that happens to have his uncle and brother-in-law on the board of directors. Now all kinds of unsavoury things are creeping out of the woodwork. Your mayor is also involved. Seems like he passed an environmental impact assessment without running it past the council. People are calling for his head. Fanie Prinsloo – remember him? – has come out and said it publicly. Corruption.'

'I don't care about any of this,' Adam says. 'What's it got to do with me?'

'But this is your friend's little project, isn't it? I wouldn't want to be him right now.'

'He's not my friend.'

'What do you mean? Just two weeks ago you were down here at his invitation for a fancy party at that criminal's house. I tried to warn you at the time, if you remember. I told you – '

'I don't see him any more,' Adam says. 'He isn't my friend.'

19

Lindile arrives in the afternoon on Saturday. He's a tall, thin man in jeans and T-shirt, driving a battered old Golf, which he parks in front of the house. He comes quickly down the path and knocks three times – a hard, clean sound – on the front door. He greets Adam with a cool nod and only accepts his handshake after a considered pause. He has a narrow face with a tight, set look to it, like a padlock.

'I am here for my parents,' he says.

'Yes, yes,' Adam says. 'We have been waiting for you.'

He stands aside to let him in. Ezekiel and Grace are waiting uncertainly in the lounge. They seem almost afraid of their son, but once he has come inside they greet each other with hesitant formality. Adam isn't sure of what kind of scene he is watching: one of reconciliation, perhaps, or just of tired filial duty. There is no way to know.

'We're very glad to see you,' Adam says.

'I'm sure you are.' The voice is low and flat, as it was on the phone, but he stresses the 'you' slightly: a possible accusation.

Adam tries to remember what he knows about this man. The bits and pieces that Canning had thrown out were either sentimental ('my first playmate') or dismissive ('he got all political later'). Neither seems to fit the self-possessed person in front of him, who shows no interest in small talk.

'Please take a seat,' Adam says. 'Can I make you some tea?'

'Yes,' Lindile says.

He goes into the kitchen and makes tea. When he carries it through to the lounge, Lindile has seated himself in a chair, a little distance away from his parents on the couch. They aren't looking at or speaking to each other, and the silence continues while Adam serves them. Then he puts himself uncomfortably down between the two old people; there is no other place. To keep the conversation moving, he says, 'What is it you do in Cape Town?'

'I'm a lecturer.' He names a college that Adam has never heard of.

'And what's your subject?'

'Political Science.'

'Oh. Very nice.' Adam's eyes go down to the front of Lindile's T-shirt, which carries an image of marching workers under a clenched fist. 'And whereabouts do you live?'

'In Nyanga. Is it an area you know?'

'No.'

'Yes, I have a house there. Four rooms. I live there with my wife and my cousin. Now my parents will be living there too. I don't know what we are going to do.'

After all the terse answers, the fullness of this reply seems to carry a message. Adam sets his cup down next to him and speaks quietly. 'Look,' he says. 'Lindile. It feels to me as if you are very angry. I don't know you, I don't know what's happened in your life, maybe you have reason for your anger. But what I don't understand is why you are angry with *me*. I'm only trying to help.'

Even as he speaks, the words turn back on him. He is responsible, after all, for what's happened to this man's parents; he isn't helping out of charity.

He tries again. 'This isn't easy for any of us.'

'*Ja*? How is it difficult for you?'

'I have a small place, as you can see. The same size as yours. But I've been sharing it with your parents. We've been living here, on top of each other.'

'Yes,' Lindile says, 'that is very good of you. You have given my parents a bed for a few nights, you have given them some food. Now you want to get rid of them. So you have called their son in Cape Town, who hasn't seen them in more than ten years, to come and take them away.'

'I didn't know there was some estrangement between you and them. I'm sorry if I've been insensitive. But still – this is your mother and father. I'm a stranger to them. They are your responsibility, surely, much more than mine. A child has duties towards his parents.'

'You say you're a stranger. But you know them, don't you, from where they work? You said you were a friend of Kenneth's.'

'Is that what this is about? Are you angry because I know the Cannings?'

With the first trace of temper to flash through his composure, Lindile cuts him off. 'If you want to help,' he says, 'if you really want to help, then give us some money. That will make a difference.'

'I can't. I'm not in a position to do that.' Adam turns in agitation to Ezekiel, appealing to him. 'I can't give you work,' he says, 'or a place to live. I wish I could. I know money is the problem.' The old man smiles and bobs his head. But Lindile speaks sharply to him in Xhosa and the smile disappears. Though Adam doesn't speak the language, the meaning is clear: don't make yourself servile, don't dance in front of this man.

Then Lindile turns back to him. '*Ja*, you are right,' he says. 'Money is the problem. Money has always been the problem. Even before this. Even when they were working, they had nothing.'

'I know that. I saw.'

'No money, no power. Very simple.'

Adam gestures at the room, with its ugly, second-hand furniture. 'I also have no money. Can't you see? I am already learning what no power means. You assume too much, Lindile. We are not all the same. I am not like...'

'Like your friends,' Lindile says.

'Yes,' he says. 'Like my friends.'

He feels that he has made a point, but in the silence that follows he knows: in the eyes of this man, he is just like his friends.

'Canning tells me,' he goes on, 'that you were also his friend.'

'He told you that?'

'He said you played together when you were boys.'

'When I was too small to know better, yes. But even then, when the playing was finished, I went to my *pondok* and he went to the big house.'

'Oh, come on,' he says. 'For God's sake. The whole country's moved on since then. Everything's changed. Can't you move on too?'

Lindile smiles thinly. 'No,' he says. 'I can't move on.' And that seems to be the truth of it. He is stuck in the past, pinned down under his anger, which is like a huge rock on his chest. Adam will never be able to do enough, give enough, to make things right.

As if to underscore this fact, Lindile jumps up. 'Let us see how you live,' he says, and before anybody can stop him he goes stalking through the house, from room to room. Adam finds himself scurrying along indignantly behind him. When they get to the bedroom, Lindile stops and turns, his arms folded. 'So,' he says. 'This is your no-money. You say you can't help us, but you have much more than we do. Even with four rooms, you are living here alone.'

'This house doesn't belong to me. It's my brother's house.' His voice rises, shrill and defensive.

'But you have four rooms,' he says again. 'Why can't my parents live here with you?'

Adam is speechless. The question is obviously outrageous, and he can see from Lindile's thin smile that he's trying to provoke him. Yet on some level inside himself he also thinks that what Lindile says isn't so unreasonable. He does have four rooms; they have none. Why shouldn't they be living here with him, sleeping in his bed, sheltering under his roof? Why should he have it all to himself?

He quells his self-doubt in a moment. Of course, this is just a perverse game, and what's being put to him is something else, something not said. He thinks he has the measure of this man. Judging by his car, his clothes, he is not too badly off; he is probably on a par with Adam. But although they're on a level for the moment, Lindile is on his way up, Adam on his way down. And it's part of their precarious equality that Lindile doesn't have sharing on his mind. No, he would like their positions to be reversed: he would like to be here with his parents and wife, and possibly his cousins too, occupying all four rooms, while Adam is outside and homeless. Better yet, he would like Adam to be far away, in another country entirely. That is what would satisfy Lindile.

Ezekiel and Grace have followed them through, looking agitated. They seem unsure of what is playing itself out here, between their son and this white man, their benefactor. They start speaking anxiously in Xhosa, but Lindile ignores them. To Adam he says coolly, almost as if their whole exchange hasn't happened, 'We will leave now, I think. Thank you very much for everything. Thank you for the tea.'

Adam walks out with them to say goodbye. The old people are obsequious, thanking him with the usual excessive pantomime, which Lindile again cuts short with a brief, explosive word. Then the car pulls away, disappearing down the road, driving out of his life.

20

He starts to pack up the house. From the supermarket he gets a few old boxes and puts his belongings into them. He has thought of it as a big job, one that will take days or weeks, but is soon reminded, all over again, of how little he owns. In a couple of mornings his life is disassembled and ready for removal.

Nevertheless, he doesn't call Cape Town and tell his brother to expect him. He's not quite ready yet to leave. There is nothing to stay for, exactly, but now that it's on the verge of turning into the past, this phase of his life takes on a sentimental glow. None of it has been too bad, really. Even staying here on his own has been something of an adventure.

So he drifts around from room to room, gazing out of the windows, saying goodbye to the furniture. He occupies himself with little missions to the municipality, giving them a month's notice to disconnect the telephone, the electricity. Preparing the house for its emptiness again. He spends a lot of time sitting out on the back steps, gazing over the valley.

Winter is ebbing away; spring is sweeping in. Each day feels a little warmer, as the earth tips its face toward the sun. On the branches of the trees outside the front door, tiny buds and shoots are showing. The first swallows have come back into the sky. And in the yard, the new weeds are growing with a fresh infusion of pace and power. They are knee-high in some places already, and each day the green carpet is discernibly taller, thickening and rising like some insidious ambition. But Adam only watches them indifferently, knowing that somebody else, at some other time, will have to clear them.

On one of the evenings that he's sitting out there, enjoying a mug of coffee, the telephone rings. In his pleasant lethargy he almost doesn't answer it. But the ringing goes insistently on and on, and in the end he gets up.

The voice on the other side is low and panicked. 'Adam,' it says. 'We have to meet.'

So distanced does he feel from recent events that it takes Adam a few seconds to recognize who's speaking. Then he's instantly furious again. 'No, Canning,' he says. 'I don't want to see you.'

'You don't understand. This is very important.'

'Important to you, maybe. But not to me. There's nothing to discuss.'

A pause, a faint burr of static. 'You're wrong, Adam. You need to hear this.'

Something in Canning's voice disturbs him, a note that carries down the line and plants itself in his head, like a tiny seed of disquiet. He hesitates for a moment, then says, 'All right. Where do you want to meet?'

*

The sun is going down as he drives through town and up to the highway, and the scarlet drama of the sky adds to his sense of intrigue and unease. Why the intense urgency of this meeting, and why at this time of day, when the long, attenuated shadows are all joining into one? And why at the old road, with its air of dereliction and decay, away from any observing eyes? When he's turned off and parked behind a line of trees, the traffic passing on the main road seems very far away. He is alone in a shadowy half-circle of gravel, littered with plastic bags and beer cans and used condoms, smelling of urine.

The old road is a curious feature. It leaks sideways off the new highway and goes under a set of barricades before disappearing into the landscape. It is recognisably still a road, but the markings and signs have faded almost to invisibility, and the tar has been cracked open by bushes and tussocks of grass pushing through. In the last light, as the afternoon tapers away, it looks like nothing so much as a ghost-road, only half-present, through which the earth is showing. It's hard to imagine that any traffic ever travelled on its surface.

While he waits, Adam walks around the parking area, kicking at gravel. The rush and roar of passing trucks carries through the trees, and the leaves vibrate. He is full of paranoid thoughts by now, and he has almost made up his mind to leave, when Canning finally arrives. He parks the SUV some way off from Adam and in just a few seconds he comes hurrying over.

Both of them, as they approach each other, are reserved. In keeping with the furtive nature of their encounter, Canning is wearing some kind of cloth cap on his head. Dressed like this, with his head pulled down between his shoulders, he reminds Adam of a tortoise. His flesh is pale and soft: like tortoise-flesh, hidden from the sun.

He says, 'Did anybody see you come?'

'I don't think so. What's this all about, Canning?'

'Let's walk. Do you feel like a walk?'

There's nowhere to go, except along the old road itself. Under a bleary half-moon hanging low in the sky, in the greenish glow of twilight, the road is a luminous stripe across the darker land. They steer over the crumbling tar, avoiding the clumps of foliage in their way. They pass an old traffic sign, listing to the left and rusted away. There is the stridulation of insects, the call of some night-bird up ahead.

'I heard you were having some trouble with the golf course.'

'Yes,' Canning says impatiently, 'but it's just a little setback. We'll get around it very soon. Contacts, contacts – it's all about who you know.'

'Well, you seem to know some powerful people.'

'Yes, yes. Actually, that's the reason we're here. I hope you realize,' he says sententiously, 'that I'm talking to you at great risk to myself. I would be in a lot of trouble if they saw me with you. I'm doing this because of what you mean to me. From the old days.'

'Well, thank you, Canning,' Adam says dryly.

'Oh, don't mention it. You're my oldest and closest friend, after all.' Their metronomic footsteps skip a beat as they skirt around a bush sprouting in the middle of the road. 'If only you didn't insist on being honest,' he says with sudden bitterness. 'If only you didn't insist on speaking up. I told you it would make him upset.'

'Who?'

'Who? Mr Genov, of course. He's such an unreasonable man. I've tried to talk to him, I've tried to explain, but he won't listen. It's just to be on the safe side, he says. I can't stop him, Adam. I have no power.'

'I have no idea what you're talking about.'

'What? Don't you understand anything?' Canning stops and faces him, spreading his plump palms in appeal. 'I'm trying to warn you.'

'About what?'

'Listen to him! They're going to kill you, of course.'

Only now does the conversation become real to Adam. His knees go weak, a white light flashes behind his eyes. The notion of murder is suddenly like something tangible, hovering close by in the air. He has entertained the idea of it himself. He has, in a theoretical way, contemplated what it would be like to kill the man he's speaking to now. But murder has a life of its own; he has sent it out into the world, and it has boomeranged back towards him.

'*Why*?' he says.

'Because you know too much. Because you made the payment to the mayor.'

'But I didn't understand what it was.'

'Yes, but that doesn't matter. I'm sorry about it, Adam, it's my fault, really, I suppose. But no use crying over spilt milk.' Canning gives a little shrug, as if they're talking about some minor oversight. 'Oh, it's all been so stressful,' he cries. 'I wish this phase of my life was over!'

They resume their walk with incongruous calm, as if none of the preceding talk has happened. And their voices, as they go on speaking, also have a disconnected composure:

'Talk to him for me. Tell him I'm no threat.'

'I told you, I tried. But it's too late. And anyway, you *are* a threat.'

'Am I so important?'

'You don't understand. It's because you're not important at all.'

'Poor Mr Genov, you said. So misunderstood. Such a bad press.'

'I suppose I misjudged him. But I'm going to cut my ties with him. I want you to know that. When this is finished, I won't see him again. Which is no consolation to you, obviously. But I'm just saying.'

He is almost curious. 'How…?' he says.

'What do you mean? Oh, yes, I see… with a gun, I think.'

'And who…?'

'I don't know exactly. They send somebody. There are people who do this sort of thing. For a living, as it were.'

'And when is this supposed to happen?'

'Tonight, of course. That's why I insisted on a meeting.'

'*Tonight*? But it's almost dark already. What am I supposed to do?'

'Well, you mustn't go home. Not under any circumstances. Leave right away. Go to Cape Town.'

By now, they are perhaps a kilometre from the main road, with deserted countryside around them. They go over a rise and in front of them is a ruined bridge, half-projecting over a gorge. On the far side the road continues, but they can't walk any further. Canning stops at the edge of the bridge, but Adam takes a few more aimless steps. He feels reckless, a little crazy. Space opens out below him; the metal struts whine in the wind. Without thinking, he lifts a foot and stamps and the sound echoes down the gorge – half-clang, half-crack.

'Er, I wouldn't do that,' Canning says. 'It doesn't look safe.'

'*Safe*?' Adam says. The word has become ridiculous. He stamps again; the echoes peal away. He's choking on all the pent-up emotion from the past months, some of it secret even to himself. He wants to laugh and weep at the same time. Is this really going to be his fate: to die because of a golf course? Tragedy and absurdity mix into a venomous cocktail and he suddenly lunges at Canning, grabbing and pulling with no clear intention. 'This is all your fault,' he shouts, 'you lying, pathetic, little… chemical salesman!'

In a moment – unexpectedly – Canning is screaming back. His bloodless face is distorted. 'Who… are… *you*… to accuse… smiling and talking… while you're *fucking my wife*!'

They are fused together for a moment in a furious embrace, balanced on the edge of the bridge, an ungainly quadruped emitting high, hysterical cries. But the huge landscape absorbs their frenzy like a sponge. Eventually they quieten down and separate themselves, finger by finger, becoming individual and apart.

They can't look at each other.

'You knew all the time,' Adam says. He's breathing heavily, while he smoothes and tucks in his shirt. He's lost some buttons in the scuffle.

'What did you think? That you were subtle?' Canning is flushed, his rapid breathing close to tears. He has a graze on one cheek. His cap has fallen off the bridge, and he keeps running a hand anxiously over the top of his head. He says, 'She's the most precious… the most precious thing I have. I notice her all the time.'

'I'm sorry,' Adam says. He has to fetch up the words from deep inside, and even then they mean nothing.

While they stand there for a long time in silence, the last sun disappears and the night takes hold. Patches of cloud drift over the moon and the earth wells up and disappears in the intermittent light. Canning says eventually, 'I don't mind you so much. With Baby, I mean. It was like sharing my good fortune with you. It's *him* that eats away at me. I keep thinking about his horrible hands all over her…' He gives a shudder.

Adam says quickly, 'But then why don't you cut him off?'

'Business is business,' Canning says. He jiggles his pockets, giving off the emphatic clink of loose change. 'Got to keep your eye on the fox. My personal life is separate. I would never cross the line, but *he* did. No, if she had to betray me with someone… I'd much rather it was you, Adam. Rather you than anybody else!'

'Thank you, Canning. I suppose.'

'Shall we walk back?'

They retrace their steps without speaking, both of them sunk in introspection. It's only when they come back in sight of the main road, with the headlights of cars sweeping past, that something else occurs to Adam. 'How does he know about me?' he asks. 'How does he know I paid the mayor? How does he know where to find me?'

'Because I told him, of course. I told him where you live.'

'But I don't understand – if I'm your friend – why you would do that. If you knew what he would do...'

'Don't you get it?' Canning says. 'I had to *stop* you. This has been my one big dream for half my life. The golf course must happen. I can't have you messing things up with your silly principles.'

'So you told him everything. And then you call me out here to warn me.'

'Yes,' Canning says sadly. 'It's weird, I know. But I couldn't decide what was more important, you or the golf course. I wanted to save you both.'

'Maybe you have.'

'I hope so.' He takes hold of Adam's fingers and squeezes them. He doesn't shake his hand so much as vibrate it, a tremor that seems to come from the core. 'I suppose we're not going to see each other for a while.'

'I suppose not.'

'It's strange, isn't it? How things work out. You think it's all going to be a certain way, and it turns out to be utterly different.'

'Yes, it's strange.'

'Take care of yourself, Adam.' He lets go of his hand at last.

'You too, Canning. Take care.'

He gets into his car and sits there for a few minutes after Canning has gone down the road. He's not thinking about anything; just trying to calm his heartbeat and his breath. He knows what he has to do, but he doesn't feel like proceeding in a rational way. Instead, he has a primitive, visceral urge to flee. Into the landscape, under the ground. He feels like a hunted animal, the focus of a carnivorous intent, that must run blindly for its life, stumbling across rocks, tearing itself on thorns. He has at last become part of nature, which he'd wanted to sing aloud in poems, and there's nothing Beautiful about it.

He forces himself eventually to take control. He starts the car at last and turns out of the dark knot of trees. Back on the road, he sees the direction ahead and begins to gather speed. This is what he must do, he tells himself: drive like this, all the way down to the city, not stopping anywhere. He'll be okay among buildings and lights; no harm can come to him there. He has almost begun to believe it. But as he comes to the turn-off that leads into the town, his mind returns to him in the form of a memory – a rootless, irrelevant fragment, which insists on being considered. Till it hardens into realization.

It's a blinding moment. He takes his foot off the accelerator and lets his momentum drop away until the car judders and stalls. In the stark wash of the headlights he sees the fork in the road floating just ahead of him, like the embodiment of a choice. He sits and stares, but he doesn't know which way to go.

A truck roars past, horn blaring, rocking the car turbulently in its wake.

'What now?' he says aloud.

Don't be a fool. Keep on going, don't look back.

'But I can't. I have to... I don't know, warn him, stop them, do something.'

What for? It's got nothing to do with you.

'But he's an innocent man.'

Hardly. Remember what he told you. Doesn't any of that matter?

'Innocent of my crimes, then.'

What crimes have you committed? You were in the wrong place at the wrong time, that's all. It was fate.

'I don't know what I'm supposed to do.'

Do nothing.

A hand extended on the cliff-face: a choice, entirely his.

AFTER

21

One day, out of the blue, Gavin told Adam that he thought he'd had some kind of a nervous breakdown while he was out in the country. 'I was quite worried about you,' he said. 'You weren't yourself for a while. You looked really scary, Ad. Thin and dirty, with a crazy stare. I got a shock when I saw you, that first time you came down here.'

'*Gavin*,' Charmaine said reproachfully, but she was playing with his hair as she spoke. They had recently got engaged, and there were a lot of lovey-dovey caresses going on between them.

'What?' Gavin said. 'It's true. Can't I be worried about my brother?'

This was a few months after Adam had got back to Cape Town, when things had settled. At first there'd been quite a bit of tension between him and his brother, especially after he'd turned down Gavin's offer of work again. But later, once he'd found another job and started earning a salary of his own and had moved out of Gavin's place into a flat by himself, the tension had eased.

'Something did happen to me up there,' he said. He was trying out the idea of a breakdown in his mind, and it fitted quite comfortably. Maybe that was what had happened to him; maybe that explained the odd way he'd behaved. 'You know,' he went on, 'I never mentioned this before, but I think Charmaine was right. There was another presence in the house with me.'

'Oh, jeez, not you as well,' Gavin said. 'What kind of a presence?'

'I can't tell you. But I wasn't alone there.'

They were sitting in a booth at an expensive Waterfront restaurant, yachts bobbing idly outside the windows. They were all a bit drunk, and Adam enjoyed the effect that his admission was having. Charmaine slid closer to him along the seat, her headlamp eyes fixed on his. 'I could sense it,' she whispered. 'I told you, remember? An old woman, very sad.'

'Oh, for the love of God.'

'I don't know about an old woman,' Adam said. 'But something listened. Something watched.'

'Something talked a lot of bullshit too.'

'No, it's true,' Charmaine said. 'If your mind was open to it, you'd understand. There are other planes intersecting with this one. There are all kinds of entities you just don't see. I really believe that.'

By now Adam was sorry that he'd started this line of discussion. He didn't believe in other planes and invisible entities, even though he hadn't felt alone in that house. But he thought of the other presence as a split-off part of his own mind, something real and imaginary at the same time, a sort of by-product of the depression he was going through.

He had certainly been depressed; Gavin was right about that, even though Adam hadn't known it at the time. He looked back now on his time in the country as a deviation from the main route of his life. He had been playing at poverty, while knowing all along, at the back of his mind, that he could go back to middle-class comforts whenever he wanted to. And now that he had picked up the thread, the whole episode caused him profound embarrassment. Sitting around doing nothing for day after day – what had he been thinking? His false friendship with Canning, and the affair with Baby too: when he looked back on his own behaviour, he didn't recognize himself. No, the entire thing was an aberration.

Thankfully, however, it was all very much in the past. Gavin didn't even own the house any more. He'd put it on the market not long after Adam had returned to Cape Town. There was no point in keeping it, Gavin said, considering he never went up there, and a pall had been cast over the idea of a rural idyll after what had happened to the next-door neighbour. It was no use Adam reminding him that the man was in hiding from a dark and dangerous past; in Gavin's mind the incident was confirmation that crime was rampant everywhere now, even in a sleepy backwater like that. The country was going to the dogs.

In the end, the only trace left of Blom was in the form of that awful metal sculpture. Adam had forgotten it existed, until Gavin and Charmaine had gone up there to clean the place out before the new owners moved in. They'd brought Adam's possessions, which he'd abandoned so hastily, back down to Cape Town with them, and the sculpture was in one of the boxes. It didn't look as powerful or repellent to him now as it had used to, but in any case he didn't want it. He was about to throw it into the bin when Charmaine stopped him. 'If you don't want that,' she said, 'I'll take it.'

'You're welcome. Go ahead.'

'Such a beautiful peacock feather. The whole thing has a very positive energy to it.' She carried it off and now it sat on her bedside table, amongst a collection of crystals and pendulums and Buddhist mandalas.

And that was it; there was no other tangible evidence of anything he'd been through up there. What he'd actually hoped to bring back with him had gone up, quite literally, in smoke. He never admitted that to his brother, of course, though Gavin kept returning to the subject.

He brought it up again now, after they'd left the restaurant and were walking, a little woozily, to the car. 'By the way,' he said to Adam, sidling casually closer, 'what happened to all the poems you wrote?'

'Oh, I'm still polishing them.'

*

His car disappeared one day while he was at work. He assumed at first that it had been stolen, but on further enquiry, it turned out that he'd parked in a loading zone and the car had been removed by the traffic department. When he went to pay that fine, they still wouldn't release the car. The computer had thrown up the traffic fines from a year and a half before, as well as the summons to appear in court. There was a warrant out for his arrest.

'But I didn't do anything,' he said.

He would have to explain in court, they told him. There was no way around it now; the warrant couldn't be undone.

He had a last flare-up of moral indignation. He would put his case, he decided, the way he'd planned to at the start. But on the day that he did appear in court, he had to sit first through a dispiriting array of sad and sorry characters, all with their own unlikely excuses. Each one had a story about why they had not paid their fine, or had failed to turn up in court before: one had been sick, another had been led astray by a series of absurd coincidences... By the time his own name was called, Adam's fount of self-righteousness had dried up. The magistrate, a weary-looking black woman, looked sceptical before he even started. And the sequence of events that he'd planned to relate – all of them true – sounded in his own head like obfuscation and lies, no different to those he'd been listening to all morning.

In the end, he didn't explain at all, beyond saying that he'd been living in the country and had forgotten about the fines. The magistrate looked relieved at the straightforwardness of his account. He should have paid in the first place, she told him, and no summons would've been necessary. Adam opened his mouth to argue, but heard himself apologizing instead.

It was all too high-up and out of reach. That was how it felt. There were principles, rules by which one should live, and these hovered in the air, shining and inviolate. Then there was the way one *did* live, which was a ramshackle construction of compromise and half-truth. Perhaps it was age, but he was learning to accept reality.

He stood in a line in front of a grimy window to pay what he owed. The woman behind the glass counted his money and stamped various forms and slid them back to him. On top of all the other fines there was now an extra one, an admission of guilt. Then he stepped aside and the next person in line took his place.

*

He had taken the whole day off work for his court appearance and now he found himself with a spare afternoon. He wandered through town and, out of habit, went into the Company's Garden. It was where he spent most of his lunch-breaks, sitting on a bench. The first white settlement had grown its fruit and vegetable supplies here and he liked the tatty remnants of history which occasionally showed through.

His usual bench was occupied, so he moved on to a different seat, under some overhanging vines. He watched the squirrels and pigeons for about half an hour, then he got bored and decided to go and retrieve his impounded car from the traffic department. He strolled back down the path and was about to walk through the gate of the gardens when he saw Canning directly in front of him. He was coming up the avenue past the parliament building, hands in his pockets and head down. It would have been easy for Adam to avoid him: he could have turned around and walked away. But he hesitated, and the hesitation became a choice.

Canning looked up and saw him and stopped. The two of them stared at each other for a moment, both very still in the flux and flow around them. Then Canning did something peculiar. His face clenched slightly, and he stepped sideways around Adam and hurried on. In a few seconds he was almost lost in the crowd.

Adam looked after him in amazement. What did it mean? The sensible thing would be to ignore it and walk on, but very suddenly, on impulse, he started to follow.

It was a weird chase. Canning never quite ran, but he was scurrying quickly along, ducking and diving, continually looking over his shoulder. When he saw Adam behind him, his body went tense with shock. For a few seconds he increased his pace, but then he seemed to give up. His shoulders slumped, he went a little slower, and when he passed a vacant bench he abruptly sat down.

Adam caught up and sat next to him. Canning was pale and breathing hard. He didn't look directly at Adam, but kept glancing sidelong, with little frightened turns of his head.

'What's the matter with you?' Adam said.

Then Canning gave a big exhalation. 'It *is* you,' he said. 'You're real.'

'What are you talking about? Who else would I be?'

'I thought that you'd gone back to the house after all. You know, after we spoke that last time...'

Then Adam finally did understand. 'You thought that was me? You thought I was dead?'

Canning nodded, blinking furiously. 'But you aren't, are you?' he asked, absurdly.

'No, of course not.'

'That's good.' Thus reassured, Canning visibly relaxed. 'I'm very glad to see you, Adam.'

Strangely, he didn't ask any further how Adam had escaped: his return from the dead had almost instantly become a fact. Instead it was general matters that they spoke about – Adam's move back to the city, the new job. It turned out that the office where Adam worked was ten minutes away from where Canning now lived. They had been here, so close to each other, for the past eight or nine months, and yet this was the first time they'd met.

'Well, we must get together,' Canning said. 'We need to catch up.'

'Yes,' Adam said, but in the pause that followed both of them knew that they wouldn't. There was no mutual future between them.

Canning had aged terribly. It was just over a year since they'd last seen one another, but a tiredness, a greyness, had come into his face. There were loose bags under his eyes, his hair had thinned even further, his mouth had started to sag. But at the same time something light and boyish had switched on in his eyes. It was that old happy spark – a throwback to long ago – that Adam had always set off in him.

'You heard about the golf course, I assume.'

'No,' he said, though of course he'd heard some things. Gavin had called him whenever a fresh item appeared in the newspapers – when the commission of inquiry had cleared Sipho Moloi, for example, or when the mayor had been forced to resign, still protesting his innocence. Or even when, in the next municipal elections, Fanie Prinsloo had become the new mayor. But it had been a while since any of this had appeared in the media.

'It opened last week,' Canning told him. 'Big song and dance, very fancy. They've kicked off with a new international tournament, the Liberty Vision cup. I'm surprised you didn't know about it – it was all over the television. I don't mind telling you, it looks magnificent. That is, if you care about golf courses.'

'I don't care about golf courses.'

'Nor do I, actually,' Canning said. 'Not any more.' He gave a barking, bitter laugh. 'No, I've given all that up.'

'Still,' Adam said, 'you got what you wanted. You managed to wipe out the past.'

'Yes. It's all gone now. None of it looks the same. The lodge, the *kloof* – oh, you wouldn't recognize any of it. Crawling with people. All built up. Gone,' he repeated, and made an abrupt gesture with his hand, as if he was pushing something away.

'You still go up there sometimes?'

'No, I cut my ties. Took the money and ran. I told you, when the deal was done, I would get out.'

After a pause, Adam asked, 'And how is Baby?'

'Oh, I think she's well. But I wouldn't know for sure. You heard she left me, of course…?'

'No.'

'Yes. She's living with *him* now. Our divorce went through a couple of months ago. I think they're planning to get married next year. But that's all right. No hard feelings. She's happy, I suppose, which is the main thing.' He glared into the distance for a while. 'I suffered over it,' he said at last. 'I loved her very badly, as you know. But I'm over it now.'

'That's good. I'm glad.'

'I called Adele the other day. My first wife, you know. I miss her and my little girl a lot. I thought there might be a chance, that we could… But she said no. Well, that's how it is. You can't go back to the past.' He reflected on this musingly for a moment, then said, 'Yes, I killed my chances there.' His voice changed abruptly, becoming hard and small:

'She destroyed my life, my whole life, just to get ahead. She won't stay with him either, you watch. Everybody's just a step on the ladder to her. I hate her guts.'

It took Adam a moment to realize that he was talking about Baby. No hard feelings, but he hated her guts: the old ambivalence was still at work in Canning, speaking its double truths.

'Yes, it was hard,' Canning said. 'But that's all past now. And I did all right out of it!'

As he usually did when he talked about money, he shook his pockets, giving off a merry, jingling noise. Money had always been a substitute for Canning, filling in the spaces left by love or friendship. And it seemed genuinely to console him, even now. But there was also a tiny strain of doubt, indistinguishable from the greyness in his face. As if to cover it up, he repeated loudly, 'Yes, I did all right out of it!'

'That's nice,' Adam said hollowly.

'I got myself a couple of vintage cars. A 1929 Packard and a 1930 Cadillac LaSalle Convertible. You must come and have a spin sometime. I also bought a wonderful house, national monument, Herbert Baker. I don't need to work again. But I might take up something, just to keep occupied. It's lonely sometimes, having nothing to do. You know what I mean?'

Adam didn't answer and a silence came again: the silence that had brooded under their every conversation, waiting to consume them, from the first day they'd met outside the coop. They became uncomfortable and started going through all the cues of departure. Canning stretched and changed position. Adam looked at his watch.

'Good to see you, Adam. We'll get together sometime.'

'Yes, of course.'

Canning stood up; in a minute he would be gone. Unexpectedly, startling himself, Adam said, 'There's something I've always wanted to tell you.'

'What's that?'

'I don't remember you from school. Not at all. I have no idea who you are.'

Canning sat down again. He looked astonished. 'I don't understand,' he said at last. 'Are you making a joke?'

Adam shrugged. He didn't know where this was coming from. The moment for such a talk was long past; there was no point any more. But the words had risen from some recess in him, charged with peculiar urgency.

'But we talked about it. You said...'

'Yes. But I was lying.'

Canning looked stricken. 'But you *must* remember,' he said plaintively. 'You were my hero.'

'So you keep saying.'

'Our talk in the cloakroom... You do remember that.'

'No, I'm afraid not.'

They stared at each other. Canning's face was working, but it took a long time for his voice to emerge. 'It was the end of term,' he said, very softly. 'I was supposed to be going home for the holidays the next morning. I'd just spoken to my father on the phone and he'd said something to me. The usual thing, about how I was useless, I would never amount to anything – how he'd prefer it if I didn't ever come home.

'I'd heard it a thousand times before, but that night was different. For some reason I just cracked. It was all too much and I couldn't go on. So I got a piece of rope and went creeping into the cloakroom. I was going to string myself up in a corner, where they wouldn't find me till morning.

'But it didn't happen like that. Because fate had sent you there to meet me. You were already there, in one of the cubicles, crying.'

'*Me*?' Adam said. He had been listening with incredulous fascination, waiting for something to be stirred – but it was like hearing about a stranger.

'Yes, you. They'd been teasing you, the other boys, about how you used to wet the bed – '

'Yes, all right,' Adam said quickly; he didn't want to dwell on that.

'And we ended up talking. You didn't see the piece of rope, I hid that away, but we were both outsiders that night. You were very kind. You were gentle to me. Nobody had ever talked to me like that before – as if I was an important person, as if I mattered.'

'Me?' Adam said again. 'Canning, are you sure you don't have me confused with somebody else?'

'No. Of course not. It was you.' Canning was both calm and adamant. 'It was one of the most important moments of my life. The advice you gave me – I've held onto it ever since. How could I forget who spoke to me? Everything changed because of you. It was the first time I didn't feel alone, the first time somebody was *with* me. I stayed alive that night because of you, and I've never forgotten. We didn't talk much after that, we were shy of each other, but I could see that it mattered to you. And after we'd left school, I always knew we'd meet again one day.'

'I don't remember.'

'But it happened.'

'Maybe. But, Canning, you have to understand... for me, it must've been a passing incident. Whatever advice I gave you... it must've been because I was upset. I've never thought about it again.'

'I've thought about it every day since then.'

'I'm sorry, Canning.'

The gulf between them had become complete. There was no bridge, no connection any more.

After a long silence, Canning went on tonelessly. 'You told me to wait,' he said. 'You told me we'd both have our payback one day. If we were patient, if we stored it all up, all our crying and anger, the right moment would come to take revenge. And now I have.'

Finally Adam understood. The destruction of Gondwana, the transformation of the pristine wilderness into a golf course: all of this was because of him. Because of some thoughtless adolescent advice a quarter of a century ago. The knowledge repelled him; he moved away from Canning on the bench.

'I don't remember,' he said again – but for the first time it wasn't true. When Canning had spoken now about revenge, something had stirred at last in Adam. It wasn't a memory; not quite. But it was like the edge of a memory: a shimmer, a tincture, a taste, in which that cloakroom from long ago was present.

It had happened; he was there. That much he knew. But the words, the gestures, the specifics of the encounter – all that had disappeared. The only thing left was that residual tingle, like a movement glimpsed in deep, dark water, a trace of something whole and complete. He had become another person entirely. And maybe – the thought occurred to Adam, at this inappropriate moment – it was what his whole life would come down to in the end: everything that felt burningly present and important would just be a tremor one day, like something that had happened to somebody else.

He pushed the thought, and the moment, away; he stood. Although he didn't have to go back to work, he was behaving as though he was late.

'We'll talk about it another time,' he said. 'But I've got to go.'

'Yes, yes, of course, I understand.' Canning had also jumped up. 'Thank you for going over this old stuff with me…'

'Yes.' He took a step back. 'Goodbye, Canning. Take care of yourself.'

'Goodbye, Adam. Nice to see you.'

They nodded at each other, and then they were hurrying in different directions, under the overhanging trees.

A little way further on, Adam stopped again. It felt as if he'd left something behind, something vitally important that he would need in just a moment. But when he patted his pockets, it was all there: his phone, his keys, his wallet, his diary. He stood for a moment longer, thinking of nothing, till he came back to where he was. Then he started to rush on, through the shadow cast by a statue, rusting and discoloured and streaked with bird-shit, of some forgotten hero.

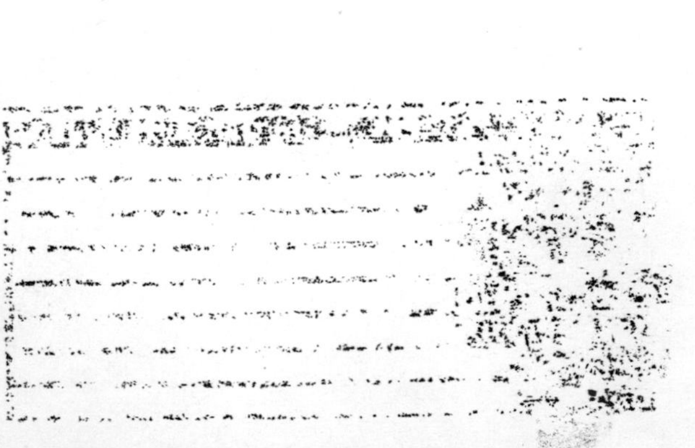